**Sometimes our costumes
reveal our true selves....**

Psyche danced as many dances as possible until at last she grew breathless and thirsty. She returned to Cassandra's side and was just about to suggest finding refreshment, when she looked up at Cassandra's gasp and saw her sister's face pale.

"What is it?" she asked. ⬚ ⬚ ⬚ the first time in her ⬚ ⬚

It was Harry. ⬚ ⬚ ⬚ ⬚ ⬚ ⬚ov-ered half his face ⬚ ⬚ ⬚ ⬚ ll. His hair blazed i⬚ ⬚ ⬚ ⬚ ⬚ ⬚t, his firm and stubb⬚ ⬚ ⬚aised in a familiar tilt, and his lips were the same finely sculpted shape she'd known for most of her life. She knew too well the chiton he wore, as well as the wings, the familiar bow and quiver of arrows he had slung over one shoulder. She would have thought he had decided to come to the ball invisible—except it was all too clear he was very visible, if Cassandra's open mouth and the gasps of various ladies were any indication....

Cupid's Kiss

by

Karen Harbaugh

A SIGNET BOOK

SIGNET
Published by the Penguin Group
Penguin Putnam Inc., 375 Hudson Street,
New York, New York 10014, U.S.A.
Penguin Books Ltd, 27 Wrights Lane,
London W8 5TZ, England
Penguin Books Australia Ltd, Ringwood,
Victoria, Australia
Penguin Books Canada Ltd, 10 Alcorn Avenue,
Toronto, Ontario, Canada M4V 3B2
Penguin Books (N.Z.) Ltd, 182–190 Wairau Road,
Auckland 10, New Zealand

Penguin Books Ltd, Registered Offices:
Harmondsworth, Middlesex, England

First published by Signet, an imprint of Dutton NAL,
a member of Penguin Putnam Inc.

First Printing, February, 1999
10 9 8 7 6 5 4 3 2 1

Copyright © Karen Eriksen Harbaugh, 1999

Author's Note

In 1815, the volcano Tambora erupted in the East Indies and caused a remarkable drop in temperature in the temperate areas of the world for at least a year. In Connecticut, for example, it snowed in July of 1816, which destroyed a huge number of crops. A similar decrease in temperature occurred in England, although since the warm-water Gulf Stream that comes up from the Caribbean tends to make England a bit warmer and wetter than the eastern seaboard of the United States, the drop in temperature (depending on the area, of course) was not as severe. As a result, it is indeed a fact that England had astonishingly cold and wet weather the summer of 1816, with destructive hail and snow into the late spring.

Of course, the reason I give for this decrease in climate temperature is complete fantasy (maybe . . . you never know), and if any of the weather conditions in my book are exaggerated, I hope my readers will understand that exaggeration is often the heart of fiction.

Best wishes,
Karen Harbaugh

Prologue

Eros's wings fluttered uncomfortably as he glanced at the four women before him, though he did his best to seem unconcerned. He did not like being confronted by four goddesses at once, for they tended to bring a great deal of force from the Great Goddess to bear upon him, and besides, it made it difficult for him to get a word in edgewise once they started.

"I don't know what else you wish me to do," he said. "I have looked and looked for her—and yes, I know, the fate of the gods depends on my finding her. Don't you think I wish it, also?" He stared off into the mist and light that surrounded them—really, he thought they would pick a more interesting place than this to discuss matters. He envisioned a green field and trees, and an orchard, not much different than those at Sir John Hathaway's estate in England, and it immediately appeared around them. There! Much better.

Demeter gazed at the landscape and smiled slightly. She waved a hand, and the apple tree became heavy with fruit. "Very pretty. But do stop fidgeting, boy, and listen!" she said, eyeing him sternly. He raised his brows and brought his attention back to the matronly goddess. "Time grows short."

"I thought I had at least twenty years or so more left in which to find my wife," he said. An ache went through his heart at the thought of his lost Psyche, she who had disappeared more than a thousand years ago. No matter that it was so long ago; he had managed to live without her, even take pleasure in day-to-day existence, but he still yearned for the woman he had fallen in love with so long ago. Did he not say, millennia ago when he had married her, that she was his very soul? Without her, he was not truly whole. He looked away briefly, not wanting the women before him to see the pain that must have shown on his face. He had tried so hard to find her!

Gray-shrouded Hecate shook her head. "No, it is much shorter than that—you have wasted your time," she said. Her voice was like the sound of a low crooning wind.

"Wasted my time?" Eros said indignantly. "How have I done that? Have I not looked the world over for more than a millennium?"

Artemis gave him a keen glance, fingering her bow impatiently. "You're spending too much time where you don't belong, friend. What the Hades were you doing on a battlefield? Zeus take it, that's not your realm! Leave it to Ares. You've weakened yourself, and it's not doing us any good. Not only that, but your aim's been off lately."

"Hardly," Eros said, nettled. "I'll wager you a golden apple that you can't hit that branch on the tree to the right at fifty paces, while I—"

"Done!" Artemis said instantly, her eyes brightening. She brought out an arrow from her quiver.

"Oh, for heaven's sake, put your bows and arrows away!" Demeter cried. "We are not here for a shooting match. Artemis, you should *not* encourage him!" Eros grinned and Artemis gave him an irritated look as she put away her arrow. "It is not as if we have much time to spare."

A laughing breeze curled around Hecate's cloaked figure. "Time has indeed grown short," she whispered. "There is only a year left, perhaps a little more."

"A year?" A creeping dread came over him. "But . . . but I thought perhaps ten, twenty . . ." He thought of the time he had spent on the battlefields protecting Kenneth Hathaway. It had weakened Eros a great deal, but he could not refuse Psyche Hathaway's urgent pleading to protect her brother. She had grown dear to him—a dear friend, she had said when they had last parted—and he found he could refuse her very little.

He valued that friendship. It alleviated the painful loneliness he often felt when he searched for his wife, and he was grateful for it, for it had kept him from despair. He smiled slightly, remembering. Psyche Hathaway was even named for his wife, and he liked to think the spirit of his wife had been present at his friend's birth and somehow influenced her parents' selection of names. It comforted him to think it and gave him hope that perhaps his wife was near.

"A year," Hecate repeated, her voice bringing him back to the present. "Then we fade altogether, never to be remembered. You must hurry. Already the effects are being felt, even on earth."

"But what must I do?" Eros said, almost groaning. "I have done everything I can—I have looked everywhere for her!"

"Men!" Artemis said and wrinkled her nose in disgust. "By the Goddess, they are helpless! What they would do without the help of women, I do not know. The so-called superior sex, the mortals say! Ha!" But a bleak look had entered her eyes, and Eros remembered when Artemis had loved a man, and a mortal, at that. She had removed herself from humankind after Orion had died tragically, and now ran only with her wolves and wild-ones in the woods. There had been a marked weakness of the gods after that . . . A twinge of remembrance, a thought just out of reach tugged at him, but he could not bring it forth. Uneasiness crept into him, but he shrugged it off.

Demeter sighed. "Sometimes I think you are as unseeing as the Romans made you out to be, boy, when they envisioned you a blindfolded infant."

"But such a darling!" Aphrodite exclaimed, and smiled brightly. "Didn't you think so, sweeting?"

"No, Mother," Eros said, grinding his teeth. Having to appear as an ineffectual infant before grown mortals had been humiliating. He had refused to be appeased for more than a century after that, and the Romans had grown cynical and decadent, and at last were conquered. His Psyche had accused him of arrogance, which had sparked their final argument. She had said he did no one any good when he removed himself from humankind. She had left him after that. He glanced at Artemis; her face was impatient, her movements restless, her eyes searching the horizon as if looking for something lost. Perhaps . . . perhaps there was something in what Psyche had said.

Again a thought niggled at his brain, but again he could not bring it forth. He drew in a slow breath as the uneasiness he felt earlier grew. Lately, it seemed that he could not bring up images and incidences from long ago that he thought he knew well. Was it because the end of the gods had indeed grown near?

"Look about you," Hecate whispered. "Then you must tell us what we must know."

"What is this?" Eros frowned, shaking himself out of his thoughts. "I must tell *you* something? This is the first I have heard of—why in Hades didn't you tell me this before?"

Demeter patted his arm in a motherly way. "We did not know until now, boy. The Delphic Oracle told us just yesterday."

"Wonderful." Eros began to pace restlessly. "First you tell me I only have a year—maybe less—instead of twenty, and then you tell me I have to tell you something you need to know. Did the Oracle give you any sort of clue about it, or where I might find my wife?"

The goddesses looked at each other and a breeze blew Hecate's cloak restlessly about her. Aphrodite gave him an apologetic look. "I'm very sorry, darling. We did try to get Hermes to seduce it out of one of the Sibyls, but I'm afraid Apollo didn't take to that very well. Or Gaia, for that matter."

Eros grimaced. One did not wish to displease the Great Goddess Gaia—it tended to have worldwide consequences, and that would never do.

Aphrodite planted a motherly kiss on his cheek. "Really, darling, I am sure you will do quite well. It is no doubt your Psyche's fault. I have never known such a stubborn—" Demeter gave her a long look, Artemis cleared her throat, and the breeze around Hecate turned into a sharp wind. Aphrodite stopped suddenly and shrugged.

"You are not telling me something," Eros said flatly, as he gazed at all four goddesses. A guilty look flickered over Artemis's face and Demeter visibly winced.

"We can't," Aphrodite said. "You know how it is with oracles, and it has grown worse over the years."

"Of course." Anger and irritation made his voice less than respectful—even snappish. Eros picked up his quiver of arrows and slung them over his shoulder. "*Don't* tell me." He grasped his bow and turned on his heel, stomping his feet the first few steps before his wings took him aloft. "I hate oracles. Devil take them all!" And with a flash of light he was gone.

The four goddesses gazed at each other and uneasily shifted their feet. "He has spent entirely too much time among mortals," Demeter said. "Did you hear him? 'Devil take them all,' he said! He sounded very much like a mortal to me." She frowned. "I cannot like it."

Aphrodite smiled reminiscently, and a sensual glow began to form around her. "Ohh . . . I don't know. Mortals can be amusing every once in a while."

Artemis cast her a scornful look. "You are thinking of Adonis, no doubt. A waste of time, in my opinion." Her lips turned down, as if a bitter taste had entered her mouth, then her expression grew thoughtful. "I should watch him. He could get into trouble. The war weakened him, and as a result, it weakened us; he should never have gone there." She gazed at the spot where Eros had disappeared and slowly pulled her quiver of arrows onto her shoulder and took up her bow. "Mortals are nothing but trouble, and he seems to be drawn more and more into their company. No, I cannot like it." She began to run, and with a long, graceful leap disappeared into a flash of silvery light.

"Oh, dear." Aphrodite bit her lip anxiously. "Do you think we should go after her? She may be right, after all."

The breeze around Hecate stilled, and with a long sigh, she pushed back her gray hood, revealing a face at once an-

cient and young. "No," she whispered. "Leave them alone.
She may be wrong."

Lady Marshall's ballroom was brightly lit with candles,
and Eros made sure to wrap the shroud of invisibility around
him tightly so as not to be seen as he watched from outside
the ballroom. The goddesses were right. Even though it was
late spring, there was an unnatural chill in the air, and he
could hear worried conversation among the more responsi-
ble landowners in the crowd regarding the strange weather.
It was clear the power of the gods was fading, and thus the
ordered ways of the earth were disturbed.

His gaze followed one bright red-haired figure, laughing
and dancing with the characteristic joyousness he'd come to
know so well. Psyche Hathaway. She had been a friend for
many years now, and he had come to care for her more and
more each year. He had not forgotten his mission of course,
that he was to look for his lost wife. But he had not had a
friend such as Psyche for . . . well, he was not sure he had
ever had one. And it was possible he would never see her
again.

It had occurred to him she might contain the soul of his
wife, but he had dismissed it. He had glimpsed his wife a
few times in the hundreds and hundreds of years he had
searched for her. At first it was in the form of inanimate objects. Later, she had taken the form of living things, and then
more recently, human shape. Each time he had had a sharp
sense of yearning recognition. But each time she had flitted
away, like a bright and teasing butterfly, his sense of her had
become less acute when he chanced upon her the next time.

Even so, each time the parting was more painful. The last
time, he had found her in the form of an old woman, full of
tired years . . . and nothing had prevented her from dying in
his arms. He had seen the spark of recognition in her eyes
just before her spirit fled the body, and he had wept in frustration and grief. Something had happened to put her into
the cycle of birth and death again, making it harder than ever
to find her.

No, he had not felt the recognition this time, not when he had first seen the little child that had been Psyche Hathaway. He could not recall any evidence that she was his wife incarnate.

She was a graceful dancer. Eros watched as she moved across the dance floor with both energy and ease, her skirts fluttering about her like silken feathers. A desirable woman, he thought suddenly. He had always known it, of course, and he had desired her once she had stepped over the threshold of womanhood. But he could not betray their friendship, and he respected the rules by which she had chosen to live. Besides, she had never given him reason to believe she thought him anything but a friend.

And, he still loved his wife. Sometimes he felt it was a curse to be the god of love, for once he had given his heart, it was not something easily retrieved, unlike the hearts of so many of the other gods. But now he must look for his wife in earnest, and it would mean he would not enjoy the company of Psyche Hathaway much anymore. He had a duty to the gods, after all.

A small, rebellious flame still burned in him, however, and he snapped his fingers, summoning fine evening clothes that fitted themselves instantly upon him. Just for a few months he would enjoy the company of his friend, and then he would continue his search. He was sure his wife was somewhere in England, for no other country called to him as strongly as this one, and he had searched the world over. The goddesses had been wrong—he had searched with weary persistence and deserved to refresh himself by enjoying the company of Psyche Hathaway.

He sighed, dropped the invisibility from around him, and stepped into the ballroom toward a small, red-haired and laughing young lady.

Chapter 1

Lady Hathaway could not help being puzzled at Lord Crispin's cheerful face, especially when her youngest daughter, Psyche, made it utterly clear she had refused his suit. It did not keep Her Ladyship from feeling more than a little despair, and after Lord Crispin took his leave, she sank into a chair and covered her eyes with one hand. Psyche stood respectfully waiting in front of her, grimacing slightly. A long sigh finally burst from Lady Hathaway, and she looked at her daughter mournfully.

"I am accursed," she said. "I have a daughter who refuses to be married. No, no! Do not speak." She raised her hand as Psyche seemed about to say something. "I am trying to think in what way I have sinned, though to be sure, I have tried to be a good mother and a good wife. Perhaps the gypsies cursed me after I tried to persuade them to go away when they stayed so long upon our land, although it is not as if I truly believe in curses. *Something* has made sure I suffer nothing but agonies when it comes to my attempts at marrying off my children! And this, so close to the end of the Season."

"I do not see how you can say that," Psyche said reasonably. "After all, Cassandra and Paul are perfectly happy, and she will be a duchess someday. And Aimee and Kenneth are so in love that they cannot be parted, and she even followed the drum when Kenneth fought at Waterloo last year."

Lady Hathaway brightened a little, but she looked at Psyche and sighed once more. "Well, what you say is true, but they went through such fits and starts before they were married. I am surprised I did not go into an apoplexy because of it all. And *you*!" She bent an accusatory eye upon her daughter. "*How* many offers have you refused? And Lord Crispin of all people! What can there be to object to in him? He is handsome and amiable, is an earl, has extensive estates, and has an income of twenty thousand pounds a year. A fortune!" Psyche opened her mouth, but closed it again as her mother continued, "Oh, I could excuse it when Sir Douglas Rackham offered for you—he is a gamester, and I did not blame you for wishing not to fear a stroke of bad luck every week."

Psyche sat gingerly upon a chair. It would take a while before her mother finished, and it could not hurt to be comfortable. She turned her gaze attentively upon Lady Hathaway.

"But then there was Lord Eldon, and Mr. Fairchild." Lady Hathaway ticked off each name on her fingers. "The Earl of Kennard, for heaven's sake—how could I forget him? And, well, if I were to name them all, I should run out of fingers!" Lady Hathaway put her hand over her eyes again. "To think I thought you would be the easiest of my children to marry off." She gave a short, sharp laugh. Perhaps the laugh had an edge of hysteria to it; Psyche could not quite be sure, but she was sorry she had disappointed her mother. She patted Lady Hathaway's hand comfortingly.

"You are not cursed, Mama, I assure you. I shall be married someday, but it is truly a good thing I refused them all, for I would have suited none of them!"

Lady Hathaway eyed her with discontent. "If *they* thought differently, do you not think perhaps even one of them was right?"

Psyche smiled. "Of course not. Why, all of them married other ladies almost immediately, so they cannot have been truly in love with me."

"Married out of pique, I daresay!"

"No, no! We are all good friends now, as I am sure Lord

Crispin still will be, especially after he marries Miss Kirkland. I am certain he is in love with her, but they have quarreled, and he was in abject despair. You may be sure I told him how Mary—Miss Kirkland, you see—wept over it. So of course I *had* to tell Lord Crispin, for you should have seen how downcast he was while he proposed to me, poor man! As if he were attending a funeral." Psyche laughed merrily. "You cannot suppose I would feel flattered to receive such a proposal as that."

Lady Hathaway raised her head and gazed at Psyche mournfully. "Well . . . I suppose it cannot be flattering, but it certainly would have been practical."

"Mama!"

"Oh, very well!" Lady Hathaway said testily. "I suppose I would not have wanted you to accept a marriage proposal under such circumstances."

Psyche smiled, took her mother's hand, and lifted it to her cheek affectionately. "Dear Mama! How I do love you!"

Lady Hathaway bent a stern look upon her. "And *don't* think you can get around me with your caressing ways, young lady!"

Psyche immediately put on a meek expression and her mother burst out laughing.

"Oh, you horrid girl!" She gave a quick kiss on her daughter's cheek. "Why I let you distract me from my intentions I do not know."

"Because you are the best mother in the world," Psyche said, grinning.

"Terrible girl!" Lady Hathaway said, but smiled. "Do go up and dress for Lady Marshall's ball. The silver gilt muslin gown, please—her ballroom will be draped in blue, and I think the dress will look very well against it." She hesitated a moment, and Psyche gazed at her attentively. "Have you heard anything from Mr. D'Amant?"

Psyche raised her brows. "Mr. D'Amant? Should I have?"

"I thought, perhaps since you did say he was your friend some years ago—"

Psyche rolled her eyes in exasperation. "Oh, heavens,

Mama! He is *only* a friend. I imagine, since the war is done with, he has gone traveling about on business. There is no reason why he should send letters to me, especially without your knowledge." She bit her lip, annoyed at herself, for she could feel her face become warm. Of course her mother noticed it; she had a smug smile on her face that said as surely as if she had spoken aloud that she was thinking matchmaking thoughts again.

"Oh, Mama, *do* stop!" Psyche said, and gave an impatient sigh. "If I am blushing it is because I know *precisely* what you are thinking. Mr. Harry D'Amant has no *tendre* for me at all."

"Of course, my dear," Lady Hathaway said complacently.

"And"—Psyche continued firmly—"I have not seen him for at least a year, and you cannot think anyone with an interest in me would stay away that long. *And* I am going to put on my dress straightaway before you say another word!" Psyche put her hands over her ears and ran out the door.

Lady Hathaway sighed and shook her head. Psyche was almost twenty years old now . . . how long was she to wait until her daughter showed a firm interest in a young gentleman, enough to form a *tendre*? She was very popular, if the number of dances the girl danced at every ball was any indication. And though her hair was a lamentably bright red, it was thick and lustrous, and her figure quite good. Her daughter might discount the number of marriage proposals she had received, but no man would ask her to marry him if he did not think of the prospect with at least a small measure of enjoyment.

She left the drawing room and slowly went up the stairs to her chamber. The girl had been on the town for nearly two years now, and despite all the marriage proposals she received, it seemed her heart had not been touched except by anything warmer than friendship the whole time. Except, perhaps, once.

Lady Hathaway entered her bedroom and saw her husband sitting at her dressing table, deep in the perusal of an old manuscript. Her jewelry box was teetered on the edge of the table, and her perfume bottle was on its side—fortunately the cork had held, although she doubted Sir John would have noticed anything so trivial to his great intellect as spilled perfume. She cleared her throat. Nothing. She coughed loudly. Slowly Sir John looked up from his manuscript and blinked.

"What, are you here, my dear?" he asked.

Lady Hathaway spread her arms. "As you see, love. This is my room, after all." She turned to the bell rope and rang for a maid.

Sir John looked about him, clearly bewildered. "But what was my manuscript doing here?"

"I have not the slightest idea, John. No doubt you brought it for some reason."

"True. I do nothing without reason," he murmured, and his brow furrowed in thought. Then he brightened. "Ah! I have it now. I have learned some Sanskrit—did I tell you, Amelia?—and General Foxworthy gave me this manuscript upon his return from India. There are some sentences I cannot quite translate, but I think it has something to do with beds." His gaze strayed to the large canopied bed and he frowned.

Lady Hathaway blushed, for the maid had just stepped into the room and looked at both of them curiously. "Never mind that, John! Do make yourself ready for Lady Marshall's supper ball. You said you would escort us to it, after all."

Sir John's frown grew deeper as he transferred his gaze to the clock on the mantelpiece. "Already? Hmph. How I came to promise such a frivolous thing I do not know."

"Aristotle, my love," Lady Hathaway said promptly. "One must divide one's time into Work, Leisure, Play, and Sleep." She selected a forest-green silk gown with a silver net overdress from her wardrobe. She had quite fancied it when she saw the design in *La Belle Assembleé,* and felt she was quite right in choosing it. She turned to her maid. "Foster, the tortoiseshell comb for my hair—or no, the silver one would be better."

Her husband's eyebrows shot up almost to his receding hairline. "Aristotle! Well, well." He gazed at Lady Hathaway suspiciously. "Have you taken any books from my library?"

She widened her eyes and laid her hand over her heart. "I? Heavens, no, John! If you must know, I procured my own copy." The maid began unbuttoning her dress.

"You?"

"But of course, my dear," she said complacently. Though she had not the superior mental faculties of her husband, she was certain she had superior knowledge of Tactics and Strategy. Where else had her son, Kenneth, inherited that ability? She had learned long ago that a surprise attack was always a useful thing, if used sparingly. She smiled at her husband. "Do close your mouth, my love—I think you should wear the Bath superfine coat and silver striped waistcoat. You look very well in them."

Sir John frowned again. "Frivolity."

"No, it is not," she replied. "I did ask you to help me find a husband for Psyche. Surely you cannot wish for a son-in-law who is a dullard!"

"Good heavens, no!" Sir John began to look concerned.

"And what if he cannot even speak Greek or Latin?"

"Good God!" Sir John began to pace, scowling dreadfully at the floor.

"Therefore, I thought it best if you came to Lady Marshall's supper ball, in case such an uneducated fellow should approach your daughter. You must admit it would never do."

"Certainly not! I am glad you brought this to my attention, Amelia," Sir John said, moving toward the door. He looked at his wife in approval. "How fortunate I am that I married you!"

"Not at all, John. As you said, you have always relied on reason to make your decisions."

A slow smile grew on his lips as he gazed at her standing

there, half dressed. "Not always," he said, and kissed her ear.

"John!" Lady Hathaway exclaimed, blushing, as he left the room. She was quite good at Strategy, but sometimes her husband took quite unfair advantage of her. As did her children! She did her best to be a good mother and wife; a little more effort on her part could possibly get Psyche more suitors before the Season was over.

Psyche sighed as her maid dressed her hair. Another ball! She liked them very well, but they did not seem as amusing as when Harry had attended them. How she missed him! She had many good friends now, but it was not like having her very best friend about.

Harry had appeared to her when she was a child, lost in the woods, and had led her home. At first she had thought him an angel, for he had worn a short white garment—a chiton, he later told her—had wings, and could fly. But he had laughed and said he was not, and had been so merry that she could not help liking him from that time on. He had appeared only to her for many years, invisible to others, her family included. But not long ago, he had decided to dispense with his wings from time to time so that he could accompany Psyche to balls and such.

She could not help smiling a little smugly to herself. Except for her sister Cassandra, no one knew how unusual he was, not even Mama. There was something quite wonderful in knowing that one had a Greek god for a friend, a delicious little secret. She had felt a bit guilty in thinking she was keeping a secret from her mother, but there could be no doubt Mama would be overset at the notion of Psyche's having such a friend. Mama was a very practical lady; she had no great opinion of the morals or antics of the Greek gods from the stories Papa had related, and as a result, Psyche could not see her approving of a friendship with Harry if she knew. And of course, she would not want Mama to be upset!

As she tried one necklace, Psyche grimaced, discarded

it, then put on another. It was troublesome enough that her mother thought Harry had been her beau. Really, she would have laughed had she not been so put out of countenance. Now Mama was forever asking after Mr. Harry D'Amant, wondering whether and when he would come to call.

However unusual a friend he was, there was nothing like having someone who entered into most—if not all—of one's sentiments. But Harry was on a quest; he had been looking for a friend ever since she had known him. She had asked him a few times who it was and if she could help, but he had only shaken his head, clearly unwilling to discuss it. A bereft look had crossed his face; it must have been someone very dear, and her heart went out to him. At the very least she could be a comfort to him while he searched. That was what a good friend did, after all.

Looking in the mirror, Psyche tugged at the edge of her bodice. The dress looked very well on her, she thought. It was the latest mode, brought from France now that the war was over: a sheer muslin dress embroidered with silver-gilt thread. She had at first thought the décolletage shockingly low, for it divided the bodice in half, almost down to the high waist, and the upper part was gathered away almost to the edge of her shoulders by silken braids. But her mother had approved the dress immediately, and in fact had had an oddly set look upon her face when she had ordered it fitted to her.

Psyche frowned for a moment, then shook her head. If Mama had raised no objections to it, it must be acceptable. She gave a satisfied nod and put on the thick cloak the maid held out to her before descending the stairs to the waiting coach.

It did not take long to arrive at Lady Marshall's house. Psyche had been here before, and had enjoyed the Marshalls' easy manners and hospitality. They encouraged their guests to roam the rooms and view their paintings—quite superb, in fact, for the collection featured quite a few Van Dycks and at least one painting by Raphael.

She glanced at her mother and father and smiled at them as they entered the house. Mama knew Lady Marshall well and was confident the company they kept was composed of the best sort of people. As a result, Psyche was sure she would be fairly free to go about as she wished in the house. A niggling impatience came over her . . . she would be glad to leave London; her freedom was less curtailed in the country. She sighed. Only a few more weeks, and they would be home.

She danced a country dance and a quadrille, then managed to bring Lord Crispin and Miss Kirkland together again. A *very* satisfying evening, she felt, and smiled to herself. She was watching the couple dance together, a bit closer then necessary in a waltz, when she felt a warm breeze briefly touch her cheek.

"Psyche."

She jumped, then turned to face Harry, her heart filling with joy. "Oh, I should have known you would come upon me in that manner!" she said, barely restraining herself from hugging him then and there. It needed only his presence to make this evening perfect. She smiled at him instead, then cocked her head, for it seemed he held his breath as his eyes flickered over her, and she almost asked him if anything was wrong. But then he looked at her in his old, familiar way, his lips turned up in a mischievous grin, his eyes smiling warmly at her, and she thought she must have imagined it. "But I shall not scold you this time, for it has been an age since I have seen you! Oh, my dear friend, how I have missed you!"

He was dressed to be seen, for he was not in his usual Greek chiton but in fine evening wear, and if the admiring glances from the other ladies were any indication, they saw him very clearly indeed. She saw the hand of Weston in the cut of his coat, and his neckcloth was neatly tied, and though his embroidered waistcoat was on the dandified side, it did not detract from the whole picture.

He smiled, but his eyes grew serious as he brought her hand to his lips. "Have you, Psyche?"

"But of course! How can I not miss my best friend, after a whole year of not seeing him?" She squeezed his hand briefly and earnestly. "Have you found your friend, Harry? I know you have been searching for such a long time."

"No," Harry said, glancing away and releasing her hand. "I have not." A tense, tight look crossed his face. "Let us not discuss it—at least, not now." For one moment he seemed to search her face, then he smiled. "I would much rather talk of more pleasant things than that."

Psyche's heart ached for him. How she wished she could help in some way. However, she respected his silence on the matter, and did not want to add to his pain by quizzing him about it. She put on a teasing smile instead. "Well, you must tell me: were you invited to Lady Marshall's ball, or did you cozen your way here?"

Harry widened his eyes, put his hand over his heart, and sighed. "You wound me, Psyche. Of course I was invited."

"After, I daresay, you flattered her in a most toadying way."

"Not at all. I am very respectable now."

Psyche snorted.

"Truly! I am now a landed gentleman, if you must know."

"Really!"

The orchestra began a lilting melody—a waltz—and Harry bowed in a very correct manner. "A dance, Psyche?"

Nodding, she put her hand on his arm, still gazing at him skeptically, however.

"You doubt me; I can see it on your face." Harry shook his head mournfully as he put his hand above her waist and swept her into the dance. "I am now the proud owner of part of Sir William Hambly's estates."

She almost stumbled, but Harry's hands held her firm. "No!"

"Yes," he said complacently. "I suppose that now makes me your neighbor. I fancied owning some property, and since I am Sir William's only relative and he wished to sell the dower house, I bought it."

Psyche gazed at him, horrified. "But you are *not* his relative! We made up that story to appease Mama when I first came out into Society. Oh, heavens! I cannot but think such a fabrication will be found out, and soon, and then both of us shall be in the basket. Oh, Harry, how could you?"

"You need not worry about it. I know how concerned you are about such things, so I made sure we were related in some way."

" 'In some way'?" Psyche asked suspiciously.

Harry shrugged. "Sir William's family is a very old one, and in fact I was able to trace it back to one of my uncles who, ah, had an alliance with one of Sir William's female ancestors. So, we are related, though distantly—he's a cousin of sorts. There is no one related in any way to him, poor fellow. Except myself, of course."

Psyche remembered her last encounter with the irritable and ancient Sir William. The gentleman was well known as a reclusive and irascible man. She had a difficult time thinking of him as a "poor fellow," and even more difficulty trying to find a resemblance between his aged and wrinkled visage and that of Harry's handsome one. But her heart warmed and she smiled at him. It was very kind of Harry to be so charitable toward Sir William, even though the connection between them was a very distant one.

Her doubt must have shown on her face, for Harry said immediately, "His solicitors were quite agreeable when I showed them the papers."

"Papers?"

"Marriage lines and birth records."

"*False* ones, no doubt!" Psyche said severely.

"No, not at all. Sir William did have a sister who married a Frenchman, and she did have a son. All of them died during the revolution. That they left behind their papers in an obscure accounting office was very convenient."

Psyche thought it was *too* convenient, but she supposed that if the solicitors were satisfied, there should be no reason why she should not be, also.

"You need not be concerned, Psyche." Harry's face turned

serious. "Sir William almost wept when he found he still had a relative."

"Oh, poor man!" she said. How horrible it must have been for Sir William, to have lost his sister and her family. She squeezed Harry's hand warmly. "Whatever the case, I *am* glad Sir William believes he still has family, and . . . I suppose it is a good thing for you to be his family. No wonder he has been such an irritable man—anyone would, with such tragedy. What a terrible thing to be so alone!"

For one moment Psyche felt his arm stiffen under her hand and she looked at him. A stricken expression flitted across his face, and then it was gone, replaced by his usual smile.

"I know," he said lightly, then looked away. "I see you have done well by Lord Crispin and Miss Kirkland. I would almost think I had shot them with my arrows the way they make sheep's eyes at each other."

Psyche searched his face—there was something amiss. She had known him too long not to see it. "What is it, Harry?" she asked. "What is wrong?"

The dance ended, and supper was announced. A few friends immediately hailed Harry and he turned away, talking and making jokes, clearly unwilling to answer her. Psyche pressed her lips together for a moment, annoyed. She would not be put off by such stratagems! She waited patiently until the two gentlemen who had stopped to talk moved away toward the supper room, and she tugged on Harry's arm as if urging him toward supper as well.

"There is something bothering you, I know, so *don't* put me off, if you please," she said.

"Nonsense! What is there to bother me? Do I look as if something is amiss?"

"Yes!" Psyche said firmly.

Harry frowned as they passed a drapery-festooned mirror and stopped to peer into it. "If anything is amiss, I believe it is this neckcloth. I do not think I have quite got in the way of properly tying a neckcloth, despite my observations of the art. It is one thing to summon a presentable suit upon one, but it seems a neckcloth is quite another thing entirely."

"Harry—" she began, gritting her teeth.

"Oh, Mr. D'Amant! We have not seen you this age. How do you do?"

Psyche almost groaned. Of course Mama would see them, and of course she would come straightaway to discover what, if anything, was between them.

Harry cast her a smiling, impudent look before he turned to her mother. "An age indeed, Lady Hathaway," he said as he bowed over her hand. "Had I not felt most acutely the span of time away from the Hathaway family, I would not know a day has passed now that I look upon you, fair lady." Psyche gazed at him, disgusted. He was not going to tell her anything at all, and was turning her mother up sweet, no doubt to avoid Psyche's questions. She had quite forgot how annoying he could be!

"Nonsense!" Lady Hathaway said, and rapped his hand with her fan, for he still had hold of her fingers. But she blushed nevertheless and smiled at him. "I daresay you have returned to England to visit your uncle?"

"Yes, and to renew old acquaintances." He glanced swiftly at Psyche, but not so swiftly that her mother did not notice it. A smug look came over Lady Hathaway's face, and Psyche almost groaned again. What was Harry thinking? He was clever and quick—surely he must know that even the slightest indication he might wish to further his acquaintance with her would lead her mother to think him a suitor.

"Certainly it is most pleasant to renew one's acquaintance with *friends*," Psyche said firmly, frowning at her mother.

Lady Hathaway ignored her. "How delightful!" she said, and smiled at Harry again. "Alas, it is too bad you have returned so late in the Season. We shall be returning to our home in Tunbridge Wells in a few weeks, or perhaps travel to Brighton."

"If you are not too tired from the travel, Mama," Psyche said, hoping desperately to turn the conversation.

"How pleasant it would be to rest at home for a while, after all our activities in London." There! That should put paid upon any idea Mama may have of more parties—and hence, more suitors—at such a fashionable place as Brighton.

For a moment her mother pursed her lips in a small frown, then her face cleared. "So true! It is not as if we cannot have house parties or alfresco luncheons, after all. I daresay you shall be at Sir William's house, Mr. D'Amant, while we are at home? After your travels, I cannot think of anything more restful than a peaceful drive in the countryside, or a walk in the gardens. Should you wish to view *our* gardens, you may be sure you are welcome at any time."

"Oh, Mama!" Acute embarrassment made Psyche feel uncomfortably warm. "Mr. D'Amant has plenty of gardens at the dower house he may view, and may be too busy with them to call on us," she said hastily.

Lady Hathaway raised her brows in question. "Dower house? You will be staying awhile in our neighborhood, Mr. D'Amant?" Psyche mentally cursed herself for blurting out the news that Harry would be so near.

"Why yes, ma'am," Harry replied before she could find a way to divert her mother. "I understand the dower house and its grounds have been sadly neglected; viewing your gardens may well inspire me to improve what I have bought."

"Bought, Mr. D'Amant?"

Harry smiled charmingly. "Yes. I wished a place to live, and Sir William was amenable to the arrangement."

"How perfectly delightful!" Lady Hathaway exclaimed, her face wreathed in smiles.

Psyche stared at Harry in consternation. What was he thinking? He had been about the mortal world enough—London, particularly—surely he knew he was implying he wanted to settle in the neighborhood, and that he was wealthy enough to afford not to hang on Sir William's coattails. His whole conversation made it clear he was an extremely eligible suitor, come to settle in their district and looking to renew an acquaintance with her. Harry turned and smiled at Psyche, and her mother's expression became odiously complacent.

Psyche bit back an irritated sigh. He was funning, of course; no doubt he would be off again on his quest. But it would never do. Mama's hopes would be raised—she would act as if a betrothal were a settled thing if he kept up his attentions, and how embarrassing it would be when nothing came of it!

The scent of rich food and spices wafted past her nose, and Psyche gave a large sigh she hoped was more wistful than determined. "Oh, the supper does smell delicious! Do let us go in, Mama!"

Lady Hathaway laughed lightly. "Do go with Mr. D'Amant, Psyche. Your father promised he would go in with me, and I must find him!" She cast an arch look at Harry. "I trust you will take care of my daughter, Mr. D'Amant?"

"Mama, I can care for myself very well. I am not traveling to the wilds of Africa after all!" Psyche hissed. She was sure her face was completely red by now.

Lady Hathaway laughed merrily. "*Such* a resourceful girl!"

"Of course I will take care of her, my lady," Harry replied, smiling, and Lady Hathaway nodded in an exceedingly gracious and pleased manner as she turned away. Psyche gritted her teeth.

The Marshalls' supper room sideboards were laden with all manner of delicacies, and Lady Marshall had set out round tables here and there throughout the room, with cards set in the middle of each. The combination of supper and card games at the same time was a new, rather odd idea that had seized their hostess, but Psyche paid little attention to that or what she was putting on her plate.

Harry was keeping something secret, and she did not feel at all comfortable about it. He did not always tell her his plans and invariably, though they caused a little excitement in other people's lives, they were more mischievous than anything else and did not really harm anyone. But she could see that lost look in his eyes that she'd seen several times before, now more pronounced, and an oddly deter-mined look about his mouth and chin as well.

She glanced at Harry. He seemed only mildly interested in the food before him. His plate filled, they went to a round table to the side of the room; she made sure to nudge him close to a small one, fit only for two. It would look very particular, she knew, and she could not like it, but there was no help for it if she was to find out why Harry was acting so strangely.

She watched him, saying nothing at first, for he would not look up from his dish as he pushed the food around on it with his fork.

"Harry," she said at last.

He raised his head and looked at her, and she swallowed. She had never seen him look like this—anger, sadness, and a loneliness so deep and ancient that it nearly frightened her.

"A year, Psyche," he said suddenly. "A year, perhaps less, after which I might have to go away forever."

Go away. Forever. A year. The words came down hard, like stones upon her chest, and for one moment she felt she could not breathe. "Go away . . . altogether?"

"Not right away," he said hurriedly. "And there is a chance— Perhaps I need not. It depends . . ."

"A chance?" She felt stupid, only able to repeat his words.

"The . . . person I have been looking for—if I find her, then the gods will not fade away. I thought I had more time, but I find only a year." His voice became low, and she could hear anxiety in it. She watched him crumble his food on his plate—a half-eaten lobster patty, his favorite, she noted ir-relevantly. Too soon, she might not ever see him eat one again. The thought made her throat close tight and ache as if she were ill.

Psyche looked up at him again, a hot resolution rising in her. Harry was her friend, and she would *not* let him fade away, not if she could help it. Had he not rescued her when she had been abducted as a child? Had he not kept her brother, Kenneth, safe in battle? He had done all these things for her, and it was only right she help him in return in whatever way she could.

"Who is she?" she said fiercely. "Tell me, Harry. I will help you find her, I swear it. Then you will not go away, and you will be my friend still."

He shook his head and his smile was wry. "How can you help me? I have looked for more than a thousand years. I am a god. If I have not had success, how can you, a mortal?" A servant came by, and Harry waved away his plate, his appetite clearly gone.

"Oh, for heaven's sake!" Irritation flared, and she was glad, for it was familiar and sure, and kept the grief at bay. "How you keep underestimating us! For all that you are a god, I think you do not know humans at all."

An odd look came over his face, and he gave a small, reluctant laugh. "*She* used to say that . . . I just remembered. It has been so long ago. Perhaps it's a sign." His voice grew more eager. "Perhaps you are meant to help me, mortal or not." Psyche rolled her eyes in exasperation, but he went on, speaking faster. "There is your name, after all. I have been thinking it might not be a coincidence that it's the same as hers. And look at how you successfully brought Miss Kirkland and Lord Crispin together—I admit it was well done, and didn't I say it was as good as if I had done it?"

"High praise, I am sure," Psyche replied dryly.

"Of course it was," Harry said. He smiled more confidently, and his hopeful eyes made her heart lift. "I must have come to your home because in some way, I sensed her influence upon you. Perhaps she wanted me to be your friend and your family's as well. Indeed, I came to care for you— for you all, to be sure!"

Psyche smiled in return, and she felt almost as happy as when she first saw him in Lady Marshall's ballroom. It had been such a long, natural, joyful childhood friendship that she had never questioned why he had decided to become her friend. How odd that such details had never been discussed! She would never take such things for granted ever again.

She reached across and squeezed his hand. "I am glad you care for us, Harry," she said.

"It's obvious," he continued. "I see it all now." He beamed at her. "*You* must be the key. *You* must somehow help me find my wife."

Chapter 2

The room seem to dim for a moment about Psyche and she grasped the table with her hands. "Wife?" she whispered, for she suddenly felt as if her lungs had emptied of air, and she could not breathe.

Harry looked at her anxiously. "Did you not know? I thought—your father, because he is well versed in the ancient stories—I thought he must have told you."

Stories . . . a flicker of memory came to Psyche. "Of—of course I remember," she said valiantly. "Papa told me those stories long ago. And I *shall* help you. Am I not your friend?"

"You didn't know—he didn't tell you." His brows drew together in a frown.

"Of course I remember—your wife was also named Psyche, and she was a king's daughter, and she married you after many adventures. As you see, I know very well."

Perhaps it was the exasperation she forced into her voice or the description of the story that convinced him. Harry nodded and his shoulders relaxed. Psyche told herself she was glad, for she did not want him to know she had not thought of him having a wife. But she should have—oh, she should have! Had not Cassandra and her father told her stories of the Greek gods when she was a girl? A terrible ache crushed her heart, and confusion too, for she also felt irritation and anger. But what use of even speaking of it? Especially at a supper-ball.

She glanced away and saw her mother moving toward them, now that they were done with their meal. "I think we

should play at cards, Harry." She smiled at him and believed
she did a good imitation of cheer, for he nodded and picked
up the deck. "Mama will not interrupt us if we play and I can
think of how I might help you find your wife." Her words
almost stuck in her throat. "*Vingt et un,* and penny points,
for I am afraid I have spent most of my pin money this quarter." She saw her mother turn to talk to an acquaintance as
Harry dealt cards, and she sighed with relief when they
began to play.

Psyche lost dreadfully, but she did not wonder at it; she
felt as if she played in a nightmare. A headache formed at
her temples, and soon she begged leave to stop the play;
when Harry looked concerned, she smiled at him and shook
her head.

"I shall be quite well, Harry," she said, and went to find
her mother.

When her mother took her home, talking animatedly
about how attentive Mr. D'Amant had been, Psyche continued to smile until she arrived home and stepped into her
room. There, she removed her dress, put on her night rail,
and when the maid left her in her bed, she turned and wept
into her pillow.

The thought that he would be gone from her life struck
her hard, taking the breath from her. Not altogether gone—
he would not if he found his wife. There was that chance, at
least.

But a wife! Psyche pushed herself away from her pillow
and sat up, staring woefully at the expanse of white cotton.
She did not know why she had not remembered until now
that he had one, or if it had ever occurred to her, why it had
not seemed to matter . . . until now. The thought that Harry
had a wife hurt almost as much as the thought he might disappear forever.

"If he found his wife he would not go away, not forever,"
Psyche told her pillow fiercely, and shook it as if in shaking
it she were shaking some sense into herself. The tears began
again, but she wiped them away with the back of her hand
and let out a short, sharp, determined breath. "You *cannot* be

so selfish as to wish for anything but Harry's happiness. He is your *friend.*"

But before she fell asleep, she knew she was indeed a selfish wretch, for she wished very much that Harry would not disappear *and* that he could be her friend as he had always been, and hers alone.

The morning was no better. Her bed was too comfortable, and Psyche did not wish to rise from it. She snuggled down into the eiderdown and the linen and pulled the quilt over her head. If she stayed in bed, she would not have to deal with any unpleasantness.

The quilt came down, and Psyche opened her eyes. It was no use. The depressing thoughts would come anyway, and besides, it was stuffy under the bedclothes and she could not breathe. She cast a look out her chamber window, glad that thick black clouds filled the sky and it would no doubt rain torrents. She did not want to see any callers and did not want to leave her house for any outing, or even leave her room.

Unfortunately, she did not even have her headache from last night, and so had absolutely no excuse to stay in bed. Psyche rose from the bed, rang for her maid, then opened her wardrobe, pushing her clothes this way and that. Oh, why did she not have any drab, gloomy colors among her dresses? The dullest dress she owned was a bronze-green round gown, and when her maid assisted her into it, it did nothing but make her hair look an even shinier red, her gray eyes turn green, and her skin look like cream. How depressing that she was in such flagrant good health.

She caught sight of the Gothic novel she had been writing—*The Castle of Horrors*—and picked it up from her dressing table. It would be very satisfying to live in an accursed castle, for it would have delightfully reflected her mood, and she was sure such a place would have had an enervating effect on a healthy constitution and she would most likely die tragically.

She swallowed, and her throat hurt, but she knew it was hopeless to think it would be a putrid sore throat, or the beginning of lung fever. Her life was not a Gothic novel, and if she were to even hint at a decline, Mama would force her to drink some vile-smelling potion that would motivate her to act in a bright and sprightly manner even if she were at death's door.

The clock struck ten, and she knew she should go down to her breakfast . . . but not yet. She picked up a pen, for the last page she had written caught her eye.

Cecelia dashed the wetness from her eyes, and when she turned to the handsome Count Ormondo there was no glimmer on her lashes, though her eyes shone with those fluid diamonds we so often call tears.

"Oh my dear Count!" cried she. "Would that I could forsake my virtue! Would that I could forsake the honor of my name! Alas! Alack! I cannot, even for the strong affection (for she could not bring herself to say the fatal word 'love,' Dear Reader, lest she lose her resolution) bounding from my heart like the leaping deer through the English woods I love so well!

Psyche let out a sob, and pressed her hand tightly upon her lips. Oh, she would *not* cry! She had done so already last night and it had done no good at all. But the book was irresistible: she pulled out the lap desk from under her bed. She curled up against the pillows on her bed again, dipped her pen in the inkwell she had brought to the bed table, and wrote on:

Count Ormondo seized his dagger and brought it to his tortured bosom. "Then, my sweet Cecelia, see my death!"

With a cry pressed from her agonized soul, Cecelia seized the dagger and tossed it aside, pressing her handkerchief over the wound he had begun to make. "No, no, my lord! Live on! Attend to your crazed wife, that I may remember you a virtuous man on my journey home, for the strength of my emotions cannot bear to see your soul tarnished with sin! Forevermore shall we be friends and friends only, and never let those passions of the heart destroy our reason or our faith in goodness!"

Psyche allowed herself to be drawn into the book, and

when she finished the chapter she felt much, much better. She sighed as she put away her pen, ink, and lap desk. No, her life was not a Gothic novel, but she could persevere, and be as full of common sense as possible. What was of the utmost importance was that Harry not fade away. At least—if his wife was not an odious creature—they could remain friends, even if it meant she would not see him as often as she would like.

She raised her chin and let out a resolute breath. One day she herself would marry an amiable gentleman for whom she might find a liking, if not a deep love, and she would find some contentment in that relationship and with any children she might have. A lump rose in her throat again at the thought, but she swallowed it down. Had that not been the purpose of a Season in London? In fact, the most noble and virtuous thing she could think of doing in this case would be to help Harry find his wife.

There! That would be the most practical thing to do, and perhaps he would return the favor by finding her an amiable husband. In fact, she would talk to him about it today, as soon as she had her breakfast.

She would have her breakfast in the library. If she was to help Harry, she should read as much as she could about him. Perhaps her father could help her—not that she would tell him that Harry was a god, of course, but her father knew more about the ancient stories than anyone, she was certain, since he was a well-known scholar of the classics.

When Psyche opened the door to the library, she saw her father was already there. A large repast, barely touched, sat on a cart next to his chair. He was poring over an old manuscript, his spectacles at the end of his nose and his brow creased in a frown. He wore a surprisingly bright and highly decorated dressing gown; Mama must have bought it for him, for he usually paid no attention to the selection of his clothes.

"Papa?" Psyche called softly.

Nothing.

"Papa?" she called a little louder.

Slowly her father's head raised and he looked vacantly at her for a moment. "Eh? Oh! Psyche! Have you brought my book?"

"Book?"

Sir John frowned. "Perhaps it was the maidservant I asked to fetch my book. Were you here a moment ago?"

"No, Papa. I have just come in to have my breakfast and to find some books."

Sir John's eyebrows rose and his gaze turned to the eggs, ham, and scones on the cart before him. "Breakfast? Is it time for that now?" He laughed, and the fog of acute concentration lifted at last. "It must be, since it is in front of me. Come, Psyche, and pour the coffee—I assume it's coffee, for heaven bless me, I cannot remember whether I ordered that or tea—and you may join me."

Psyche served the coffee, and they ate in companionable silence until her father seemed about to take up his manuscript again. Quickly she put her hand on his arm.

"Papa, I was wondering if you could help me. I need to find some record of Greek myths, one in particular."

Sir John's brows rose. "That is—"

"The one about Har—Eros and his . . . his wife."

"Mmmm." Her father frowned, but his eyes had a far-away look. "I am surprised you do not remember—you have the same name, you know."

"Yes. I am sure you named me, for Mama would not have thought of it," Psyche said.

Sir John smiled and for one moment he looked mischievous. But the smile disappeared, and Psyche thought she must have imagined it—her father was a serious scholar and mischievousness was not something she associated with him.

"It's true that Psyche was a king's daughter, the youngest, and the most beautiful of his three daughters," he said. "Hesiod, a Roman, related this story, but I believe it to be older than that."

Psyche settled in her chair more comfortably. Her father's

voice fell into a soft, rhythmic rumble; it was the voice he used to tell her stories when she was a little girl.

"She was so beautiful that suitors from many lands wished to wed her, and when she traveled anywhere in her father's kingdom, the people bowed down to her as if she were the Goddess of Beauty herself. It was unfortunate, and it mattered not that Psyche feared and hated her own beauty because of it; Venus—Aphrodite in the Greek, my dear— grew angry. When she sent a plague upon the land, and when the king sought the reason for it, he found to his horror that his youngest daughter was to be sacrificed to a dreadful monster at the highest mountain in his kingdom . . ."

Psyche listened intently, absorbed by the tale of her unfortunate namesake. The Greek Psyche went bravely to her fate, only to find love in the arms of an invisible lover, and later, husband. But then, because of fear and the whispers of her evil sisters, she lost the love of the God of Love, Eros, himself. That long-ago Psyche was strong and courageous, and accomplished the dangerous tasks Aphrodite set her.

"Thus Psyche and Eros were united again, and Eros swore he'd never leave her, for her devotion was more than proven. Psyche was made immortal, and their marriage in Olympus was celebrated by all the gods." Sir John took a sip of coffee and smiled at his daughter. "Would you like to hear another?"

Psyche sat silent for a moment, struggling with despair. "That is all," she said at last, and managed to return her father's smile. "Thank you. Or wait—" She hesitated. "I was wondering, is there any truth to the story? Could it be real?"

Sir John shrugged. "Perhaps there was such a princess with that name—some of the stories have some basis in fact. But most scholars agree this story is allegorical; Psyche means soul after all, and Eros is the God of Love. There is even a hint of their belief in life after death—Psyche goes into the underworld, after all, and is brought back to life."

An odd feeling uncurled in Psyche's heart—if she were to name it, she would say it was a sort of recognition. But she dismissed it; the sensation had nothing to do with the story her father told. "I suppose they, like us, believed in such things."

Her father nodded and pushed up the spectacles on his nose. "Yes, but differently, too. Some of their heroes may have gone to the Elysian fields—their version of heaven— but Plato mentions the belief that souls are born again in new bodies and I believe . . ."

Psyche's attention drifted, thinking of the story her father had just told her. If Harry's wife was truly like the woman in the story, she *deserved* to have him, for she was beautiful, brave, clever, strong, and virtuous, even if she did make the mistake of believing her horrid sisters at first. Of course Harry would search for her for so long. Psyche only wished that she did not feel so low about it.

"I believe I have a few translated myths should you wish to read them for yourself," her father said at last.

"What? Oh! Well, perhaps I might," Psyche replied. She smiled wryly. "I fear you named me wrongly, Papa. I am not like the Psyche in the story, you know."

Sir John patted her hand. "But of course you are, my dear."

"My dear, sweet, *fond* Papa!" Psyche laughed, kissed his cheek, then left the library.

After she closed the door, she leaned against it for a moment and sighed. She definitely would do her best to help Harry find his wife. He had helped her many times and it was only right she return the favor.

She went to the parlor—no one was there—and played a little tune on the pianoforte. She wondered when she would next see Harry . . . in the past few years since she had grown up, he had not come when she called. Psyche frowned. Yes . . . it *had* started when she began to grow up. She had been used to Harry suddenly appearing in her chambers ever since she was a child and first discovered him. But these days he had gained a certain circumspection, and he appeared only in the more public rooms—the parlor, the library, or the drawing room.

She blushed. It was just as well he did—quite improper for him to appear in her bedroom, to be sure! It did not seem to mean much when she was a little girl, but now that she was grown up, it was quite a different matter.

"Psyche."

She started, and her fingers played a sour note, for Harry's voice had sounded just above her head. But her heart thumped more with joy than surprise, for when she turned to look at him, he smiled at her fondly, and she could not help thinking how much she so dearly loved her friend. She shook her head.

"Harry, for heaven's sake! I would think that startling me would have become quite tedious to you by now, for you have done it any number of times over the years." He was dressed in his chiton again, and his wings fluttered as he slowly descended from just a few feet above her. He obviously did not mean others to see him; otherwise he would have worn a gentleman's coat and trousers and dispensed with his wings. It was a good thing she had thought to close the door. She would not want anyone to overhear and think she was talking to the air.

He grinned. "But you startle so delightfully, Psyche, in a bounc—"

"Yes, I know! I bounce! You have said that many times. That is not at all flattering."

Harry looked her up and down, and if she had not known him to be married and devoted to his lost wife, she would have thought his gaze lingered on her in a most improper way, especially when his grin grew wider. "But I think it is very *attractive* when a lady bounces," he said. "How can that not be flattering?" He sat next to her on the pianoforte bench.

She blushed, and grew annoyed with herself. "That is neither here nor there—and you should not be talking in such a manner, for you are supposed to be looking for your wife, you know."

Immediately he sobered, and glanced away, a frustrated

and angry look flashing on his face. "You are quite right, of course."

Psyche felt sorry, for she knew he must be saddened by his loss, and she put her hand on his, squeezing it comfortingly. "I am so sorry, Harry. But I am quite glad you came this morning. I think we should talk of how we might go about finding her. Two heads are better than one, after all."

Harry sighed impatiently and rose from the bench. "I have looked the world over, and the only thing I can conclude is that she is somewhere here in England, for I am drawn here time and time again. This is where my dreams of her are strongest, but by the gods I cannot think where she might be!"

"Well, what does she look like?"

"I don't know!"

Psyche stared at him. "But she is your wife!"

Harry hunched a shoulder in clear irritation. "It has been more than a thousand years since I lost her. My memories have faded in that time. She has shape-changed so often, I cannot be sure what she looks like."

"Shape-changed?"

"She was made an immortal, though she was born a mortal, and we are able to change our shape whenever we wish. I don't do it much, for I like my own shape well enough, but she found it amusing and did it often."

"Oh!" Psyche said. "What did she change into?"

Harry sighed. "When she first left, I thought I saw a stone that reminded me of her, and then a mirror, a butterfly—she loved butterflies, I remember."

Psyche thought it *would* be very amusing to be able to turn into different things, but she did not say so, and brought her attention back to Harry.

"But in the last century or so, she has taken human form." He closed his eyes tightly then opened them, and she shivered, for there was that forlorn look once again. "Indeed, I think perhaps she has become a mortal again in some way . . . the last I saw her, she was an old woman." He swallowed. "It was too late. She died before I could claim her."

"Oh, Harry!" Psyche cried, and took his hand in hers, held it tightly, and pressed it to her cheek. "I am so sorry!"

He looked down at her, and for one moment became very still. She could not look away, for it seemed his eyes searched deeply into hers. Then he sighed, and his hand slipped slowly across her cheek, almost a caress, then fell away.

It was as if a spell had broken, and Psyche stepped away hastily, feeling awkward. She had never felt the need to step away quickly before. She put her hands behind her.

"If she did . . . die, Harry, how do you know she is alive now?"

There was a short pause, and Psyche looked up to find him staring at her. He shook his head in a puzzled, dismissing manner. "Though she might now be mortal, I can still sense her occasionally. More than that, she is my very soul. I would *know*."

His voice was full of longing, and Psyche had to turn away, lest he see the pain and envy that must show on her face. She would *not* be jealous! Indeed, she remembered she would ask him to help her find a husband, too. She drew in a deep breath and let it out again, but did not feel much better. It was not as if she would be alone for the rest of her life. She would be married, too, just as Harry was.

She turned back to him and made herself smile. "I am glad," she said, and if there was more than the necessary emphasis on the word "glad" she could not help it. "Is she in mortal form this time, too?"

"I am fairly certain of it," Harry replied. "Every time I've glimpsed her in the last three hundred years, she seems to have been so."

"Well, how do you recognize her, then?"

Harry sighed impatiently. "I just *do*!"

"That is not of much use to me!"

"I can't help that," Harry said staring stubbornly at her. He sighed again. "When I think I see who she might be, the sensation sometimes disappears. The last time . . ." A miserable look came into his eyes. "The last time I held her and she looked at me, I swear we both knew, as if she recognized me, too. Too late, of course."

Psyche felt an odd, troubled feeling, as if there were something important she should know, but could not quite remember. "Could it be that she does not remember you, either?" she said slowly. That was not quite it, but it was a good question, she thought.

Harry frowned, clearly offended. "No. Impossible."

Psyche rolled her eyes heavenward and sighed. "How vain you are! I daresay if you can forget, she can, also."

His frown grew deeper. "Would you?"

"Of course not! I *never* would!" she said instantly.

"See?" he said, his voice triumphant, and he grinned.

"Oh, for heaven's sake!" she cried. "I would not forget because my life is short. I daresay an immortal might forget because a great deal of time has gone by and who knows how long one's memory of a face might last?"

Harry gazed at her, troubled at last. ""Perhaps there might be something in what you say . . . I don't remember everyone I have encountered." His smile turned wry. "You have had a very humbling effect on me, Psyche. First you make me admit my mistakes—not that I make many—and now you make me think it is possible for my wife to forget me."

"Perhaps she did not mean to forget, Harry," she said comfortingly. "Besides, you did say that she remembered you the last time. I am sure she will again. You need only find her and surely she will recognize you." She frowned. "But how to find her? You say that your sense she is near is strongest in England and in London. Can you be more specific than that?"

Harry pursed his lips in thought. "There have been a few times at different balls that I thought I felt her presence."

"That should make it easier," Psyche said. "If she has been present at a ball, then it may be she is someone with whom we are acquainted. You must attend as many balls as possible. When the Season is over, you may come to Turnbridge Wells and we will have a house party and you may meet ladies there as well."

A frustrated look came over Harry's face. "I cannot—" But then he stopped, and his chin took on a mulish angle. "I don't care what they say."

" 'They'?" Psyche asked.

"The goddesses," Harry said shortly, and a wild and angry look came into his eyes. "I have looked the world over for hundreds and hundreds of years and have a little time left. I have as good a chance to find her going to balls as anywhere else." He caught Psyche's hand in his and looked at her earnestly. "You have been my best friend, so I will say honestly I do not know what will happen to me if I do not find my wife. But if I must fade away, I wish to spend at least some of the time I have left with you."

Psyche swallowed and shook her head. "No, no, Harry, you must not fade away, I won't have it! We *shall* find your wife, and . . . and I will always be your friend." She closed her eyes for a moment, then gazed at him again. "But I must say, I shall be glad . . . very glad . . . if you spend a little of your time with me."

Harry gazed at her, smiling gently. "My dear friend," he murmured, and touched her cheek with his finger.

She could not help staring at him, and he stood suddenly still, his smile fading. The silence between them grew long, and finally Psyche forced herself to look away. She felt awkward again, and gave herself a mental shake. This was *not* the time to have such stupid feelings, and she would make herself as cheerful as possible.

"I am going to Almack's this Wednesday. It might be a good place to start." She heard him sigh and step back from her.

"Yes," he said. "I suppose so."

A thought made her chuckle. "I could even let it about that you are looking for a wife. That should bring you much attention from every widow, spinster, young lady, and matchmaking mama for miles around, and you will have plenty of ladies to look over."

"Gods!" Harry shuddered. "I think not."

Psyche laughed. "You deserve it, you know, for all the trouble you caused in Almack's once."

"I?" Harry said indignantly. "I caused no trouble. It was your bad aim that started it all. Besides, it may have produced some consternation at the time, but I assure you Lady Jersey was quite pleased with the result."

"I am sure she was, but it was highly improper at the time, you know. You need not worry that some lady would become overly attached to you. You can bring your love darts and cause her to fall in love with someone else, after all."

Harry nodded. "There is that."

"I could help—my aim is *much* better now, truly!"

"No!"

"It is so better!"

Harry grimaced. "Not that. We quarreled afterwards and . . . I don't want us to quarrel this time."

"I won't, I promise," Psyche said. "Besides, you tricked me into shooting the darts. That was what made me angry."

"I?" Harry put his hand over his heart, his expression incredulous. "I did no such thing. If I recall correctly, you insisted on using the darts—begged, in fact."

"I did not!" Psyche cried. "You implied I couldn't shoot them at all, and you *knew* that would make me want to do it, and I am sure you planned all along that I should throw the darts and hit the wrong people, all for your own amusement!"

Harry raised his brows and frowned. "Even if I did, you should not have lost your temper. If you had not, you would not have insisted on throwing the darts."

Psyche could not help feeling guilty, for it was true that she had a hasty temper, but her irritation grew stronger and she replied, "It does *not* excuse you from provoking and manipulating me, however. Heavens! If *that* is how you treated your wife, I am not at all surprised that she left you."

Instantly she regretted her words and bit hard on her lower lip; her words were inexcusable. The angry and despairing look on his face increased her feeling of guilt; she had let her temper get the best of her again. A dangerous glow began to form around him. and she could not look at him out of shame.

"You are right, of course." Psyche looked up at him to see the glow was gone, and that his wings drooped. "It was because we had quarreled that she had left. And here I am, quarreling still, when I said I would not."

Deep remorse forced Psyche to speak. "Oh, no! My temper—I know it is bad—I should not have let it get the better of me."

"It would not if I did not provoke you so," Harry said with a rueful smile. "We are a pair, are we not? How we remained friends when we have quarreled through the years, I don't know."

"I suppose . . . I suppose that is why we are friends," Psyche said. "Quarrels are nothing compared to what I—what we—that is, our friendship." She turned slightly away from him, hoping her face was in shadow, for she was blushing again.

There was a brief silence, and when she turned to him again, he was looking at her curiously.

"Is there something amiss?" she asked.

He shook his head slowly. "No . . . nothing is amiss. I thought for a moment . . . no."

"What is it?"

"Nothing," he said, and shrugged. "For a moment I thought there was a familiar presence—but not, I think, my wife." He stood up and stretched. "I suppose you are right; I should begin my search at Almack's, although . . . are you going to Lady Sandringham's masquerade ball tonight? Her son, the Honorable Freddy, has invited me, no doubt because he has a sister just come out this year." He grinned. "Perhaps I will let you toss some darts at her and have her fall in love with someone."

"Oh, please do! I shall show you I am much improved at throwing them."

"I'll be glad to see it," Harry replied promptly. "If you've improved, then it will be interesting to see who you think would be good matches." He began to glow and his form faded a little, but his mischievous grin was still clear. "And if you haven't," he continued, "then I shall be given a great deal of amusement once again."

"Harry!" Psyche exclaimed indignantly.

But it was too late for argument, for he had become a formless glow that flew quickly out the drawing room window. Psyche let out an exasperated breath. How irritating he could be! It was a wonder she agreed to help him at all; no doubt he felt not one bit of gratitude. But that was the way with Greek gods; they were quite arrogant, and seemed to believe mortals were still ignorant shepherds instead of the sophisticated beings they had become.

Yet, Harry had admitted to his mistakes in the last few years . . . and yes, he had even admitted he had been provoking. He was not as insufferable as he'd been when she first met him, but had improved. He was still a terrible tease, but she did not mind that much. Truth to tell, she did not mind even his arrogance, now that the possibility of his loss was so great.

She drew in a determined breath. No, she would not let her thoughts go down that road again. In fact, she would not wait until Almack's on Wednesday, but would start at Lady Sandringham's ball tonight. She looked at the mantelpiece clock. It was just past noon. There were a few things she needed to get done before the ball, and she might as well start now. She allowed herself one more sigh, and with a firm step, left the drawing room.

When the door to the drawing room closed, a silvery glow formed around the mantelpiece clock and it began to shift and move. Liquid light flowed from the mantelpiece onto the floor, and slowly it took shape.

Artemis, Goddess of the Hunt and the Wildwood, stood in the Hathaways' drawing room, and frowned as she gazed from the door through which Psyche had gone to the window through which Eros had disappeared. What she had heard, in her opinion, boded ill for the gods. Instead of finding his wife as he should, her cousin was indulging in frivolities—in London of all places! It was a city, and nothing good came of cities. The forests and woods were preferable—full of innocent animals, not stupid, distracting humans. Eros would bear watching, and it was clear where Artemis's duty lay, as distasteful as it was.

Eros and that Hathaway girl would be at a masquerade ball—Lady Sandringham's, she recalled. Very well! She would go there, and stop Eros from being so foolish.

Her form shimmered once more and with a long leap through the window, she disappeared in a flash of silvery light.

Chapter 3

Psyche watched her maid's reflection in the mirror affix the butterfly wings to her fairy costume. The ensemble looked very fine. She had designed it herself; the wings were painted India silk stretched over thin, light wires, and were attached to straps that went over her shoulders and crossed between and under her breasts, then tied at her back. She wiggled her shoulders and nodded in satisfaction. They did not shift at all, and were more comfortable than she thought they'd be.

It suddenly occurred to her that Harry had not said what his disguise would be at Lady Sandringham's masquerade ball. She frowned. How was she to find him and speak to him if she did not know what he was wearing?

"Is anything wrong, miss?" her maid asked.

"What? Oh no, you have done very well, thank you." Psyche smiled at the girl and dismissed her. She looked into the mirror again and gazed, frowning, at her hair—well, she supposed that if she could not find Harry, he would no doubt find her, for very few people had hair as red as her own. She sighed. At least there was one useful thing about having red hair: one could be easily identified. Unfortunately, one usually did not want to be identified at a masquerade ball.

She shrugged, and her wings fluttered behind her, which made her smile. Really, she had done quite well in designing her costume. It had been enjoyable making it up; She loved needlework of any kind and preferred making her own costumes. If one could not hide one's identity, at least one could be admired for one's workmanship. Psyche held up her mask and looked through it—yes, she even looked just a little mysterious in it, which was just as satisfying as having created a pleasing costume.

She waited only a few minutes in the drawing room. Her sister Cassandra, Lady Blytheland, was always quite prompt. When Lady Hathaway tried to pass off as insignificant a clearly painful headache, Psyche had stated then and there that she would not go to the masquerade ball, but that had only made her mother even more determined to go. Fortunately, Cassandra had called on them and had volunteered to escort Psyche, and it was with clear relief that Lady Hathaway had retired to her bed again.

"Psyche how charming you look! I must say I had my doubts about the costume, but you have done quite well, very well!"

"*Fond* sister!" Psyche said, and hugged her. She gazed at Cassandra and cocked her head, trying to think of whom her sister's costume reminded her. She was dressed as a Greek lady with a harp, and had to be one of the Muses, for she could not think of any of the other goddesses who had a fondness for music. She sighed. She wished she could look as beautiful as Cassandra.

"Euterpe, the Muse of Music," Cassandra said in response to her look, and she shook her head, smiling. "For the daughter of a classical scholar, you do not remember the myths very well."

"It's horrid of me, isn't it?" Psyche replied cheerfully. "I am afraid I have no talent for such things. It's a good thing *you* did, for at least Papa has had one offspring to whom he could pass on his knowledge." She motioned to the maid who had arrived with her cloak. "Do be careful, Betty—I don't wish my wings to be crushed."

"Hmm," Cassandra murmured.

"Besides, you know my talents lie elsewhere. I dance fairly well—"

Cassandra pursed her lips disapprovingly, and Psyche grinned, knowing her sister thought dancing a frivolous thing to claim as an accomplishment, and she could not help teasing her by mentioning it.

"—and there is the novel I am writing." She felt the maid carefully draping the cloak over her wings.

"A Gothic novel," Cassandra said, her voice still holding a faint disapproval, but then her expression became interested. "How is it progressing?"

"Very well, I believe, although I am afraid it becomes a little overwrought at times." The cloak was now tied under Psyche's chin, and she and Cassandra left the drawing room for the coach outside.

They talked of Psyche's novel and then of Cassandra's charities as the carriage rumbled to their destination, and soon the conversation came around to heroes and then, somehow, to the guests who might be at the ball.

"I suppose Mr. D'Amant will be there?" Cassandra asked, a hesitant note in her voice.

"Mama has been speaking to you of him, hasn't she?" Psyche asked. "I think you know it would never do."

Cassandra gave a brief grimace, showing that she knew very well what Psyche meant. She patted Psyche's hand. "I know and I am very sorry, love. If he were not who he is—"

"A god," Psyche said flatly. "And he is only a friend, after all, so I wish Mama would stop insinuating things."

"Yes, well, er, yes." Cassandra shifted uncomfortably on her seat. "How odd it is to have one among us," she said. "I never would have thought it if I hadn't seen him myself—wings and all—so many years ago."

"He is married, too," Psyche said.

Cassandra shot a keen glance at her sister. "I thought he might be."

"You knew?" Psyche stared at her.

"I know the stories," Cassandra said simply. "I thought there was the possibility he had a wife."

"He does not have his wife now," Psyche said. "He has been looking for her for about a thousand years . . . and I am helping him find her."

Cassandra looked at her. "You are in love with him, are you not?"

Psyche glanced down at her lap, then shrugged. "Don't be silly. We are just friends." Her sister gazed at her for a long, thoughtful moment, provoking Psyche to exclaim, "For goodness' sake, I have known him since I was a child—he seems more like a brother to me than anything else!"

"More than a thousand years is a very long time," Cassandra said after a brief, uncomfortable silence, and frowned. "I think after seven years of abandonment a man may claim his wife dead."

"She did die," Psyche said, and despised herself for feeling just a little hopeful.

"Well then, he is a widower!" Cassandra said triumphantly. "I remember the marriage vows said 'till death do you part' and if she died, then they are no longer married." She frowned again. "Indeed, if she has died, I cannot see why is is looking for her. Perhaps he is joking. He seems to be the sort who might."

"No, I am sure he is not. He *is* still looking for her."

"That makes no sense whatsoever!"

Psyche cocked her head, thinking. "I don't pretend to understand all of it, but it appears she shape-changes."

Cassandra gave a disbelieving if unladylike snort. "Shape-change or not, if one dies, one stays dead. It would not be death, otherwise."

Psyche shook her head. "But even so, he is a god, and such a union would be quite ineligible. Any ideas Mama might have put in your head about either of us being romantically in love are utter nonsense."

"It has been done before, if I recall the myths correctly," her sister said.

Psyche gave her a skeptical look. "In England?"

Cassandra sighed. "*Not* in England."

"And not among the *ton*. I cannot think even Lady Sefton would approve, for all her kindheartedness. And can you imagine what Mrs. Drummond-Burrell would say about it?"

Her sister shuddered. "*Not* proper. And 'quite out of the

common way,' she would say, and in *that* tone—you know, the one she used with Sally Cantrell when she ran off with Lord Worthley."

"There, you see?" Psyche said, oddly wishing that she had not argued so rationally. "The best thing I can do is remain his friend and help him find his wife. Perhaps I can even ask him to make a match for me, so that I may find a husband."

"Is that what you want?"

Psyche shrugged, took in a resolute breath, and let it out again. "It's what I must do."

Cassandra said nothing, but took her hand in a comforting grasp, and held it until they arrived at Lady Sandringham's house at last.

I *will* enjoy what I can, Psyche told herself as the footman took her cloak and as she entered the ballroom. There is no use feeling sorry for myself. She smiled at Cassandra, who gave her a reassuring squeeze on her shoulder. Did she not have the best sister in the world? And did she not have a good family and good friends? Certainly there were people so much less fortunate than herself, and she should remember that.

She felt a little better, and danced as much as possible until at last she grew breathless and thirsty. She returned to Cassandra's side and was just about to suggest finding refreshment, when she looked up at Cassandra's gasp and saw her sister's face pale.

"What is it?" she asked. She turned, and for the first time in her life she felt faint.

It was Harry. Though he wore a mask that covered half his face, there was no mistaking him. His hair blazed in golden waves in the candlelight, his firm and stubborn chin was raised in a familiar tilt, and his lips were the same finely sculpted shape she'd known for most of her life. She knew the chiton he wore too well, as well as the wings, the familiar bow and quiver of arrows he had slung over one shoulder. She would have thought he had decided to come to the ball invisible—except it was all too clear he was very visible, if Cassandra's open mouth and the gasps of various ladies were any indication.

She'd grown used to his mode of dress throughout the years and as a result had never thought it shocking, but she now knew it was quite shocking indeed. Where other gentlemen's arms were covered in cloth, Harry's arms were bare, showing every athletic muscle from shoulder to wrist. Where most gentlemen's necks were covered up to their ears, Harry's was not, the chiton draping low enough to show a broad and solid chest.

Psyche's eyes drifted lower and she blushed as she never had before. Harry's chiton only came down to his knees—she had always know it had, of course! But she could not help seeing that his legs were also bare and muscular. Heavens, why had she not noticed it before? Hastily she averted her eyes and met Cassandra's accusing stare.

"I knew *nothing* about it, Cassandra!" Psyche whispered frantically. "Oh, how *dare* he! I hope he will not cause a scandal." She groaned and looked distractedly about her. "Oh, dear, he has recognized me and is approaching. What shall I do? How dreadful Lady Sandringham did not think to decorate the room with heavy draperies! There is absolutely no place to hide. Perhaps no one will recognize him, and oh, I hope no one laughs at his clothes, for he will become angry, and I do not know what he will do if someone were to offend him."

"Little chance of that," Cassandra said dryly.

It was quite true. Harry wore his costume naturally, totally at ease, as if he wore it all the time—which of course he did. The guests parted before him as if he were the Prince Regent himself, and if anyone thought of scandal, it was not apparent on the awestruck or admiring faces in the crowd.

Psyche rolled her eyes. Of course they would accept his outrageousness. He was completely shameless, and showed not one bit of self-consciousness or guilt; if he had, they would have turned their backs on him, and his reputation would have been shredded between the teeth of every gossip. She watched as a dowager brought a lorgnette to her eyes. The lady gasped, but Harry merely bowed in a very elegant manner before her and kissed her hand, causing the woman to blush and smile, and flutter her fan like a young girl. Psyche's earlier alarm turned to disapproval. How very vain he was, to be sure!

At last he bowed before them. "Lady Blytheland, Miss Hathaway." When he rose, he gazed at Psyche and grew pale. "Why are you wearing that costume? Where did you get it?"

"You have no cause to question me on my costume!" Psyche whispered indignantly. "Not when you are so scandalously clothed. Why are you not wearing a proper costume?"

Herry lifted his chin and looked down his nose at her and Psyche's temper rose. "Of course I am wearing a costume," he said. "I have a mask, and obviously I have come dressed as the god of love."

"But you *are* the god of love! How can being yourself be a costume?"

He grinned widely. "You are free to tell everyone in this room the truth, of course."

"Oh, you are impossible! You know very well that I can do no such thing. Cassandra, tell him!"

Cassandra broke out laughing. "I am afraid I cannot, Psyche, for you *are* perfectly free to tell the truth . . . but whether you will be believed is another thing entirely."

"Traitor!"

"Not I!" Cassandra said. "Indeed, I believe it is the perfect costume, for it suits him. No one would believe he is anything but Mr. D'Amant—should he stay for the unmasking. I believe even Lady Cowper and Lady Jersey are looking more amused than anything else."

"You are as wise as you are beautiful, Lady Blytheland," Harry said, and bowed over her hand. He cast a sly look at Psyche. "May I have this dance, my lady?" he asked Cassandra.

She gazed at Harry for a long moment, then smiled ironically. "Depending on my friendship with Lady Cowper, are you, Mr. D'Amant? Clever. And I suppose you wish me to speak with her directly after our dance, so that you may enter into a conversation with her?"

Harry widened his eyes innocently. "I? Have I said such a thing?"

"No, but I am sure you would have come round to it, Harry, I know you would have!" Psyche said instantly.

Cassandra laid her hand upon Psyche's arm. "Really, Psyche, it probably would quiet any gossip later on." She turned to Harry. "No thanks to you, Mr. D'Amant," she said severely.

Harry heaved a great sigh and looked despondent.

"Incorrigible." Cassandra shook her head. "No wonder you are so inclined to argue with him, Psyche." Harry only grinned, and Psyche's hand itched to slap him. "Come, Mr. D'Amant. The dance is about to begin." He took Cassandra's hand and led her out onto the dance floor.

"Your Mr. D'Amant has captured quite a bit of attention," said a familiar voice.

Psyche looked up at the masked and dominoed figure beside her and smiled. "Lord Blythe—Paul, I mean. I am glad you are here! Cassandra did not tell me you were coming to the ball."

"She did not know I was coming, because I didn't think I would." His smile widened. "The idea of my wife dancing with everyone except myself did not set well with me, so I came to claim a few for myself." He glanced at his wife dancing with Harry. "A remarkable costume. One wonders how the wings stay attached."

"Oh . . . w-well, Mr. D'Amant has always been very clever," Psyche stammered. Heavens, Cassandra never said whether she had told her husband about Harry. A change of subject was definitely in order. "And he is not 'my Mr. D'Amant,'" she said, frowning.

"No?" Lord Blytheland said politely and raised his brows.

"My, how I long to dance!" She smiled sweetly at him. "I cannot imagine why anyone would wish to stand and converse when there is such lively music playing."

Lord Blytheland's lips twitched upward. "A set-down! Very well. Shall I dance with you, or shall I ask—oh, my dear friend Eldon to do so?"

"You must know that it is not the thing to dance with one's brother-in-law when there are so many eligible gentlemen about. I cannot let anyone think I am desperate, you know."

"In other words, you want me to go away." Lord Blytheland grinned and put his hand over his heart. "You have wounded me, sister-in-law. As you wish; I shall bring the lamb to the slaugh—that is, I shall hint Eldon your way."

"Odious!" Psyche said, but could not help giggling. There *was* something lamblike about Lord Eldon. It was not his appearance, for he was quite tall and good-looking, and he dressed impeccably, for he was an acknowledged Pink of the *Ton*. He was well mannered and amiable, and the bow he made over Psyche's hand as he asked her for a dance was exquisitely elegant.

Perhaps it was the ruminative air he had about him, as if at any moment he would crop grass, that made Lord Eldon seem rather sheeplike. Psyche liked him very well, and though he had formed part of her circle of suitors at one point, she was quite sure he had done so because at the time it was considered fashionable. Regardless, it was pleasant to have a friend who danced well and conversed amusingly.

He looked her over critically and nodded. "Very well done; the colors suit you, and the wings are quite clever."

"Why, thank you, my lord," Psyche replied. "I see however that you only wear a mask and domino."

"'Only'?" Even with his mask, Lord Eldon looked pained. "My dear Miss Hathaway, this ensemble was made by Weston. One does not apply the word 'only' to Weston's tailoring."

Psyche chuckled. "I stand corrected," she said. Her former irritation fled, and she could even smile when she saw Harry conversing with Lady Cowper and Lady Jersey, winding both around his little finger.

When the dance ended, they were very close to where

Harry was standing after speaking to Lady Cowper and Lady Jersey. Harry glanced up and saw Psyche immediately; he stepped toward her, clearly intending to speak with her.

And then there was a sudden hush from their corner, near the entrance of the ballroom. Psyche looked up and took in a quick breath, and so, it seemed, did many of the other guests—male, mostly, she noted.

The lady was tall, with black hair and flashing dark eyes. On her head was a coronet of silver, with a crescent moon made of mother-of-pearl set in the center of it. She wore no mask; it would have been a shame to have covered such wild beauty, for her skin was pearl-colored, her cheeks lightly touched with pink, and her perfectly formed lips were the color of coral.

Her dress—a chiton like Harry's—was so scandalously short as to show her ankles and the lower part of her calf, her arms were as bare as Harry's, and below her generous bosom her slim waist was cinched in with a silver stomacher. On her back was a quiver of arrows, and she carried a long silver bow, and her feet were encased in silver sandals.

A long breath was released from beside Psyche and she turned to see Lord Eldon, mouth agape, fumbling with his quizzing glass before he put it up to his eye. "By Jove!" he murmured, and a dreamy smile formed on his face.

"No," came Harry's voice to the other side of Psyche. "Diana." Psyche looked up at him. His mouth was grim and his eyes furious. "Or, more accurately, Artemis."

Chapter 4

Psyche watched Artemis searching the ballroom, ignoring the guests around her with barely concealed disdain. Anxious, Psyche touched Harry's arm. "Is it really—"

"Artemis," he said shortly. "A cousin of sorts."

His cousin did not look as if she was in a pleasant mood. Psyche remembered some stories about Artemis, and wondered if she might turn anyone into a deer. How awkward it would be! She had often thought it might be enjoyable to run as fast as a deer, but she remembered the goddess had sent wild beasts after such transformations, and she was certain being savaged in such a way would be most upsetting, especially at a ball. She gazed at Harry, and saw him look quickly about him, as if for escape.

"Don't you *dare* leave, Harry!" she said in a low, fierce whisper.

"You need not worry. If I leave, I shall make sure to take you with me."

"That is *not* what I meant!"

He smiled crookedly, then shrugged. "It is too late now." He looked at the goddess coming toward them and his jaw hardened. "She has no business here; she belongs in the wildwood." Psyche could see a faint angry shimmer about him. "So be it," he said, just under his breath. "If she wishes to interfere in another god's realm, then she will learn what it means when she interferes with mine."

Psyche grew alarmed, and whispered fiercely, "Harry, I do not think—"

"There you are!" Artemis said, rudely ignoring Psyche

and Lord Eldon. "You neglect your duties, cousin. I suggest you leave this place and attend to them."

For one moment it seemed Harry's smile turned vengeful, but it was quickly gone—and Psyche did not know how it happened, but it seemed his nature changed suddenly, and he was not her Harry but someone else in Harry's clothing. Instead of his usual direct and mischievous gaze, his eyelids lowered as if he was about to fall asleep, and his chin lifted so that his nose was in the air. He shifted his shoulders back and his whole demeanor spoke of bored and elegant insolence.

Harry was acting unwisely, she thought, for an angry glint came into Artemis's eyes and a dangerous silvery light seemed to glow around her. Psyche glanced at Lord Eldon, but other than a quick upward twitch of his lips, he seemed not to notice anything unusual. He maintained an air of polite interest, and only occasionally did his gaze stray toward Artemis before he dragged it reluctantly away.

Harry chuckled, a sound so odiously indulgent that Psyche would not have blamed Artemis if she had wished to slap him. He glanced at both Psyche and Lord Eldon and smiled pleasantly. "You must excuse my cousin, Miss Hathaway, Lord Eldon. She is somewhat naive of town ways and very duty bound." His smile was amused. "As if I were not engaging in business tomorrow, at a most unpleasantly early hour, as well!" He bowed toward Lord Eldon. "Lord Eldon, Miss Hathaway, may I present Miss Diana"—he glanced at the crescent moon on Artemis's headdress—"Knightly. Miss Knightly, Lord Eldon and Miss Hathaway."

Artemis appeared taken aback. "I—I don't—"

"Don't have your mask, I see," Harry said quickly. "How unfortunate. Did you lose it?"

Lord Eldon stepped forward; his mask was already off. "So very pleased to meet you, ma'am," he said, and bowed over her hand in an almost reverent manner. "As much as it would pain me to hide such beauty, it would pain me more to know your pleasure in tonight's festivities would be diminished without a mask." He lifted her hand to his lips briefly, and offered his mask as if it were a rare and precious gift.

Psyche gazed at him, surprised. Lord Eldon was not known as a ladies' man; they sought him out for his opinion on fashion rather than for anything amorous. He was, as he had once told his friend and Psyche's brother-in-law Lord Blytheland, not much in the petticoat line. His conversation was chatty or terse, depending on how well he knew a person, and though he had great address and exquisite manners, Psyche had always suspected these attributes hid an innate shyness.

And yet, here he was speaking more eloquently than she had ever heard him speak, and gazing at Artemis as if she were a goddess—which she was, of course, but Lord Eldon could not know that. Psyche cast a suspicious glance at Harry, but he only shook his head slightly and looked extremely innocent, which made her even more suspicious than ever.

Artemis's startled gaze softened a little at Lord Eldon's words, and she gave a haughty nod. "Your gift is accepted, mortal one." She held the mask gingerly, and looked uncertain, as if she did not know what to do with it.

"Allow me," Harry said, and deftly plucked the mask from her hand and began to tie it upon her head.

"By Zeus, Eros, you go too far!" Artemis exclaimed, and her hands rose up to snatch away the mask. She gave a small painful gasp, and her eyes widened. "No!" Her voice came out in a groan, and she paled, moon-white.

"Tsk, tsk." Lord Eldon shook his head. "Thought you had more address than that, D'Amant," he said. He turned to Artemis and bowed elegantly. "If you would allow me, fair lady—?" He held out his hand and Harry's smile turned smug as he gave the mask to Lord Eldon, for the goddess now stared at his lordship as if she had found something long lost and dear. Where she had been pale as the moon, her face was now delicately flushed, and her lips parted with a quick half-sobbing breath.

Artemis had indeed found something long lost, and agony

overcame her in that moment: Eros had taken his revenge and pierced her with one of his darts, just as she lifted her eyes and looked upon Lord Eldon's handsome face. Returned again were all the emotions she had banished upon Orion's death: tenderness, love, a liquid softening of her body . . . and grief.

Anger, too, for she knew Eros had chosen to make her fall in love with a man who was clearly the antithesis of all she cared for: a man of the town, a man of manners and words instead of action. One who, no doubt, took more care over his clothes than his horses—if he dared dirty himself by riding horses at all. She did not know what to do, and looked helplessly at the man before her. The room, the walls, seemed to close in upon her. She did not belong in a town, she belonged in the open air of the countryside and the woods, not in a roomful of people, not here, falling in love with a type of man she despised.

"I don't—I want—I cannot stay here," she said, and hated the note of desperation in her voice. She glanced at Eros, but his eyes were merciless; he would not forgive her interference, not for a while at least.

A concerned look crossed Lord Eldon's face. "Are you ill? Do you wish to retire to another room?"

She could feel some of her goddess strength leave her, and she almost wept at the kindness in the man's voice. Kindness. She was a goddess, and needed no kindness from anyone, much less a mortal. But the concern in his voice melted her to her bones, and she craved the sound of it again. Gods. No, she would not. She could not be falling in love with him.

But the sound of the crowded room and the cold lifeless walls began to press upon her. "Out," she whispered, and despised sounding so weak. "Air. I need to be outside."

The look in Lord Eldon's eyes became a little alarmed. He took her by her elbow and after a brief bow in Eros's and Miss Hathaway's he excused himself and led her through the crowd before them. "You are ill," he said softly. "Room's dashed too warm, is what it is." He thrust open the

windowed doors that led out onto a balcony overlooking a
small garden. Artemis drew in a deep breath and the scent of
new-budded shrubs and flowers came to her. She could feel
the faint beams of the crescent moon enter her flesh, and her
strength returned a little, but she knew she could not stay in
the city for long. Why she thought she could have influenced Eros in any way, she did not know—he was one of the
few gods who could affect even the oldest and most powerful of gods, for he ruled over love, and that was a power not
limited to any one place, as hers was.

"I am a fool," she said. She found her hand taken and patted kindly, if a little awkwardly.

"No, no, I assure you, Miss Knightly," Lord Eldon said.
"The air—too warm. Forgot your mask. Anyone might do
that. Have done it myself."

She felt comforted in spite of herself, but she pulled her
hand away. It was the love dart that weakened her so, and
the fact that she was not in her natural realm. She lifted her
chin. "I thought Eros was not doing as he ought—and he
still is not. He is neglecting his duty."

Lord Eldon frowned for a moment, then his face cleared.
"Eros? Oh! Harry D'Amant. Clever costume, eh? Devil take
me if I can see how he attached those wings—looked dashed
real, by Jove! I shall have to ask him who his tailor is. Devilish fine dresser is D'Amant—a bit off on his waistcoats,
and his neckcloth could be tied with more precision, but I
have never seen him stint on his coats or his boots."

Artemis stared at him, dismayed, and mentally cursed
Eros. She would *not* be in love with such a fop as Lord
Eldon. She was Artemis, the Goddess of the Moon and the
Forests. She would have a man of action if anything, and
certainly not a mortal. She wished not to have anything to do
with them, especially not a man like Lord Eldon, even if he
was handsome and treated her as the goddess she truly was.
She did not need the concern that showed in his eyes, and
especially not his kindness.

Kindness again. Her throat closed at the thought. No! She
had no need for it, for she was a powerful goddess . . . Ah, but

she had not seen such a thing from anyone since . . . Orion. He who loved her, who died in her arms, accidentally shot through the heart by her own arrow. Her own had frozen in that moment, and she had vowed she would never love again, for love caused only agony. She had been successful; so much so that she was called chaste and virgin, for no man had touched her from that time on.

But Eros had caused her to love again, and to this unworthy successor to her long-dead lover, this Lord Eldon, who was surely not even half the man Orion was. Ah, gods, she could not love him! She was as cold as the moon; she had made herself so.

"I . . . I need to leave," she said suddenly. She could not stay here, not so close to this man. The hand he had touched tingled, and it made her wish he would touch her again.

"Of course," he replied politely, then hesitated. "May I call on you tomorrow, to see if you are recovered?"

He had stepped closer to her, and she felt his breath on her cheek. She could not look at him. If she did, he would be close enough to kiss. She *must* leave! "Please—" was all she could say, and she fled the balcony, barely managing to cast the shadow of invisibility over her as she ran through the ballroom and out of the house.

"Harry," Psyche said fiercely as she watched Artemis and Lord Eldon go to the balcony. "I need to *speak* to you!"

"You *are* speaking to me," Harry said, a very self-satisfied smile on his face. "Shall we dance?"

Psyche let loose an exasperated breath. "The next dance is a country dance, and we shall be separated too much for a decent conversation. I wish to speak to you where there is no chance anyone will hear, somewhere private."

"Tut, tut," he said, raising his eyebrows. "So important that you are willing to risk your reputation by being alone with me, hmm?"

Psyche blushed, suddenly conscious again of his costume, or rather, relative lack of one, and was annoyed at herself. The way he dressed had not mattered to her before;

there should be no reason why it should matter to her now. She pressed her lips together in what she hoped was a no-nonsense way.

"You know that is ridiculous. I shall go first to the library here, and I expect it will be empty since Lady Sandringham's guests are not at all bookish except for Cassandra, and she is dancing with Paul. You will follow after you have danced with . . . oh, there is Miss Cody. I shall introduce you to her. After your dance has finished, you will come to the library, where, if we are at all disturbed, you shall become invisible, so it will seem I am quite alone." It was a good plan, and she was sure he could not object to it. "You need to dance with more ladies, you know. How else will you be able to determine if one of them is your wife?" She was pleased with herself for speaking with a good deal of firmness.

Harry looked at her for a long moment, his lips turned down in a discontented line. Then he shrugged and nodded. "Very well," he said.

She led the way toward Miss Cody, a very pretty blond girl, just out for her first Season, who blushed and stared with awe at Harry when Psyche introduced him, and who looked about to faint when he asked her to dance. When Harry cast a mischievous grin at Psyche, she did not know whether to laugh or be annoyed, for she knew he had exerted immense charm when he asked, just to provoke Miss Cody's reaction.

Psyche found Cassandra and let her know where she would be. Perhaps her feelings showed too much on her face, for her sister watched her for a moment before she said, "I assume you wish to talk to—"

"Yes," Psyche said, hurriedly. "It is nothing, really."

"The young woman—?"

Psyche grimaced. "His cousin."

Cassandra's eyes widened. "You don't mean—is she who I think she is? That is, it was not a costume?"

"*Not* a costume," Psyche replied.

"Oh, dear." Cassandra paused, then said, "Will you need any help? Perhaps I should come with you."

Psyche thought for a moment. "No, not at this time. It is only Harry, after all, and he has always treated me like a sister." An odd depression followed her words, but she squashed it firmly. "But I might ask you to help, later. Especially if Artemis may need to stay somewhere while she is in town."

"Stay?" Cassandra eyed her sister in alarm. "I don't know—I think I might—oh, dear."

Psyche gazed at her encouragingly. "Only think, Cassandra! She must know ancient Greek very well, and you may practice it with her so as to become more proficient in it."

"Well, I admit that is a very attractive prospect, but—"

"*Thank* you, dear, dear sister!" Psyche said, and smiled brightly at her. With a last grateful squeeze of the hand, she left Cassandra sputtering half-protests behind her.

Psyche found the library quickly. When she had been a girl, her father had come to Lord Sandringham's library to buy a rare copy of Sophocles, and he had taken Psyche along with him. The room was large, and well apportioned, and though darkly furnished, it also was warm; a fire had been lit in the fireplace and comfortable-looking chairs and sofas had been arranged around it. Though the ballroom and dancing had made her quite warm, the hallway had been cold and she settled herself on the sofa closest to the fireplace and extended her hands toward the fire.

She sighed. She was proud of herself for introducing Harry to Miss Cody, even though she could not help hoping the girl was not his wife in disguise. She knew Miss Cody was a very good sort of young lady, but somehow she did not seem quite worthy of Harry. Surely, someone less young and unsophisticated would be more suited to him.

Certainly someone with more common sense than Harry! She grimaced. Well, he did have it; he simply did not seem to think he needed to apply it. He was better now than he had been when he first decided to appear in society. Perhaps it was the way of the gods . . . certainly Artemis had not showed any common sense whatsoever when she entered the masquerade ball. Psyche wondered how the goddess had got admission into Lady Sandringham's ballroom, but reflected that as a goddess, Artemis could probably find some way of intimidating someone into compliance.

Psyche stared into the scarlet-and-yellow flames. *That* was a problem. How was she to explain Artemis's presence? It would be awkward if she were asked! Then there was Lord Eldon to think of . . . she was certain the besotted look in his eyes meant Harry had caused him to fall in love with the goddess, and that would never do! Harry might have been angry at Artemis, but he should not have involved such a good-hearted gentleman as Lord Eldon.

"Psyche."

She could not help letting out a squeak of surprise and starting quite violently at the sound of Harry's voice whispering in her ear. "Will you *stop* doing that?" she said indignantly. "And yes, I know you like to see me bounce, which is not at all flattering, for it implies an overall plumpness that I have tried very hard to keep to a minimum."

Harry opened his eyes innocently wide. "I never said you were plump overall, only plump in the right places."

Psyche's face grew hot, and she pressed her hands on her cheeks to cool them. "I wish you would not say such things!"

"You do not like me admiring the way you look?" Harry asked, and leaned back against the sofa, gazing at her contemplatively. "You never seemed to mind much before."

Psyche looked away from him, and her hands twisted together. "I was a child then . . . and it is different when one has grown up.

"Is it?" Was there a softer note in his voice? She glanced at him, but he only looked politely concerned.

"And you are married, after all, and an unmarried lady must not allow herself to be familiar with a married gentleman, or any gentleman for that matter, unless they are betrothed."

"Do you not wish to be my friend any longer?"

This time there was real hurt in his voice, and Psyche impulsively took his hand, holding it tightly. "Oh, no, no, you must not think that!" she said earnestly, gazing into his eyes. "I shall always be your friend. *Always!* That shall never, never change, Harry, no matter what happens."

His smile was warm, and clearly relieved. He lifted her hand to his lips. "I am glad. I do love you, Psyche, and I always will."

She stared at him with sudden confusion, and saw that except for a slight trembling of his wings, he had become very still.

"As . . . as a friend, of course," he said, and his voice sounded strained.

"Of course," she replied. She had embarrassed him—she should not have stared at him so, and made him think she felt more for him than she really did. "One may love one's dear friends. Have I not always said so, myself?"

There was silence for a few heartbeats.

"Have you?" he asked.

"Yes, of course, surely you must have heard me say it." She glanced away.

He released her hand—he had held it all this time, but she could not seem to move it from him—and she continued, "And how fortunate for you as well, for I shall be able to introduce you to many ladies, and perhaps among them you shall find your wife."

She raised her eyes to his, and found him gazing at her, as if searching for something in her expression. She put on a smile—a crooked one, she feared. "It was a good thing I learned matchmaking from you. Now I may help you find your wife." She closed her eyes for a moment. It would be best if she said it now, while she was talking of matchmaking. "And . . . I suppose it is time for me to think of getting a husband." She laughed wryly. "Certainly Mama has been after me about it for more than a few years now. Perhaps you could—" She must say it. It would prove she would be *happy* when Harry found his true love. "Do you think you could matchmake for me, as well?"

She dared look at him, and if the firelight had not shown otherwise, she would have thought him a statue, so still was he; his eyes looked more lost than she had ever seen them.

"You . . . you wish to be married?" He seemed to stumble over the words, as if they were foreign to his tongue. "Who is he?"

"I have not settled on anyone," she said carefully. "I thought I would, eventually. I have a fondness for children, and I do very well with them, or at least I do with Cassandra's." She smiled slightly. "Certainly Mama expects it."

"You wish me to help you find a husband?" There was a bewildered note in his voice, and he looked as if he thought the idea absurd or impossible, for his expression was one of surprise and consternation.

"Have I not said it?" She could not help replying a little sharply; surely she was not such an antidote that he believed her unmarriageable. "If you must know, I have had ten proposals of marriage so far, so it cannot be such an impossible task."

"Ten?" His brows rose, and there was such surprise in his voice that her sense of insult and irritation grew.

"It is not as if I were a hideous crone, after all!" she exclaimed. "Really, Harry, is it so impossible to think that gentlemen might find me even remotely marriageable?" She jumped up from the sofa and stared angrily at him, her fists on her hips. "I am twenty years of age—I have grown up! Have you not noticed it?"

A slow smile grew on his face. "Yes," he said, and she blushed, remembering his "bouncing" comments.

"Well then, if you have noticed it, is it not reasonable to assume other gentlemen have also?"

The grin disappeared and he stared steadily at her. "Do you like having other gentlemen notice?"

"I suppose if I wish to be married, then it would be a good thing for them to notice."

Harry frowned. "Who has proposed to you?"

Psyche lifted her chin. "I shall not tell you—and they are married now anyway, most of them, except for Lord Eldon."

"Eldon!" An angry look flashed across Harry's face.

"If I had accepted him, he would have made an admirable husband, for he is a very pleasant, good sort of gentleman."

"But you did not."

Psyche shrugged and smoothed out a fold of her dress. "I did not think we should suit . . . which brings me to the thing I want to say to you, Harry." She had been diverted from what she had come to the library to talk about, and she was relieved she remembered it now. "How dare you make Lord Eldon fall in love with Artemis! What did he do to you, after all?"

Harry stared at her stonily for a moment before he said, "I did not do anything to Lord Eldon." He rose from the sofa and went to the fireplace. He leaned his forehead against the mantelpiece and stared into the fire.

"How can you say that?" Psyche asked. "If ever there was a case of love at first sight, he has it. How else could it have happened? He had never shown such particular attention to any lady before this."

Harry turned his head at her words and his smile was ironic. "But enough so that he felt he must propose marriage to you."

"Nonsense! I was fashionable for a while—as strange as it may seem to you. You must know how attentive he is to fashion."

"Is *that* all?" Harry still smiled, but his voice lost its edge. "It must not have been a very strong affection, indeed, for he is clearly in love with Artemis now."

"Because of you, I am sure!" Psyche retorted.

"How little faith you have in your own kind! Must I always be the cause behind such an attraction? Sometimes one soul calls to another, and I know better than to stop such a thing."

Psyche groaned and leaned back against one end of the mantelpiece. She closed her eyes, trying to rein in her impatience. "Harry, it is totally ineligible. A goddess and a mortal? Impossible! How will they get along?"

"It has happened before."

She opened her eyes and stared into Harry's, close now, for he put his hand against the mantelpiece, so near her she could feel its warmth. His gaze drifted from her eyes to her lips. "Do you think it cannot happen? We have hands to touch, after all." His finger touched a curl of her hair that had fallen against her cheek. "Lips to kiss." His finger traced a line from her cheek to her lips, and gently feathered across them. "And hearts—" He paused, and his brows drew together.

Psyche drew in a short, trembling breath, watching him; she was unable to move or speak, for she felt very strange—at once frozen and full of melting heat. His finger had traced a shimmering line along her skin, and she wished to feel it again.

"Why did you wear this costume?" he asked abruptly.

"What?" Psyche stared at him. Why was he asking about her costume?

"Your costume. Why did you choose to wear it? Why *this* costume? The butterfly wings, the dress."

Psyche swallowed and resolutely shrugged off the tension that had built up inside her. "I do not see why you should care what I choose to wear to a masquerade."

He seized her chin in his hand and stared sternly into her eyes. "No arguments this time, Psyche. Tell me."

"I fancied disguising myself as a fairy," she said after a short, defiant silence. "For all the good it did me, for you recognized me straightaway."

He released her chin and stepped back. "A fairy? That's all?"

"Yes, that's all." She gazed at him curiously. "Is something the matter?"

"No." But Eros stared at her, confused. Hope faded, and disappointment replaced it. It would have been very convenient if it had been Psyche. But she had dressed as a fairy, not as the popular manifestation of his wife, and as he looked into his friend's eyes, there was not the recognition he believed would signal the existence of his wife's spirit in Psyche Hathaway. Yet, for one moment, he had longed to kiss her—not a friendly peck on the cheek, but on her lips in a lingering, tasting sort of way. He looked at those lips again, and saw them part in a quick breath, and the urge overcame him again.

He moved away and gazed out the window. He needed to keep his mind on his quest, and dallying with Psyche Hathaway was not wise. It would distract him and he had not much time—much less than the one year he had hoped for. Already the forces of nature were disturbed; a few flakes of snow drifting lazily past the window mocked the late springtime that should have been in full flower.

"Are you well, Harry?" Psyche's voice startled him, and Eros realized the silence between them had been long. He turned and smiled reassuringly at her, for she had sounded anxious.

"Of course." He waved his hand at the window. "I am merely concerned about the weather."

Psyche gazed at him warily. "Are you trying to distract me? If you are, you shall not succeed, I assure you!"

He shook his head. "No, and I wish I were only trying to distract you. The weather is a serious matter. This continued cold even into late spring means the power of the gods is starting to fade." Psyche's eyes widened, and he took her hand, wishing to comfort her. "The sooner I finish my quest, the better." He sighed. "I suspect Artemis will probably call on you, possibly to harass you or perhaps even to ask you to intercede with me to reverse the arrow's effect on her."

"You used your arrow on *her*? I thought you said—"

"That Lord Eldon's love came into being without my help. Artemis, on the other hand, needed a great deal of it." He grimaced, thinking of the shocked and dismayed look on the goddess's face.

"Oh, Harry!" Psyche groaned. "What is Lord Eldon going to think when she reveals her nature to him?"

Eros shrugged. "Lord Eldon has more common sense than he is given credit for. He will deal with the matter well, I am sure."

"But—"

He held up his hand. "No, I will not reverse the arrow's effects. Artemis needs to learn a lesson, and I believe it will heal her as well."

Psyche scowled briefly. "I cannot like it, and I think it is arrogant of you to assume she needs to learn a lesson. But . . . well, if she does indeed need healing, and if your dart will help her do it, then I suppose it cannot be all bad." She gazed into the fire, a thoughtful look on her face. "I suppose if she becomes persistent, I can always call upon Cassandra. She will take Artemis in, if need be, and I am sure they will get along famously. There is nothing like conversation with a kindred spirit to divert one from one's original purpose."

Eros grinned. "No doubt."

"Of course," Psyche continued, this time more slowly, "I will help you to the best of my abilities, Harry." She gazed at him earnestly. "I don't think"—she paused, as if to gain control over some deep emotion, and then gave him a crooked smile—"I don't think I could bear it if you were to fade away and if I could not see you again. You have been my dearest friend. I—I could not wish for a better one."

He saw tears in her eyes, and wanted desperately to comfort her. It could not hurt to hug her, and the fact that she did not pull away when he did showed how much she trusted him. "I, also." He gently wiped away a tear on her cheek. "Don't cry, Psyche. I will do my best to look at the ladies you bring before me, and then when I find my wife, I will not disappear." She moved a little away from him, an uncertain smile on her face. "I'll also make sure you are well taken care of and matched with a good gentleman, whatever happens."

A heavy ache settled somewhere in his chest, different from the one he felt when he thought of his lost wife. The sooner he found her the better; he realized the thought of fading away did not hurt as much as the thought of never seeing Psyche Hathaway again, most of all because he knew she would be unhappy. Her happiness had come to mean a great deal to him. "It is the least I can do," he said.

Psyche gave another quick, crooked smile. "Thank you," she said. There was a short silence, then she looked at him, her smile suddenly mischievous. "Well, shall we go back to the ballroom again? It will be amusing to see how many people you can scandalize without incurring the wrath of Lady Jersey, Lady Cowper, or Lady Sandringham."

He smiled, relieved that her manner had lightened. "None of them shall be wrathful, whatever I choose to do," he said.

"Hmph! I doubt that!"

"Never doubt, Psyche. I have flattered Lady Jersey with exquisite grace, and have appealed to Lady Cowper's kindness of heart. Lady Sandringham will feel nothing but gratification that her ball was a sad crush and that it will be discussed for months to come. She and her daughter will be invited everywhere after this, I am sure."

"How annoying that you are probably right," Psyche said. "Will you stay for the unmasking?"

"Yes."

Psyche grimaced. "I do *not* think I shall stay for it, then."

"Coward."

"I am not!"

"Yes, you are." Eros knew his words would provoke her, and he grinned when her eyes flashed irritation. He preferred her irritated rather than sad; her tears made him feel heavier than his wings could lift. She stared at him angrily and his smile grew wider.

"I am not, and I *shall* stay for the unmasking, just to show you I am not."

"We shall see," he said, and pulled invisibility over himself.

"Harry!" Psyche called.

He said nothing and watched her in amusement, while she twirled around, looking for him. She stopped, and with an irritated stamp of her foot, flounced out of the room.

Eros grinned. He had to admit, even though he had been only teasing before, he did indeed like to see her bounce. She curved in all the right places, and had become a lovely young woman. She did not seem to understand her attractiveness at all, basing it upon some nonsensical fashion for brunettes. It was just as well, he supposed. Her lack of conceit and her merry nature were part of her charm. She would make some lucky man a good wife.

Eros stared out of the window and watched more snowflakes drift down to join the layers of snow below, starkly white against darkness. He shivered, though he did not feel the cold, for the fireplace was well stoked, and even if it was not, he could generate enough warmth himself. He wondered what it was like to fade from the minds of men, to drift into oblivion. He could not imagine it; he supposed mortals might know something of it, for they lived always close to death, and had an acute awareness of it, however they might try to ignore it.

Did Psyche Hathaway know? His mind fluttered away from the thought, then came gingerly back. She was mortal, therefore . . . therefore, a day would come when she would be gone. And he would still go on, without her.

A chill seized him, and he suddenly wished he could make her immortal. The gods did not do it often; it was granted to those closest to their hearts, or those of great virtue or courage. Psyche Hathaway was virtuous, although since she had never gone through any great trials he was not sure if her virtue or courage were of the heroic kind. She was, however, very close to his heart. Eros put up his hand against the window and stared out into the night. He had given the gift of immortality once already, and that to his wife. It was not something given lightly, even for a friend.

A friend. Eros grimaced. To be honest, Psyche Hathaway was more than that. He desired her; he knew he should not, for he loved his wife, and it was his duty to seek her.

He sighed. Immortality was not something he could give now, certainly not before he was done with his quest. The gods' powers were fading; it was almost June, but the bleak sky wept torrents of rain when it did not snow or hail. It was not as bad here in England as it was elsewhere; it must be a sign he was very close to finding his wife, that she must be somewhere near.

Eros sighed again and moved toward the door. Artemis did not understand: it may have seemed to her he was not seeking his wife, but he was, and the search often drained him. Being around people engaged in the business of encouraging men and women to fall in love or at least marry—as these particular mortals did at their balls—restored him, for where love existed, he thrived.

Yes, he did thrive here, especially since Psyche Hathaway had taken upon herself the role of matchmaker, and had even thrown his darts, however much they might go astray when she did. He laughed softly. With or without darts, she had done very well, although it was more amusing to see her *with* the darts.

He snapped his fingers and a handful of darts appeared, floating in midair. He considered them, and nodded. They fell into his outstretched hand and he tucked them into his belt. Psyche had said it might be amusing to see how many people he could scandalize without incurring the wrath of his hostess or the patronesses of Almack's. He could not make her immortal, but the least he could do was grant her a wish from time to time, even if it did not turn out the way she thought it might. But that was what made it amusing, was it not? Eros chuckled, and his step was light as he left the room.

Chapter 5

Clothes, neckcloths, and hats were scattered on the furniture, and the beam of sunlight that peeped from behind the clouds into Eros's room at Grillon's did not make it look any better. Eros frowned. Perhaps he needed a valet after all. Somehow the things he had acquired since his decision to live among mortals did not want to stay neatly in their places, and it was annoying when none of his neckcloths were creaseless enough to tie in a satisfactory manner.

He could summon some clothes and make them disappear again when he did not need them. However, he had made some friends in the past few years, and it would be inconvenient if a suit of clothes he fancied at Weston's or Scott's belonged to one of them. One did not allow one's friends to appear naked at a ball or rout, however amusing it might be for a moment or two.

He eyed a particularly fine waistcoat and jacket, selected a linen shirt and pantaloons, and snapped his fingers. Instantly, the shirt and pantaloons were on him, and they fit very well. He made a mental note to visit that tailoring shop again the next time he wanted to buy more clothes.

He felt a wild and silvery presence behind him suddenly, and he turned. Artemis, of course. He eyed her grimly. She looked a little haggard, and her eyes held a despairing look.

"Ah. My dear cousin, what brings you here?"

She raised her chin, a poor attempt at preserving her pride, for her lips trembled while she did it. "You know why I am here," she said, her voice low. "Stop it. I want it to end."

Almost he felt pity for her, but he remembered the thousands of years in which she had scorned everything over which he ruled, and how much pride she had taken in the invulnerability of her heart. Then, too, she had spoken with disdain about his mortal friends, including Psyche. He raised his brows. "It? End? I can't imagine what you are talking about."

Artemis took a threatening step toward him, her face angry, and the energy around her sizzled.

"It will not work, cousin." He turned to a mirror and began wrapping a neckcloth around the collar of his shirt. "Your power is much reduced, whereas mine has remained strong. If you strike me, you strike down any chance the gods have of surviving."

He watched her shudder, and again felt pity. It was for her own good; ever since the loss of Orion, she had turned potential lovers away, sometimes with a curse and with violence. He remembered what Psyche had once told him, that the gods had weakened because they had become removed from mortals; perhaps she had been right. His powers remained strong since he consorted with them, unlike the other gods. He frowned, his hand pausing over a loop in his neckcloth. Had it been his wife or Psyche Hathaway who had said it?

"Please . . ." Artemis's voice came out in a halting whisper. "I cannot bear it. I am drawn to him, and I cannot stay away from him no matter how much I try. The humiliation of being in love with such a man, a mortal—"

He made his voice stern. "You do Lord Eldon an injustice. He is good, kind, and more intelligent than you think. You should look beyond the surface he presents before you judge him."

"But a mortal—"

"You did not object to that when you loved Orion."

Artemis pressed her hands over her eyes. "He was different!" she cried, anguished. "Not like Lord Eldon—"

"Enough!" He turned to her. "Did it ever occur to you that

perhaps you might become stronger if you walked among humans once again?"

"No!" Her voice was full of revulsion.

"Then think of it. Try it. Perhaps if your efforts are sincere enough, I will reverse the effect of the dart."

"No, please—"

"I believe Lady Blytheland is willing to house you and show you the ways of this world; her sister graciously requested it of her. Be grateful she did." He pulled the end of the neckcloth through another loop. It looked very well, he thought, or at least as well as could be expected when one was distracted.

"It is easy for you to say," Artemis said angrily. "It is merely an excuse to stay near your mortal lover."

His hand froze over the neckcloth as a cold anger overcame him. "Leave me. If you say any word disparaging Psyche Hathaway, you will know a madness the like of which no one has ever experienced. I could choose to make you form a passion for someone quite different than Lord Eldon. Think of it."

"You love her, admit it!" Artemis spat out the words. "I have seen how you watch her, it is why you have not even bothered—"

He turned swiftly and faced her, and at last she stepped away from him, fear evident in her eyes.

"You will leave. Now."

With a last wild look, Artemis disappeared in a flash of silvery light.

Eros stood looking into the mirror for a long while, then closed his eyes. It was true of course. He loved Psyche Hathaway, though he had told himself it was merely friendship, perhaps even lust. He knew it when he had blurted it there in the Sandringhams' library. She was lovely, down to her very soul, and he had seen it ever since she was a child. It was why she had attracted so many suitors, he was sure. A woman was always more beautiful when beauty lived in her heart.

Impossible. He loved his wife; he could not love someone

else. He needed to find her, and could not be distracted from his quest. A young woman like Psyche Hathaway was not that unusual; he had seen more beautiful women in the past who had charmed through sheer joy of life and goodness of heart. But, of course, he had not known those women as he had known Psyche.

Eros drew in a deep breath and as he let it out he opened his eyes. He would not deny the love he bore for his friend. He was the god of love, after all, and knew the emotion well. But he had a duty, and when he found his wife again, no doubt his love for her would overcome anything he felt for Miss Hathaway.

It was best he remember it, and remember, too, that he had promised he would help find her a husband, just as she promised she would help him find his wife. He smiled slightly—it seemed impossible that she could do anything to help him, but he was sure she was a key to discovering his wife's whereabouts.

Well, he would treat Psyche Hathaway as he had always treated her: teasing, comforting, arguing. He could do it; he need only focus on their long friendship, and remind himself of his wife when necessary.

He had promised to call on Psyche this afternoon; it was near the time. Eros turned away from the mirror and selected a hat from the ones he had left on the bed. Frowning slightly, he sighed. He really should get himself a valet. He had no notion what to do with a hat when it was not on his head, and it would be much easier to have a servant handle it.

With an adjustment to the brim that pulled it into a rakish angle, he nodded, satisfied, at the mirror and left the room.

Psyche had expected Artemis would come immediately to see her, but she did not. It was just as well; she had been busy introducing every eligible lady to Harry in the last remaining weeks of the Season. He had turned his nose up at all of them—or no, not exactly. He charmed and dazzled every one of them. But it seemed his wife was not among them, and Psyche could not help feeling selfishly pleased, though she castigated herself over it daily, and rightfully so.

She shook her head at her own contrariness, and continued playing the pianoforte in the drawing room. A sudden rattling of the windows caused her to look up; hail was falling. The Season could not end soon enough for her. The continued bad weather had curtailed the *ton's* activity quite severely. A few routs and balls were still held, but the alfresco luncheons to which she had looked forward had been canceled. She liked balls, but liked variety, too . . . and she longed to be away from tiresome gossip. Especially since the gossip seemed to be centered around her and Harry.

The intensely irritating truth was that Harry's constant attendance upon her caused comment, and more than one acquaintance quizzed her about a possible betrothal. Psyche had managed to keep her countenance and even look surprised. How could anyone think they were betrothed if she always introduced him to heaven knew how many eligible young ladies at every ball? Psyche was certain she was not to blame—she had always been very careful to behave in a friendly manner toward him and to divert his attention from herself at every turn. If she had to deflect one more innuendo or ignore one more smirk, she would scream.

A distant clock tolled the hour, making Psyche look up at the one on the mantelpiece. She frowned and ceased her playing. It was a silver ormolu clock, and she was certain they had a gold one, not silver. How had she not seen it before? It wasn't working properly, for it showed the hour to be a quarter past noon, not two o'clock. Psyche rose from the pianoforte and inspected the clock. Ah, definitely, it had not been wound; she could not hear any chain movement in it. She picked up the key and opened the glass face cover.

The clock *melted*. Psyche dropped the key and barely suppressed a scream. The glass dissolved and the silver metal poured over the edge of the mantelpiece to pool on the floor. She stepped back quickly and almost tripped on a footstool before gripping a side table, her heart thumping madly as she watched the silver pool rise from the floor and take shape.

She let out the breath she was holding. "Artemis."

The goddess stood staring at her in silence, and Psyche began to feel uncomfortable. It could not hurt to be hospitable, however, so she smiled. "How good of you to call," she said, hoping she did not sound inane. How did one entertain a goddess? It was not like entertaining Harry, for she had known him forever. Perhaps she should pretend it was Lady Jersey or Lady Cowper; certainly such respect would not hurt. "Would you care for some refreshment? Tea, perhaps, and some biscuits? My mother has gone out, but I am sure she will return soon."

Artemis's lips trembled, and she took the lower one firmly in her teeth before replying, "I thank you. I do not require refreshment."

"Not even a bit of tea?" Psyche coaxed. It was clear the goddess was repressing some strong emotion, for one hand grasped her bow tightly and the other opened and closed in a nervous gesture. She remembered that Harry had stuck Artemis with an arrow and her heart went out to her. If it was anything like the effect it had had on Lord Blytheland or her brother, Kenneth, it was a confusing and terrible thing to bear. She smiled sympathetically. "Do have a little. There is nothing like a refreshing cup of tea to put one in better spirits."

Artemis let out a low groan and suddenly covered her eyes with her hands. "Gods. It shows. I cannot stand it. I begged him to release me from this . . . this humiliation, but he would not. I, Artemis, reduced to begging!"

"Oh, poor dear!" Psyche's heart melted and she patted the goddess on her back in a comforting manner. "Harry can be horrid, can he not? But he was very angry at you for interfering with him."

Artemis's hands came down, and her chin thrust out stubbornly. "He was not doing as he ought. He should have put more time into his quest instead of in frivolous activities."

Psyche opened her mouth to protest, but decided it would

do no good. "It is not wholly frivolous . . . it is the way we mortals go about looking for husbands and wives. I have been helping him, you know. He is certain his wife is somewhere among us."

Artemis frowned. "He is blind! If *I* were to look for a husband—" She paled, shivering, and an anguished look came into her eyes.

Poor thing! Psyche took the goddess's hand and led her, unresisting, to the sofa. She patted her hand. "I cannot know what it is like to be shot with one of Harry's darts, for he has never done it to me, but I know it must exercise one's emotions in quite a violent manner. My poor brother-in-law acted like a madman when Harry shot him, and he is the most amiable person imaginable! Of course, he was shot more than once—"

"More than once?" Artemis stared at her in horror, looking almost ill.

"—but that is neither here nor there!" Psyche said hastily. The goddess gave another shudder, and this time Psyche noticed gooseflesh appeared on her skin. "What we must do is get you other clothes than what you are wearing. You look very well in your chiton, but you cannot be very warm." And it would be very awkward if anyone saw her here, she thought. It was very well to look like a goddess at a masquerade, but one could not dress like that otherwise. Indeed, what if Mama should return?

Artemis's mouth turned down bitterly and she shook her head. "I am out of my realm. My powers are not what they should be these days." She rubbed her shoulders with her hands. "I feel the elements more than I should."

Psyche patted her arm in a comforting manner. "I believe you are of a height with my sister Cassandra. I shall get one of her old riding habits for you."

The goddess gave her a grateful look. "You are very kind." She seemed to choke for a moment, then continued. "I shall remember to reward you before I leave this mortal world."

Psyche shook her head and smiled. "There is no need to talk like that. One does not die from love, you know."

"What? Oh!" Artemis's puzzled frown cleared and she laughed slightly. "No, I promise you, I shall not die. I am immortal after all."

Psyche was glad she could make her smile at last. She nodded. "Can you make the dress appear on you? It's in the attic, in a large brown trunk. It is dark blue with white trim, and silver epaulettes, and made of light wool."

Artemis closed her eyes for a moment, then waved her hand. The dress appeared immediately upon her, molding itself around her figure. It was a bit snug, since the goddess was built on slightly grander lines than Cassandra. But she looked exceedingly well in it: the dark blue made her skin look luminescent and the highlights in her black hair shone like stars.

The goddess frowned. "A clumsy piece of clothing. How can anyone move their arms freely in it? I doubt I can stretch my arms out enough for a proper shot with my bow."

Psyche chuckled. "You sound like my sister. She did not care for it for the same reason—she thought the sleeves too constricting, though it is very much in fashion."

"Fashion! Hah!" Artemis's lip curled in scorn. "I care nothing for such things. It is a bondage upon the bodies and spirits of women."

"Definitely, you will find Cassandra amiable," Psyche said. "You will like staying with her, I believe."

Artemis looked at her in consternation. "But I do not wish to stay—"

A knock on the door sounded, and the butler entered. "Lord Eldon," he announced.

Psyche let out a sigh, annoyed at herself. She had forgotten to tell the butler they were not receiving callers at the moment. She glanced at Artemis's hunted, yet hopeful expression, and she felt very sorry she had forgotten. The goddess had stepped back near some curtains when the door opened, and she stood in shadow, not visible from the door. Perhaps Artemis was afraid—fear seemed to flicker over her face. No doubt it would be best if she let Artemis come forward on her own, rather than bringing her to Lord Eldon's notice.

Lord Eldon stepped into the drawing room and smiled when he saw Psyche, then bowed over her hand. "Pleased to see you, Miss Hathaway," he said. They went through the formal pleasantries, he with his usual ease of manner, and yet there seemed a little hesitation in his voice, and his expression had lost its ruminative vagueness and had taken on an intent look.

"Is there something you wish to say, Lord Eldon?" Psyche asked after a short awkward pause.

"Miss Hathaway, I understand you are acquainted with Miss Knightly?" Lord Eldon said.

"Miss— Oh, yes, Miss Knightly. Yes, I am."

"I had promised to call on her—she seemed ill at Lady Sandringham's ball." He smiled wryly. "But dash it all, I'm such a looby that I didn't get her direction. Stupid of me, but there it is."

Psyche smiled and patted his arm in a comforting way. "I daresay she left too quickly for you to inquire."

Lord Eldon looked relieved. "I'll be your servant forever if you could tell me—if you know, of course. I thought you might since she is your betrothed's cousin."

"My—my what?" Psyche stared at him.

"Your betrothed—"

"I am not betrothed!"

Lord Eldon rocked back on his heels and his expression became alarmed. "Devilish sorry! Er, that is, I always thought the two of you were well suited and thick as thieves forever. Pity it isn't true. I heard it from Hetty Chatwick that you and D'Amant—well, I thought it was a settled thing, for she said she had it straight from Lady Hathaway."

Psyche groaned. "Oh, for heaven's sake!" She knew her mother was ambitious and loved her dearly, but sometimes Psyche wished her mother had chosen to show her love in a completely different manner than insinuating something that was not true.

"Of course if it's a secret, you may depend on me to be as silent as the tomb," Lord Eldon said promptly.

"Very kind of you, my lord, but if Hetty Chatwick has hold of the notion then we can be sure half the *ton* has heard it."

Lord Eldon rubbed the side of his nose contemplatively. "Can't see yourself going along with it anyway, hmm? Harry's a good man, friend of your brother, and a devilish fine shot. Saw him at Manton's the other day, and I won a pretty penny betting he'd shoot the pip out of the ace of hearts. Twenty-five paces, give you my word! What's more, he did it twice. Amazing, that." He smiled modestly. "I've always had a good eye for a matched pair, you know. Knew from the moment I set eyes on your sister she'd be perfect for old Blythe, even when he didn't know it himself. I picked out the grays I gave them for their wedding present, too. Looked dashed handsome pulling their honeymoon carriage, I thought."

For one moment Psyche was distracted by an image of Lord Blytheland and Cassandra pulling a traveling coach, but shook her head, and his lordship obviously meant the grays. "That may be, Lord Eldon, but one's ability for choosing horses is not necessarily a sign that one can choose marriage partners." She wished he would not talk of any romantic connection between herself and Harry, for she was sure she was blushing. It was embarrassing to think rumors of it were being bruited abroad the whole of society.

"You might give it some thought," Lord Eldon said, nodding wisely.

"I can hardly do so when he has never asked!" Psyche exclaimed. "Besides, we would not suit. It would never do."

"Hmm." Lord Eldon gave her a skeptical look.

"She is not betrothed, I can assure you of that," came Artemis's voice.

Lord Eldon looked up and Psyche's irritation faded completely, if not for Artemis's intervention on her behalf, then for the opportunity to see true love in the flesh. If ever there was a man in love, it was Lord Eldon, for he stepped forward, took the goddess's hand, and brought it reverently to his lips.

"Miss Knightly," he breathed. The goddess gazed at him, her lips parted in a hesitant smile. "I hope you are well? You had left—I could not find you—"

Her smile widened. "I am well. You were very kind."

There was silence as the two stared at each other as if nothing else existed in the drawing room, which was quite romantic, thought Psyche, but rather tedious, for she could not help feeling useless and as if she intruded upon something that should be quite private. And . . . wistful. She was honest enough about that. It would be pleasant to have someone so very in love with her as Lord Eldon clearly was with Artemis. She thought, suddenly, of Harry, and sighed. He would find her a husband sooner or later, and she should be happy with that.

She looked at Lord Eldon and Artemis and how their faces had a strangely hungry look to them; perhaps they might like a bit of refreshment. She pulled the bell rope and when the maid entered the room, the two started and moved away at last.

"Tea, please," Psyche said to the maid. "And some biscuits—perhaps some macaroons and some cakes." She looked at her guests in a friendly manner. "Well," she said, covering up the awkward silence, "do you go to Lady Maxwell's rout, Lord Eldon?"

His lordship pulled his gaze away from Artemis with marked reluctance, and made a worthy attempt at looking politely interested. "I had been invited, but was not at all certain of attending." He cast a wistful look at the goddess. "It depends, I suppose, on whom I might meet there." He hesitated, then said, "Do you go, Miss Knightly?"

An alarmed expression flashed across Artemis's face. "I—no. I have other plans, and I am not partial to such gatherings."

"Ah. And to what sort of gatherings are you partial, Miss Knightly?"

Psyche took pity on the goddess, for Artemis was looking

extremely uncomfortable. "She is very fond of sport, I do believe, Lord Eldon. She hunts, and is as good a shot as her cousin Harry."

"Are you, Miss Knightly?" Lord Eldon said, looking pleased. "Might I interest you in a ride at Hyde Park tomorrow, if the weather is not as nasty as it is today?"

"I . . . have no horse."

Lord Eldon's brows rose in surprise, obviously taking in her riding habit.

"Oh, that is Cassandra's dress," Psyche said quickly. "I am afraid Miss Knightly's own dress was sadly muddied—ruined in fact—when she arrived here. A drunken horseman splashed mud upon her, so of course she had to change her clothes."

"Dashed cur!" Lord Eldon scowled. "If you will tell me what he looks like, I shall—"

The door opened and Lady Hathaway entered. "Psyche, can you imagine? An invitation from Lady Comfit to her daughter's betrothal ball! I cannot imagine why she—" Lady Hathaway caught sight of Lord Eldon and Artemis and stopped. "Lord Eldon! What a pleasure to see you." She extended her hand, smiling, and his lordship bowed elegantly over it. "And this is . . . ?" She raised her eyebrows at Psyche.

"Miss Diana Knightly, Mama. She is Mr. D'Amant's cousin, a friend of Cassandra's, and newly come to London."

Lady Hathaway nodded to Artemis, who inclined her head regally instead of curtsying. Lady Hathaway looked a little affronted at Artemis's lapse in manners and protocol, and shot a questioning glance at Psyche. Psyche mentally sighed. She did not like lying to her mother, but what was to be done? It would be horribly awkward to explain Artemis's situation, and certainly not in front of Lord Eldon.

"She is an old friend of Cassandra's, Mama, recently arrived from Greece and has lived there most of her life. She has been telling me how different Greek manners are from English ones."

"Ah." The sound was disapproving.

"Her father is very well connected and a scholar, like Papa, only more so. He taught her everything, including hunting and shooting with a bow and arrow—is that not marvelous?" Psyche said hurriedly, hoping her fabrication was not too far from the truth so as to be a complete lie.

"More of a scholar than my husband?" Lady Hathaway's face softened and she moved forward, extending her hands to Artemis in greeting. "My poor dear child! No wonder you have had such an unusual upbringing. I know just how it is. My own daughter Cassandra was taught at home by my husband, and though he is a dear man, she came out of it more naive than I could wish."

Artemis drew her hands away. "I am not naive!"

"Tut, tut, child, I did not say you were!" Lady Hathaway replied. "No doubt your mother had a sensible influence upon you, and there is nothing wrong with a bit of charming naïveté."

"Yes, but—"

"Well, there you are!" Lady Hathaway said triumphantly. "How else to account for the lack of scholarly slouch? But clearly you did not know how to comport yourself at a ball—not that you did anything irretrievably scandalous, of course! Do you stay with my daughter?"

"I—"

"Yes, she does, Mama," Psyche said quickly.

Lady Hathaway gazed at Psyche sternly. "I believe I was speaking to Miss Knightly, my dear. I do not know what has got into you lately, especially where Mr. D'Amant—"

The door opened. "Mr. D'Amant," announced the butler, and Harry entered the drawing room.

"Speak of the devil," Psyche muttered. She noticed from the corner of her eye that Artemis started and clasped her hands nervously together, and just a flicker of amusement crossed Lord Eldon's face before it became placid again. She almost groaned. That put paid to any attempts she might make at scotching rumors of a betrothal between Harry and herself.

How could Lord Eldon believe they were not betrothed when Harry went immediately to her after greeting her mother and Lord Eldon? Especially when he held her hand for longer than usual, and gazed at her in such a warm way? Oh heavens. She could feel her cheeks heat—*not* because she was in love with Harry or because she was betrothed to him, but because Mama had such a smug smile on her face! But she could not say that, oh, no. Psyche gritted her teeth.

"I hope you are well, Miss Hathaway?" Harry said politely.

"Yes, I am well, thank you," Psyche said, grimacing and jerking her head slightly in Artemis's direction.

Harry turned to look at the goddess. "Ah, yes. You are looking a little pale, cousin." His eyes had cooled, and his smile held a hint of anger. "Are you not well?" He sat on a chair to which Lady Hathaway had waved him, leaning back with an easy, negligent air.

Artemis raised her chin. "A slight affliction of the heart, cousin. Soon cured if I give it time—speedier if the doctor I seek will give me the right remedy." She smiled grimly.

Lord Eldon looked concerned. "A heart affliction! Miss Knightly, I hope it is not serious."

Artemis turned to him, and her smile faded. "I—no, not serious. As I mentioned, easily cured, given time."

"Do not be so sure of that," Harry said, crossing his legs. He tapped his finger against his lips in a meditative manner, smiling slightly. "Some illnesses do run their course, and the patient never recovers from it, living the rest of their lives trying to accommodate the . . . change it has made in them. And sometimes the doctor one seeks will only make it worse. You should be very careful about how you approach doctors."

Artemis shuddered, then looked at Harry. "There is one doctor with the immediate cure, but it is difficult to persuade him to give it."

Harry stared at her just as gravely. "You are mistaken. There are two doctors, but you refuse to see the other, the one quite willing to give you the cure."

Karen Harbaugh

Psyche looked from Harry to Artemis. She was not sure what this talk of doctors had to do with either of them, for the gods never became ill so far as she knew. But she could understand that Artemis spoke of the effect of Harry's dart on her, and she looked to Harry to cure her of it. It was, however, something Harry did not want to do. It was horrid of him, of course, for the goddess did not want to be in love with Lord Eldon.

She could not chide Harry or speak of these things in front of others; she wanted to speak to him in private. But how to do it? He would not come to her lately unless it was in the ordinary human way—at balls, in their drawing room, or some other place where they could easily be interrupted. Heaven knew how the rumors of their supposed betrothal would fly if they were constantly seen to leave together.

Psyche gnawed her lower lip, thinking. She would have to get rid of Lord Eldon, Artemis, and her mother before the allotted time for Harry to call was over. How fortunate he had arrived much later than the others. It would be a little awkward, but she could do it.

She rose and put a concerned look upon her face. "My dear Miss Knightly, you never told me you were ill! To think how that horrid horseman drenched you on your way here. How dreadful if you caught a chill, even with the change of clothes. You simply must go upstairs to my room and rest for a while until you feel ready to return to Cassandra's house."

Artemis looked confused. "But I never catch illnesses—"

"My daughter is quite right, Miss Knightly," Lady Hathaway said, a concerned and interested light growing in her eyes. "A heart condition is nothing to be trifled with. Indeed, I cannot see how Cassandra let you leave her house when you are in such a weakened state."

Psyche hid her smile. How convenient. Mama fancied herself something of an amateur physician. Being of a generally strong constitution herself, she spent much energy on other people's illnesses—bothersome when one was feeling perfectly well, but appreciated when one was feeling quite poorly. Psyche glanced at Artemis's outraged expression and tried desperately not to laugh.

"I am not weak!"

Lady Hathaway patted the goddess's hand kindly. "Of course not. But you will be if you do not take care of yourself."

"Truly, listen to Lady Hathaway, Miss Knightly," Lord Eldon said. He looked at Lady Hathaway and smiled. "I assure you her advice is quite sound. She gave me one of her salves once and it did wonders for a putrid sore throat, give you my word!"

Artemis gazed at him, and her mouth opened and closed before she blurted, "I am not ill in that way, truly!"

"If you are well enough, you could go home to Cassandra," Psyche said quickly. She frowned. "Only, you are without a carriage . . ."

"Miss Knightly, if you would do me the honor of taking my carriage, I would be most pleased to escort you," Lord Eldon said, looking deeply into Artemis's eyes.

"I—I . . ." The goddess's voice faded away as she gazed at him. Lady Hathaway raised her brows and Psyche gave her a bland look, causing her mother's lips to twitch upward for a moment.

"Indeed," Psyche said, "I have a message to give to my sister—could I possibly impose on you to deliver it?"

"But of course," Lord Eldon replied, reluctantly looking away from Artemis.

Psyche walked to the escritoire, hurriedly writing to Cassandra about Artemis's plight. Dusting the letter before she folded it, she gave it to Lord Eldon. She could feel Harry's gaze on her, and a quick glance at him showed his eyes dancing with amusement before he returned to his conversation with Lady Hathaway. She wondered what he was saying and hoped it was nothing that would raise her mother's hopes any higher than they already were—as if they *could* go any higher!

Lord Eldon bowed to Lady Hathaway, to Psyche, and nodded to Harry. "Good afternoon, and I thank you for a delightful time." He turned to Artemis, and his face softened. "If you are ready, Miss Knightly?"

Again the goddess hesitated, but Psyche touched her arm lightly. "Really, Miss Knightly, it would be best for you. I do think your cousin"—Psyche gave a quick frowning glance at Harry—"should take better care of you. I believe I shall talk to him regarding your—your heart condition."

Artemis gazed at her intently, then nodded. "Very well, Miss Hathaway. I shall do as you say." She turned to Harry and nodded curtly. "Cousin. Until next time."

Harry bowed elegantly, and Psyche could see the slight mockery in his smile. "Until next time, cousin."

Lord Eldon gave a last bow, and tenderly taking the goddess's hand, escorted her out of the room. Releasing a sigh, Psyche turned toward Lady Hathaway.

"Oh, heavens, the time!" Lady Hathaway said before Psyche could open her mouth. "I quite forgot I was to call on Mrs. Matchett. How silly of me!" She gave a bright, tinkling laugh, startling Psyche, for it was unlike her mother to laugh in such an artificial way. "I shall have to change so that I may call on her straightaway—do excuse me, Mr. D'Amant. My dear daughter will have to entertain you in my place; I cannot disregard my obligations this time."

Realization dawned: Psyche remembered her mother had said Mrs. Matchett was an encroaching, squeeze-crab of a woman. Why Mama promised to see a woman she detested when there was clearly an excuse to stay, she did not know—unless it was, once again, to push Harry more in her, Psyche's, company.

She was spared the chance to retort, however, for her father entered the drawing room, looking more distracted than usual, for his neckcloth was untucked, his hair mussed, and his spectacles sat slightly awry on his nose. Psyche sighed again. This was a day for interruptions!

Sir John looked around the room, gave a brief bow to Harry and a quick smile to Psyche. His gaze fell on his wife and his brows drew together. "Amelia, I need to speak to you." His usual vague but thoughtful demeanor had fallen from him, and his eyes were sharp with concern.

"Is there something wrong?" Lady Hathaway said anxiously.

He hesitated. "Nothing that cannot be remedied in time."

Lady Hathaway cast a quick look at Psyche. "But I was to see Mrs. Matchett in a few minutes."

"Mrs. Matchett?" Sir John raised his brows. "She is a miserable woman—so you said just yesterday. Why should you wish to see her?"

"Oh, for goodness' sake!" Lady Hathaway cried impatiently, clearly avoiding looking at Psyche. "It is not as if I cannot be wrong and change my mind, after all."

Her husband gazed at her from above his spectacles. "You need not change your mind; you are quite right. I have conversed with the woman more than once and each time my good opinion of your perspicacity increased. Therefore, there is no need to see her, but every need for me to speak to you privately."

"But Psyche—our guest—"

Sir John turned to Harry. "Do you read and speak Latin, young man?"

"Yes, sir."

Sir John eyed him sternly. "Fluently?"

"Yes, sir."

"And Greek?"

Harry gave a modest smile. "Like a native, sir." Psyche choked, and her father absently patted her back until she caught her breath.

"Very well." Sir John gazed at him keenly. " '*Divina natura dedit agros—*' "

" '*—ars humana aedificavit urbes,*' " Harry replied. "Marcus Terentius Varro." He wrinkled his nose.

"You do not like Varro?"

"I prefer the Greeks, actually," Harry said, and grinned.

"Hmph." Sir John turned to his wife with a pleased smile. "As you see, I am doing as you asked. So far this young man has done quite well, though his accent is different than what

I am used to." He turned back to Harry. "Well, you may stay with my daughter while I speak to my wife, and if your Greek proves to be as good as your Latin, I may let you court her."

"Oh, Papa!" Psyche groaned.

"Good heavens, John!" Lady Hathaway cried.

Sir John's gaze was bewildered. "But I have determined this young man—you call yourself Mr. D'Amant, yes?"—he smiled benignly when Harry inclined his head—"is not an idiot. You yourself said it would be a shame for a potential son-in-law to be less than intelligent. Thus far he has proved to be at least adequately so."

Harry put his hand over his heart and bowed. "I am moved, sir. Positively touched." Psyche suppressed a gasp and could feel her face growing warm from the effort. She pressed her hand over her mouth and turned away.

"I believe that is enough for now, at least until after I have spoken with you, Amelia. A serious matter."

Psyche watched as Lady Hathaway covered her eyes with her hand and moaned, moving weakly toward the door.

Her father patted her on the back in a comforting way. "Never fear, my dear. It is not all that bad, though as I said, quite serious." He put his hand under his wife's elbow and guided her out of the drawing room, shutting the door behind him.

Chapter 6

They were alone at last, but as Eros gazed at Psyche, she stared at him, her face slowly turning beet red. He lifted an eyebrow and gazed at her quizzically. She usually spoke to him at once when alone, but she was having difficulty saying anything at the moment, for her mouth opened and shut, and she turned even redder. "Are you well, Psyche?" he asked.

"I—I—oh, dear!" With a sudden leap at the sofa, she seized a pillow and buried her face in it, her shoulders shaking.

Eros bit back a grin and patted her shoulder as if in profound sympathy. "I hope nothing has upset you?" There was a short silence. Then she emerged from the pillow at last, gasping for breath, and wiping away tears.

"Upset?" She gasped again, and burst into giggles. "Oh, no! But you should have seen Mama's face—oh, dear, oh, dear!"

Eros smiled widely. "I did."

"And when Papa said you were not an idiot—!" Psyche clapped her hand over her mouth, but let out a snort instead. "Oh, goodness!" She dived into the pillow again and let out an audible wail of laughter.

"A very perceptive man. I have always thought so. How gratifying to think he believes me to be intelligent."

"Oh, not *intelligent*," Psyche said, emerging from her pillow. "J-just not an idiot."

"*I* distinctly heard him say I was adequately intelligent," Eros replied. He bit the inside of his cheek to keep from laughing, for she had put on a wide-eyed innocent expression.

"Oh, *adequately. Such* an improvement over idiocy."

His attempt at twirling his quizzing glass in a nonchalant manner failed and he whacked his leg. She gave him an ironic, triumphant look, and he burst into laughter at last.

"Gods, Psyche, we are a pair. Laughing at your parents—inexcusable!"

"I know, and I do love them, so it is even more wrong of me to do it." Psyche sighed. "How difficult it is to be a good daughter." She glanced at him, and it set him off laughing again, especially when she retorted, "I do not see what is so amusing about trying to be good!"

"There is nothing amusing about it at all," he replied. "It's you who are amusing, and no, you need not become irritated at me. I like to be amused."

"Oh, so I am your personal jester, am I?" But her lips lifted in a brief smile for all that she was trying to frown.

"No, only my dear—friend." Eros barely restrained himself from saying what he felt, and he was certain she did not notice the hesitation, for she smiled at him.

"I don't see why you settled upon me as a friend, Harry, but I am glad you did." She sighed, and there was silence between them for a moment. A clock chimed the hour, making her glance at it. "That reminds me—and I wish you had not distracted me from thinking of it!" she said, holding up her hand as he opened his mouth to protest. "I do wish you would release poor Artemis from the effect of your dart. She is miserable, you know."

He shrugged. "*She* makes herself miserable. If she would let herself love as she should and as Lord Eldon deserves, then she would be happier than she has ever been in the whole of her immortal life."

"Oh, Harry, it cannot work, as I have said before! How can it be at all a happy match?"

"It has been done before, as *I* have said before."

He watched her, satisfied, for indecision was in her eyes,

and he was certain at least for now she would not bother him about Artemis and her suitor. She sighed and shrugged.

"Yes, we are a pair. Laughing and arguing, and altogether stubborn, both of us." She gave him a rueful glance and shook her head again. "I do not know how many young ladies to whom I have introduced you, and you turn up your nose at every one of them."

"None of them are my wife." He smiled and cocked his head at her. "And you cannot say I turn up my nose at them. I found them all very pleasant, indeed."

Psyche attempted a disapproving look, but her lips trembled upward instead of down. "You mean you flattered them terribly and they turned instantly into your adoring slaves."

"No, not slaves." Eros put on a considering air. "Worshippers. I am, after all, a god."

"Oh, for heaven's sake!" Psyche said, frowning fiercely, then bursting into giggles. "You are incorrigible!"

"Not I! When one is a god, one naturally attracts worshippers." He stared at her then, at her raised brows and skeptical look, and knew she had never seemed inclined to worship in any way. An odd thing—not that he wished her to, of course. "I wonder . . . *you* have never done so."

Psyche rolled her eyes. "Of course not. I know you too well for that."

"Do you?" He wondered if that were all . . . the thought that she might be his wife flickered in his mind again. But why had he no hint of it before, if it were so? There seemed not to be any recognition on her part, either.

"Of course. Have I not known you almost all of my life?" Psyche shook her head again. "Besides, one cannot worship a person and be his friend at the same time." She stared thoughtfully at the flames in the fireplace for a moment. "No, I believe it would ruin a friendship, and I would not wish that."

Was that all, however? Eros hesitated, and the silence between them grew awkwardly long. He took a deep breath. "Why have you not accepted any man's offer of marriage, Psyche?"

She shrugged. "I have not felt we would suit." She rose from the sofa and went to the fireplace, putting out her hands toward the warmth. "Do . . . do you think perhaps there is something wrong with me?"

"Wrong?"

She turned to him, a rueful smile on her lips. "I should not have complained that you turn up your nose at the ladies. I have done that to all of my suitors, after all." She sighed. "I have even kissed some of them, and do you know, I have not wanted to continue the experience with any of them."

"Kissed some of them?" Eros said. A quick pang of jealousy overcame him, though he suppressed it. He had no right . . . or at least . . . A jumble of thoughts and emotions welled up in him, and he forced his attention back to Psyche instead of his own confusion.

Psyche blushed. "Perhaps I shouldn't have—although other, quite respectable girls have done it! In public, too, for it has become quite the fashion, although Mama says such displays are much too fast. I have been very discreet, however, and you are the only one I have told. *You* shall not tell anyone, I know."

He could not suppress his anger when he said, "You may be very sure I shall not!"

"You are angry at me." Psyche gazed at him, her eyes wide with guilt and sadness. "I suppose I should not have done it." She hung her head and her hands clutched the folds of her dress. "But I have seen Mama and Papa kiss, and think married people do quite a bit of it. I *shall* be married someday, but what if I did not like to kiss my husband?" She sighed. "It must be uncomfortable to dislike kissing one's husband. And I did not like to kiss any of my suitors!" She gazed at him earnestly. "It could not be anything wrong with *them*—they were all very gentlemanly. So I thought . . ." She hesitated. "I thought there might be something wrong with me." She looked bewildered and Eros's anger faded instantly. He took her hands and pressed them.

"No, of course not." He smiled at her and kissed her fingers. "There is nothing wrong with you at all. Your parents love each other, which is why they find it pleasant." He chuckled. "I'm sure they have had a bit of practice as well."

Psyche looked relieved. "Practice! That must be it." She frowned, however. "But how is one to know whether it is love that makes it a pleasant thing, or whether it is the practice?"

Eros shrugged. "When it is love, then you don't care whether the kiss has much practice behind it. When one has practiced, a kiss can still be very pleasant, even without love."

"Well, that does not help at all!" Psyche said indignantly. She was silent for a moment, her brow creased, clearly thinking, and Eros suppressed a grin. He had never seen anyone take such a small thing as kissing so seriously.

"I think I should practice," she said suddenly. She smiled confidently at him. "I should think if kissing is pleasant when one is not in love, then it should be extremely pleasant when one *is* in love. *That* is how I shall tell the difference." She nodded in a satisfied manner. "Papa was quite right about the importance of logic. I never thought one could apply it to matters of the heart, but apparently one can."

"No!" Visions of Psyche locked into an embrace with various gentlemen burned in Eros's mind, and his hand tightened on hers.

She looked at him, clearly surprised. "Was Papa wrong? Does not logic work in these matters?"

"No—yes—" He stopped and took a deep breath. "You must be careful. Not all men who are friendly or seem to be pleasant are gentlemen. They might—they might try to take advantage of you, or ruin you."

"But I don't wish to marry a man I won't like to kiss, and since there is no guarantee I shall love him when we marry—for you know, I might marry for respect rather than love—I still think I should practice. Then perhaps it would be pleasant."

"No."

Psyche let out an impatient breath. "You are of no help!"

she said testily. "At least you could offer to help me practice."

He looked at her, not quite wanting to decipher her meaning, and the silence of the room was a sound itself, echoing between them. She blushed but looked at him steadily, raising her chin.

"You said you might help me find a husband—I do not see why you can't help me find someone with whom to practice."

He let out a long breath. "It is not as easy as that." His gaze skittered over her lips, and he thought about the kissing she wished to practice—no.

"Why not?"

"It is not always comfortable with people you do not know."

Temper flared in Psyche's eyes, and she stamped her foot. "For heaven's sake! I am sure it cannot be that difficult. People start not knowing each other, and then they *do* know each other. How long can it take to become comfortable?"

Eros shrugged again. "Oh, a few months, a few years. Sometimes less than that." He did not wish to think of kissing—ironic, considering his occupation. He twirled his quizzing glass on the end of its ribbon, this time more successfully. It soothed him somewhat, for it took his mind away from the possibility of Psyche kissing some gentleman. He should disappear; that would put an end to their frankly unproductive discussion and perhaps it would help him stop thinking of it.

She let out another impatient breath. "Impossible! Why, the only man I have known and with whom I am comfortable is you."

The twirling quizzing glass flew from Eros's hand and crashed into the fireplace. "What?" He turned to stare at her.

"Oh, dear! Your quizzing glass! I hope it was not a favorite?"

"Never mind the quizzing glass," he said. "What did you say?"

Psyche cocked her head, her brow furrowed in thought.

"That is an idea, you know. It had not occurred to me before, but it cannot be of any significance if you kiss me, for it would be between friends, like one I might give my brother, except I have always kissed his cheek. It says in the *Mirror of Graces* one may kiss 'the friend of our heart's care,' which I am sure you, as my best friend, must be." She looked at him solemnly. "It is a very strict book on manners—by A Lady of Distinction, so I am sure there cannot be anything wrong with our practicing."

Eros opened his mouth, then shut it. He closed his eyes for a moment and sighed a sigh he barely kept from being a groan. Ironic. So very ironic. He, the god of love, about to refuse a kiss. He ached with want and denial, but he turned away.

"No!" It was all he could say. He shuddered. Not kissing Psyche went against his nature; yet he knew he should not. Even now he could feel a weakening, though whether it was in power or in his will to resist her, he could not tell. He shook his head. Something was wrong with him; lately he had felt confused, unable to separate his wishes from reality, from what he knew he must do. He loved Psyche Hathaway, but shouldn't, not if he valued her friendship or wished to keep the gods from fading away.

Friendship. He breathed a sigh of relief. He concentrated on it and the confusion slipped away. That was what he had with Psyche and what kept everything reasonable and sane for him.

"Is there something the matter, Harry?"

He turned to her and smiled. "Nothing is wrong, Psyche. You need not worry about me."

She looked relieved. "Well?"

"Well, what?"

"Are you not going to kiss me?"

He rolled his eyes. "I thought I said no."

"Yes, but you did not say why," Psyche said reasonably. "It isn't as if either of us is in love with the other, so I am sure we will not act in the silly way lovers do when you shoot them with your arrows." Her lips pressed together primly, almost shyly. "It will only be a kiss between old friends, and I am sure it will be comfortable, even if I may not like it at first."

"Well, it's—I—" Friends, she had said. And she might not even like it, she had said. There was that. Eros gazed at her earnest and curious face. True, they had been friends for a long time. It would be nothing like the feverish desire one felt when under the influence of his arrows.

An uncertain look crossed her face. "If you think it would be unpleasant, you needn't do it. I only thought you might oblige me this once, even if it might be distasteful to you."

Distasteful. Eros gazed at her mouth, at her full and curving lips, and thought it would not be distasteful at all. He had never kissed her—brief brushes on the cheek—brotherly actions only. Who was to know if it would be truly distasteful, if he never tried it? A kiss between friends, she had said.

"No . . ." he said slowly, still staring at her. "A friendly kiss . . ."

Psyche nodded. "Yes, that's it. A sensible sort of kiss, just for practice."

There could be no harm in such a thing, could there? Eros wondered. He had concentrated on their friendship before— it had eliminated his confusion and given him focus. He could do the same thing now. A kiss between friends. That was all. It was even in her book of etiquette; he knew enough of mortal society to know that such books were considered guides to proper behavior. If a kiss between friends was considered proper, then surely there would be no harm in it. He stepped closer to her.

"Are you going to kiss me now?" Psyche asked, her eyes wide.

"Yes," he said, and brought his lips down to hers.

It was a brief brush of lips, Psyche thought, like silk across her mouth. It was pleasant, a friendly kiss, he had said. Her heart beat fast, perhaps because she had felt a little bold asking Harry to kiss her. But it did say in the book her mother had given her that it was allowed to kiss a dear friend, and was Harry not her dearest friend?

Then he kissed her again, and it was not like the first one, although she could not say this one was any less friendly than the last. His lips came down lightly, like the wings of a butterfly, touching her upper lip, then drawing on the lower. She heard him sigh and felt his arms come around her, pulling her close—the Lady of Distinction had said nothing about hugging.

But she had no time or thought to spare for such things as hugs, for Harry's lips came down on hers once more, more firmly now. Psyche could not help touching his cheek and putting her hand behind his neck, threading her fingers through the soft curls there. A wash of warmth rose up from the pit of her stomach, but she shivered as if with cold, and moved closer to him, for he seemed to glow with heat.

Harry groaned and pulled her tightly to him, causing her to gasp. But her gasp was smothered by yet another kiss, deeper, exploring, so that she gave a long, low moan from the sheer sweetness of it, and his body pressed so close that she could feel the beat of his heart and smell the scent of clean spring air that surrounded him.

"Harry . . ." she murmured, closing her eyes, as his lips went from her mouth to her cheek to just under her chin.

A sudden rattling of the windows—hail—made her start and open her eyes.

"Harry!"

He released her suddenly, so that she almost stumbled backward. She looked at him and he was staring at her, breathing heavily, a look of confusion in his eyes, as if he saw a stranger in front of him instead of a friend.

"Harry," she said, and raised her hand to touch his face. He flinched and moved back. The heaviness so ever-present in her heart lately came to the fore, and she felt a little like crying.

He took in a deep breath, turned away to look at the mantelpiece mirror, then began to adjust his neckcloth. "I think"—his voice sounded strained—"I think perhaps that is enough practice for now."

Did he think it distasteful? Psyche touched her lips with

her fingers—she had not found it so. To be honest, she wished very much that he would kiss her again. For all that it had felt so strange, it had also felt quite wonderful. The kisses she had experienced with other men were nothing in comparison to this. Perhaps it was because Harry was her friend . . . but if this was a friendly kiss, then she would not be able to survive a lover's kiss, for surely it would be too overwhelming to bear.

"That . . . that was a friendly kiss, then?" she asked, wanting to be sure.

His hands stilled over a fold. "Yes," he said, and continued to adjust his neckcloth. "However, if any other gentleman kisses you in that way, you should slap him soundly."

"Harry, that makes no sense whatsoever!"

"Only because I, as a friend, am allowed to kiss you that way. You can't be sure that a gentleman would not . . . do more after such a kiss."

"More—?"

Harry's face turned grim. "Much more."

She had a feeling her mother would not approve of "more," and Harry definitely disapproved of it. Shooting him a quick look from the corner of her eyes, she asked, "If gentlemen would do more after such a kiss, then why would not you?"

"Because-I-am-your-friend." The words were bitten off, as if forced from his lips. His lips moved again, as if he said something under his breath. She could read lips a little—it looked as if he had mouthed, "and an idiot."

"Shall we practice again sometime?" Psyche asked hesitantly; she could see a shimmering glow around him, similar to the one that sometimes surrounded him when he was angry.

Harry dropped his hands from his neckcloth at last and stared at her, his eyes full of bitterness.

"Harry . . ."

He disappeared.

"Harry!"

Invisible hands seized her, and invisible lips pressed her

own, fiercely, until she parted her own lips, her body melting under the heat of the invisible arms that crushed her close. And then the presence was gone, so suddenly that she stumbled.

"That's the end of it," came his voice close to her ear. "I will ruin you, Psyche, if we practice any more. And that would be the end of me, as well. I lied—you should have slapped me."

The windows opened, letting the wind and hail pour into the room, then shut once more.

Psyche trembled and sat slowly on the sofa near the fireplace. She brought up her fingers and touched her lips again; they felt a little bruised from the last kiss Harry had given her, but oddly, she did not mind. It had made her want more kisses—she melted into butter just thinking of it.

Her mind was in a fog, her body heavy with liquid heat, and she sat very still. How stupid she had been. How very, very stupid. She drew in a long, shuddering breath. She had thought Harry her friend—and he was, of course. She had thought she would be safe with him—and of course she was. She had thought she had felt only the love of a friend for him. And she was afraid she did not.

A pleasant, friendly kiss, she had asked for, and he said he had given. What a fool she was. It had been more than pleasant, and more than friendly. It had been wild and hot—as hot as midsummer noon, instead of like the freezing unnatural spring that beat hail upon the windows. He was the god of love—of course he would know all about kissing and probably had practiced it a great deal. But if he were only a friend, then she would not have—her mind skittered away from the thought—been fearful.

The door opened again, and Psyche looked dully up at her mother's worried face. Another interruption. She was glad this time, for it would keep her from thinking.

"Psyche, I am afraid we will need to leave before the end of the Season—I am very sorry!"

Psyche straightened and made herself pay attention.

"London is thin of company anyway, Mama. Is there something amiss?"

Lady Hathaway wrung her hands. "It looks as if the crops have failed—it is this horrid weather, for it has hardly stopped raining at all!" She paced about the drawing room. "If only the new bailiff had not run off with what money was made on the rents and the income he collected—I felt there was something wrong with him, for he never would look at me in the eyes, Psyche!" She sighed and wrung her hands again. "It has reduced our funds, and your father does not know the full extent of the damage. It is best, he says, to go home now, just in case."

Psyche nodded and stared into the fire. A soft touch upon her shoulder made her look up into her mother's concerned face.

"Is there something the matter, Psyche?" her mother asked, taking her hand and patting it. "If you wish to stay in London, I can arrange to have Cassandra keep you, although I understand she and Paul intend to leave soon themselves."

Psyche gazed at her mother, remembering the times she had given her comforting hugs when Psyche was sad or hurt. She swallowed, and made herself smile. "Mama, if one is kissed, and the kiss is not pleasant, then it means one is not in love, yes?"

Lady Hathaway became still and looked intently into her daughter's eyes. "Yes, I believe that is true."

"What does one feel if one is in love with the person kissing her?"

Her mother smiled gently and squeezed her hand. "Quite wonderful, my dear. Sometimes even overwhelmed, if one is very much in love."

Psyche stared at her mother, stricken. "I was afraid you would say that," she said, and burst into tears.

Lady Hathaway took her sobbing daughter in her arms and stroked her hair, sighing. It was obvious what had happened to her daughter: Mr. D'Amant had kissed her, and it seemed Psyche found it quite wonderful. Lady Hathaway had deliberately left them alone—yes, even connived to bring them together whenever possible. She knew it needed only a bit of prompting for them to fully understand their feelings for each other. They were very much in love. She had seen them gaze at each other for more than a few minutes once; if she were at all a fanciful woman, she would have said they had exchanged souls in that moment. What existed between the two was much more than the friendship her daughter had always insisted it was. Theirs would be a marriage made in heaven if they could ever come to admit it.

And yet the girl wept, still resisting. Lady Hathaway sighed again. Another difficult one—all her children were difficult when in love. But she could not help feeling that her youngest would be the most difficult of all.

Chapter 7

Psyche sighed and looked out the coach window at the dreary landscape, full of grays and muted greens, and listened to rumble and splash of their carriage wheels trundling through mud and almost flooded roads. She did not see Harry during the week in which she and her family packed their belongings for the journey home. She felt quite low, and it did not help that the weather was just as gloomy and gray as her state of mind.

She glanced at Lady Hathaway and tried to pretend she did not see her worried look. Her mother had tried to jolly her into better spirits, and Psyche did try to cooperate, for heaven knew she didn't wish to be so depressed, and hated to be such a dull travel companion. But her mind drifted, and she would forget the thread of conversation, and her mother's plans for entertaining guests at their own home—should the damages to the crops and cattle not be severe—did not secure her interest long enough for her to make a sensible response.

Then, too, she was very tired. She had not slept well lately, first from weeping, and then from the odd dreams she kept having. They included climbing mountains, strange fire-breathing sheep, and Harry. She could not understand the mountains or the fire-breathing sheep, but she could understand dreaming of Harry.

She bit her lip to suppress the sob that wanted to burst from her. She dreamed of him every night, as she never had before. Harry laughing and teasing, smiling in that mischievous way of his. Harry in his chiton, holding her close, car-

rying her through the air. Most of all, Harry kissing her, as
they had a week ago. She shivered, not with cold, and her
mother put a shawl across her lap. Psyche smiled in as reassuring a manner as possible, but it still did not dispel her
mother's worried look. Psyche sighed and looked out at the
gray landscape again.

She loved him, of course. Not as a friend as she had always claimed, although that was still there. She was *in* love
with him. How stupid she had been! The signs had always
been there: her wish that he were not married, her depression of spirits lurking deep below the surface, even losing
her temper at him. And always she had missed him dreadfully when he was not about. She had castigated herself for
being selfish in wishing to keep his friendship all to herself.
It had not been selfishness, but jealousy. She had not wanted
to share him with any other lady, despite how honestly hard
she had tried to introduce him to every eligible woman of
her acquaintance. She *had* tried hard! Yet, she should have
known every objection she had listed in her mind to each
young lady was not from any real imperfection, but from the
hope that none of them was his long-lost wife.

She wished, desperately, that *she* were his wife, but that
could not be. He had eliminated the possibility from the
start. If she were indeed his wife, would she not know it?
She did not know how such transformations worked, but she
could not imagine how anyone might forget Harry.

It was useless wishing it, and she must be practical. She
must act as if nothing had changed, and recommit herself to
helping him. It was the only thing she could do; she loved
him, and more than anything she could not wish him to fade
away. Perhaps she would remain a spinster, devoting herself
to the care of her parents in their old age. Or perhaps . . .

Or she could ask Harry to select an amiable gentleman for
her, and cause her to fall in love, using one of his arrows.
She shuddered again. She preferred to love in the way she
loved Harry. But she doubted she could love anyone else
like that.

Anything would be better than watching Harry go off

with his wife. She did not think she could bear it. Psyche would help him until that point, but she wanted him to make her fall in love with someone else before that. It might not be so painful, then.

Psyche took in a deep breath. She would tell him this, the next time she saw him. She was resolved on it.

She turned to her mother and put on a smile. "Mama, you have not told me—who do you intend to invite to our house party, should we have one?"

Lady Hathaway gazed at her keenly, as if she were about to speak about Psyche's state of mind rather than a party. But she only hesitated for a moment before smiling in return and saying, "Whomever you wish, my dear. There is Cassandra and Paul, and any of their friends they might wish to invite. Aimee and Kenneth, of course, will already be there. I suppose Lord Eldon will come—which reminds me, is it true that he has been courting Miss Knightly? I have not seen her outside Cassandra's house at all after she called on us . . . which is just as well, for I must say she is an odd young woman! Her manners were quite strange, although her demeanor was good if a little stiff and haughty. I cannot see what Lord Eldon sees in her—except of course for her undeniable beauty—since his own manners are quite elegant and exacting. I hope she is no longer Cassandra's guest, for then I should not be obliged to invite her."

Psyche rolled her eyes. "Really, Mama! I shan't care if she comes or not—and so should you not. Besides, I like her very well." She sighed. "She is all alone in the world except for Mr. D'Amant. Not a mortal soul knows where her parents are." It was not a lie—no mortal knew where the Greek gods truly resided, and Harry was the only relative she had here.

"An orphan?" Lady Hathaway sighed. "Poor child, to be without a mother or a father! I would not be surprised if they disappeared in the recent conflict with Bonaparte. So many have, you know! No wonder her manners are so strange. I suppose it cannot be altogether inconvenient if she also comes to the house party. If she does come, I shall make sure she feels welcome, and perhaps even hint to her the right way to go on."

Psyche gave Lady Hathaway a hug and smiled at her. She truly was fortunate to have a kind and understanding mother, whatever other quirks she had. Her mother patted her cheek and beamed.

"You are very generous, love. Not many young ladies would countenance the presence of a beautiful girl at her own party."

Psyche smiled, and if it had a bitter edge, she could not help it. "Oh, not at all, Mama. I am sensible enough not to want to look like a fool. How should it look if I were only to invite ladies who have less countenance than I? Such a thing cannot reflect well on me at all."

There was a short silence, then Lady Hathaway took and pressed her hand. "I wish you would tell me what is wrong."

Psyche stared at her, barely keeping the tears of frustration and grief from rising in her eyes. How was she to tell her mother? How could she say, "Mama, I am in love with a Greek god"? She would think her mad, and rightly so. Who had ever heard of such a thing? There was no use revealing something that was unresolvable, much less unbelievable.

She shook her head. "I cannot, Mama. It is something I shall get over, and be happy again, you shall see."

Lady Hathaway sighed testily. "You are an impossible girl, Psyche. I know you would feel better if you tell me. I am not so blind I cannot see it has to do with Mr. D'Amant."

"I have said he is only a friend, Mama."

"And more," her mother said firmly.

"So your loving ambition says," Psyche replied, smiling fondly at her and kissing her cheek.

"Impertinent!" Lady Hathaway's lips turned up nevertheless. "Your caressing ways shall not keep me from seeing you are in love with him. There is nothing to object in him, Psyche! He is amazingly handsome, quite well-to-do, heir to a large property that adjoins ours, and extremely charming."

Psyche shrugged as if she did not care about these things; in truth she did not. She cared only for Harry, himself.

"For heaven's sake, do not shrug. It is a nasty French habit and quite inelegant . . . and you cannot tell me you do not care for him. Why not even your father objects to him— he has deemed him quite intelligent."

An involuntary chuckle burst from Psyche. "No, Mama, only *adequately* intelligent." She remembered what had happened after that particular conversation with Harry, and the memory quickly deflated the bubble of laughter inside her.

"At least you can laugh a little—I am glad of that," Lady Hathaway said gently.

There was silence, or as much silence there could be with the rain drumming down on the coach and the wheels rumbling over ruts in the road. Lady Hathaway sighed.

"I shall not speculate upon what has happened between you, though I *suspect*—well, never mind. But you must know you cannot avoid him. He is our neighbor, and your brother's friend, known now to all our acquaintances. It will be most peculiar if we were to exclude him from our house party."

"Perhaps he will not come," Psyche said, trying to sound as nonchalant as possible.

Lady Hathaway shook her head, and her lips turned up in a small, confident smile. "Depend upon it, my dear, he shall. I doubt he could resist."

Psyche pulled the carriage blanket up to her chin, and wished she could pull it up over her ears. She did not want to hear anything more of Harry. But she doubted she would get her wish. There was still about twenty miles more to go before they arrived at their home, and it was clear Mr. D'Amant and the state of Psyche's heart was her mother's chief concern too.

But Psyche was quite wrong. Lady Hathaway had succeeded in making her daughter laugh at least a little, and it was enough for now. She could see grief haunting Psyche's eyes, and would not press further. If there was a young lady more in love than her daughter, she did not know of one. And if there was a gentleman more in love with Psyche than Mr. D'Amant, she had never seen him. She had done what she could to bring them together as much as possible and was wise enough to let it alone, and let love take its course. Though her heart ached for Psyche, she said nothing more.

Instead, she took her daughter's hand in hers, holding it until they arrived home, and only once did she need to offer a handkerchief when Psyche could not find her own.

Hail and chill rain stung Eros's face and shoulders as he flew through the gray skies. It did not hurt as much as the persistent ache in his chest that told him he had made another mistake, a grievous one. He gathered together his power and pierced through a cloud, feeling imminent lightning sizzle on his skin. He pushed onward, then emerged into sunlight at last.

He should not have kissed Psyche Hathaway. He knew there might be problems with it, but her reasoning had lured him; he'd hoped perhaps in certain cases it was allowed. Truth to tell, he'd been lured by his own desires, and would have taken any excuse given. When Psyche had said the etiquette book allowed it, he had told himself that Lady Hathaway would not give Psyche a book that encouraged her to do anything improper.

He smiled reluctantly. No doubt Psyche had misinterpreted what it had said, or taken literally some sentence or other. For all her cleverness and good-heartedness, she was still very much an innocent, and inclined to trust people more than she should.

Including himself. She had every reason to trust him . . . he had made sure of it throughout the years, and did his best to protect her as well as he could. Mortals, even gods, in general, did not trust love, and their resistance leeched him of his energy. But Psyche—she might suspect him of trickery, and at times she was wary, but she did indeed trust him. She had never resisted his friendship, and had always greeted him joyfully after he returned from his travels. It was more than anyone—god or human—had done in more than a millennium.

Perhaps that was why he never became tired in her company, and why he maintained his strength when the other gods had weakened. Except for Ares, of course. He grimaced. It was odd how mortals trusted violence and war more than they did love. Eros was still stronger, however, for there was never much energy to be gained from death.

But death was something he had to consider. He floated above the clouds, letting the light and warmth of the sun seep into him. Gazing below, he could see a mass of dark clouds covering most of the earth. The energy of the gods had lessened every year, and there was the evidence. The earth itself was disturbed, with upheavals so violent that it caused unnatural weather and suffering. Soon, if he did not find his wife, the power of the gods would fade altogether, and the order that existed in the seas, the land, and the air would be gone.

Eros sighed, and began to descend. Cold tendrils of mist rose up from the clouds and covered him until he went below; then freezing rain soaked him again. Perhaps Artemis was right. Psyche Hathaway was a distraction—a beloved one—and he had a duty he needed to fulfill. Psyche had asked him to find her a husband . . . Eros made himself relax the grip he had on his bow.

He loved her, of course. How ironic it was that he, the god of love, should have to deny it. But he would not let her know; if she brought up their kiss, he would tell her it had indeed been practice, and that he had done it to show her how a man might react to a kiss—he had been, in other words, pretending.

Eros scowled. It was a sorry excuse—an outright lie, and he did not like to lie to her. An experienced woman of the world would know it for one. Psyche had asked for only one kiss, and he'd given her more than that. It had taken only a brief touch of her lips to make him discard all caution, and kiss her with all the skill and love he felt for her. He groaned, remembering it. Had she not stopped him, he might have taken her then and there, and he'd be forced into a marriage he'd have to betray.

He pressed his palms over his eyes—a useless attempt at pressing back the images of both Psyche and his long-lost wife. By all mortal measures, his wife was dead and gone, and he had every right to marry again. But by the measure of the gods, it was different, and his nature forbade him to love anyone but his own wife. With any luck, Psyche Hathaway's naïveté and inexperience would convince her that he had merely obliged her request for a practice kiss, and that he had felt nothing at all.

The Hathaway mansion loomed below, its gray stone blending with the cloud-filtered light. A glowing window drew him down—he knew it was Psyche's room. She was probably there, for the Hathaways had arrived earlier that day. He had not stepped in her room for a few years now; that, at least, he knew was not proper according to the rules by which Psyche lived.

He should not, now, of course. But he did wish to see she was well. He had left her abruptly, not able to bear being in the same room with her without making love to her that day, and he knew if he did not stay away at least for a while, it would be difficult to keep to his resolve.

His foot touched the floor of the small balcony outside her window, and he made his wings come up over his head to keep off the continuing shower. Wiping the rain away from his eyes, he peered through the windowed doors.

The firelight cast a golden glow on Psyche's face as she stared into the fire. She was curled up on her bed, hugging her legs and resting her chin on her knees. The palm of her hand came up and stroked her cheek; a sparkle transferred from her face to her hand, and she wiped it off on the bedclothes.

Eros closed his eyes against the ache that grew in his chest. He would not be surprised if she wept because of him. He had not heard of anything disastrous occurring to her or her family. True, the crops had been damaged, and some of the newborn lambs had died from the unnatural cold and hail. But he had asked for Demeter's help, and she had done what she could to make sure the damages were not as great as Sir John Hathaway had feared, despite the new bailiff's theft.

No, Psyche's tears were because of him; whether she had been frightened by his kiss, by her own reaction to it, or she felt her friendship had been betrayed, he did not know. It did not matter; he had made her weep, and had to do what he could to make it up to her. He owed her that, at least.

When next they met, he would grant her whatever wish she asked. It was something he could do, and had done for mortals in the past. She had never asked anything for herself, only for her family. As a friend—and one he loved—Psyche deserved that he do at least this thing for her, something for herself.

He watched as she rose from her bed, and went to her escritoire. She opened it, took out a sheaf of papers filled with her handwriting, and began to write. It was no doubt the novel she was writing—he had read it, found it amusing, and had encouraged her to continue. Sometimes she wrote when she was upset or disturbed—and was clearly absorbed in it now, for the sad look on her face fled. But then her pen halted and skittered across the page, and she stopped. Tossing down the pen, she covered her face with her hands, and her shoulders shook.

The ache in Eros's heart grew, and he desperately wished to comfort her. But for all his care of her for so many years, he did not know how, now that he was the cause of her sadness. All he could do was watch while she returned to her bed, crawled under the covers, and at last, slept.

He lowered his wings, spreading them out, and lifted his face to the rain again. His feet came off the floor of the balcony—and then came down again. He could not leave, not yet. He had not come to her room for a long while, respecting her society's rules. But he needed to make sure she was well before he left for the house he had bought from Sir William Hambly.

Quietly, he made the window latch lift, and opened the

door. Carefully he shook out his wings, drying off as much of the rain as possible, then stepped in. The candles had been doused, but enough firelight came from the hearth to illuminate the bed.

He went to Psyche and watched her even breathing. One tousled red curl fell across her forehead and another across her cheek. Gently, he pushed them aside and just as gently kissed her. She did not awaken, but let out a deep sigh. He was glad she had stopped crying before she slept. Thinking she had wept herself to sleep had made him feel lower than Hades itself.

She let out another sigh, and murmured something—Eros frowned. It almost sounded like something in Greek, but of course it could not be. Psyche had not learned any Greek from her father, unlike her older sister Cassandra.

He shook his head. It was best he left; Lady Hathaway had sent a message inviting him to dinner in two days. He had not been sure if he would accept. But now that he had decided on his course of action, he would; then he would tell Psyche that she could wish anything of him and he would grant it. Then he could continue his quest, and that would be that.

Quietly, he went through the windowed doors out onto the balcony again. As he lifted into the air, he took a last long look at Psyche's room. He was beginning to doubt he would ever find his wife; perhaps he, and the other gods would fade, after all. Whatever happened, he would always remember Psyche Hathaway, and love her too, for as long as it was possible.

Chapter 8

The only noise in the chamber was the crackling of embers in the fireplace, the ticking of the clock on the mantelpiece, and Psyche's slow, even breathing. In one corner of the room a small gray statue began to glow with a cool light. The statue grew until it became the size of a tall woman . . . and Artemis stepped from the shadows.

She stood gazing at Miss Hathaway, then stared at the window out of which Eros had left. There was no doubt Eros loved the girl; he had always been quick to sense Artemis's presence, despite her attempts at concealment. This time he had not. She suspected the girl loved him in return; it would not do, unless the girl was his true wife. It seemed she was not, however, for Eros had said nothing about it. Hecate said he would be the one to identify his wife, and during all his frivolous activities, he had not identified anyone at all.

Papers peeking out from under some books on Miss Hathaway's writing table caught her eye, and she pulled them out.

Cecelia's hand weakly touched the Count's cheek—she could allow herself this familiarity, now that she was on her deathbed. "Live on my—my dear—love. Though I die, I die a virtuous woman, tried by temptation but never succumbing to it."

Count Ormondo turned his face away, hiding unmanly tears, but his love's nobility moved him; tearing his hair and gnashing his teeth, his face was ravished by the anguish of his soul. "No, Cecelia! You must not die! My wife has died at noon—you cannot leave me—I will not see you become Death's bride!"

Artemis snorted—the girl was attempting to write some sort of story—what arrant nonsense. It would be better if Miss Hathaway spent her time persuading Eros to reverse his spell. She pushed the papers back beneath the books on the desk . . .

However, it could not hurt to see if Count Ormondo managed to marry Cecelia before she died, and besides, what did his wife die of? Could he have murdered her? It was a possibility, and certainly not beyond the mortals she had known in the past. Artemis snapped her fingers and a branch of candles nearby lit with flame. She sat down at the writing table, and shuffling the papers to the beginning of the story, began to read.

"Who—what are you doing?"

Artemis jumped guiltily, then turned around. "I—well, I—"

Psyche leaped down from her bed and took the papers from her hand. "You were reading my story! How dare you!"

The goddess rose, frowning. "You are impertinent! I am a goddess. I *dare* nothing—I merely *do* and it is enough."

"That may well be, but my writing is quite private! And so is my room. You should have knocked before you came in."

The goddess stepped forward, looming over her, but Psyche crossed her arms and stood firm, though she felt very, very small in comparison. She had seen Harry in this mood, and it did no good to give in.

"You dare oppose me?" Artemis murmured menacingly.

"No," Psyche said in a reasonable voice. "But I think since I asked my sister to offer shelter while you are afflicted by one of Harry's arrows, and since I have been trying to convince him to reverse the spell, you might be more considerate."

An indecisive look crossed Artemis's face, and Psyche pressed her advantage. "Harry is still angry at you. If you were to put a curse on me, he would be *very, very* angry at you."

The goddess shuddered and sat on the chair again. Turning, she gazed at the glowing embers in the fireplace. "I am sorry—you are right. I have violated the rules of hospitality and have been an ungrateful guest to you who have been so gracious."

Psyche patted her hand kindly. "No, no, you need not go into the doldrums. All will be well, you'll see."

Artemis gave a bitter laugh. "It is not well—when Lord Eldon escorted me to your sister's house, he kissed me. Just as the maid stepped down from the carriage, before I could leave."

"Was it horrible?" Psyche asked, thinking it was clever of Lord Eldon to take advantage of the moment; his sense of address had always been very fine. She herself had been in carriages with gentlemen, but such a thing had never happened to her. Perhaps her brother's chaperonage had made a difference—Kenneth could be quite fierce. A draft of cold air chilled her feet and she went back to her bed, tucking them under the bedcovers.

"No." The goddess groaned and covered her face with her hands. "It was *not* horrible. It was ecstatically wonderful."

"Ohhh," Psyche sighed sympathetically. "Isn't it horrid how wonderful kisses can make one feel so low?" Artemis gave an echoing sigh, and both ladies contemplated the unfortunate fact in silence.

"You, however, are more fortunate," Artemis said after a while. "At least you are not compelled to be around Eros, as I am regarding Lord Eldon."

"Oh, yes, most fortunate," Psyche said, thankful that the light was dim enough to hide her blushes and that her voice did not tremble too much. She fiddled with the bedclothes for a moment, then looked up. "You know that Lord Eldon will come to visit. I don't think you can avoid him—unless you go away, back to Olympus or wherever it is the gods come from."

Artemis smiled slightly. " 'Or wherever.' The mountain is

where we have the most power, but we go where we wish, according to our attributes. I am best suited to the country-side, the woods and forests, and the night air; I draw most of my power from them." She twisted her lips discontentedly.

"Why don't you go back to Olympus, then?" Psyche asked.

Artemis spread out her hands on her lap and looked down at them. "I could not stay there. Eros's arrow is a curse upon me. I run through the woods at night, and the image of Lord Eldon distracts my thoughts: instantly I am by his side. It takes only a thought, an image. I have found myself in his room many times, much to my shame, and have just man-aged to keep invisible, my hands aching to touch him." Her hands clenched in her lap. "Gods! It is humiliating—I am acting no better than a whore."

Psyche wrinkled her brow in thought. "I do not think it is as bad as that. Lord Eldon is a complete gentleman; should you show any inclination, I daresay he would declare him-self and ask to marry you. There can be nothing disreputable about that."

"I shall not agree to it," Artemis said grimly. "It is wholly ineligible."

Psyche wished the goddess had not spoken with such em-phasis; it made her spirits more depressed than ever. She nodded, however. "Yes, I suppose so. Have you tried to re-pulse him?"

"Yes—but it has no effect."

Psyche raised her brows. "I did not think Lord Eldon would press his attentions upon you if he thought them un-welcome."

Artemis stood up abruptly. "He doesn't! I try, but there is something about Lord Eldon's smile I cannot resist. By the gods, if I did not know my feeling arose from the arrow, I would think there was sorcery in that man's smile." Her lips turned down sourly. "I half suspect Lord Eldon knows it, too, for he smiles too much in my presence."

He smiles because he loves you, you peagoose, Psyche thought bitterly, *but you cannot appreciate that fact, can you?* She wished she were in Artemis's place, and that Lord Eldon were Harry. She sighed again. "Perhaps if you told him the truth, that you are a goddess, it would make him leave." A drastic action; it would no doubt make Lord Eldon think Artemis delusional. It might, however, make him less of a temptation to Artemis if such a condition was enough to dampen his ardor.

The goddess shrugged. "I do not know. I suppose it would at least keep him from asking to marry me."

"Then you must do so," Psyche said. "When he arrives tomorrow you may tell him it is impossible." Artemis looked unconvinced, as if such an action would be to no avail.

But Psyche was growing tired and did not wish to have further conversation with the goddess. She needed to sleep—heaven only knew she had slept very little because of all her troubling dreams. She had just woken up from one such, and again it featured Harry, except it also had horrid little ants crawling all over the floor.

"Really, you should do it. Tomorrow." She deliberately yawned, covering her mouth, and hoped it would hint Artemis away.

"And so should you," Artemis replied, showing no inclination to leave. She sat on the chair by the desk instead.

"Lord Eldon is not enamored of *me*," Psyche said. "When he proposed to me last year, I refused and he was not at all heartbroken. Indeed, he never has shown any inclination to kiss me, which would indicate something more than liking." She wished suddenly she had not mentioned "more than liking"; it was not an idea she wanted to entertain about Harry; it would cause her even more pain.

Artemis's smile twisted sardonically. "But Eros is more than inclined to kiss you. He was here some minutes ago."

Psyche's hand went up to her cheek . . . the dream she had—so real!—of cool breezes, and the warmth of Harry's kiss on her cheek. She had awakened clutching her pillow, and knew it had been a dream. She gazed steadily at the goddess. "He can't have been. Surely I would have awakened."

The goddess waved at the windowed doors that separated

Psyche's room from the balcony. "You may see for yourself. The floor there is wet with rain that came in when he entered. *I* did not come from there; as you see, I am quite dry."

Slowly, Psyche slipped off her bed. Taking the branch of candles near Artemis, she walked to the balcony. Her foot encountered dampness and she lowered the candles. Faint, almost dry footprints marked the wood floor, larger in size than her own or any woman's. A bright gleam near the doors caught her eye: a single feather lay against the wood floor. She picked it up. It looked almost like a seagull's, but few came near her house and certainly not in this weather. The feather was pure white, with a shimmering overlay of mother-of-pearl. It lay in her palm, rocking gently in a stray draft, and an odd elation and wrenching agony stirred in her heart. It could not be anything but a feather from Harry's wing, dislodged, perhaps, by the force of the storm outside. She turned to look at Artemis, but glanced away at the goddess's ironic expression.

"It means nothing," Psyche said. "He is merely my friend, a dear one, to be sure, but no more than that. Perhaps he wished to see if I were well, or had arrived safely home. He has done so in the past, and it is no more than any friend might do."

"He could have done that without kissing you."

Again Psyche's hand went to her cheek, and it heated beneath her hand in a blush. She lifted her chin, however, staring firmly at the goddess. "Anyone might do that—my parents and my brother and sister have kissed me any number of times."

"Eros is not your relative," Artemis said. "He has no excuse to kiss you except that he desires it."

"Oh, stop it! What nonsense!" Psyche cried, her heart burning at the idea and wishing the goddess had not mentioned it. "He is married, is looking for his wife, and I am not she." She turned away, refusing to see satisfaction on Artemis's face.

"Good. I am glad you are aware of it." The goddess paused, and her voice became gentler. "It is not only for his good, but for your own, and that of mortals everywhere. It is imperative he find his wife and join with her once again. You have seen the disturbance in the weather, have you not?"

Psyche glanced at her, then nodded. "Yes . . . Harry had said it is not as it should be."

"More than that," Artemis said. "Should he not find his wife, the Oracle has said that the whole of the world will suffer. Many crops have failed—have not your father's? It is worse elsewhere; spring has not come upon the earth, and I fear summer will not arrive as well. The earth herself has protested, throwing fire and clouds into the air. Should the gods fade away, nature itself will fall into chaos, for we gods move the ebb and flow of the tides, the warmth of the sun, the fall of the rain, under the One who oversees us all."

"Harry . . . he only said the weather was awry, he never said—"

"I am sure he did not wish to worry you," Artemis interrupted. "He was probably confident he would accomplish his quest soon, and thought it unimportant to let you know how urgent his mission is." She smiled slightly. "You must know how confident he can be of his own powers."

Psyche nodded slowly. "Yes." A leaden feeling seeped into her . . . any hope she had had that Harry might be able to stay at her side faded. It would be selfish; the fate of the world depended on him finding his lost wife. She could not keep him from it, regardless of her feelings. If he did indeed desire her as Artemis said, it was her duty to dissuade him from it. She sighed. "You are right, of course," she said.

"I am glad you understand," Artemis said. "I hope . . . I hope you continue to persuade Eros to take the effects of his arrow from me. I shall be sure you are well rewarded." The last was said as if offering some consolation.

Psyche said nothing and did not even turn back to look at Artemis, but she felt a strange sensation, like the ebbing away of a tide of water. She looked behind her at last after a few minutes of silence, and saw the goddess was gone.

The feather in her hand tickled her palm, and she opened

her hand and looked at it again. Harry had been here, and he had kissed her. Slowly, she moved to her bed and set down the candles on the table next to it. Dark descended as she blew out the flames one by one; the only light left came from the hearth fire's orange embers. Psyche got into bed and rubbed her feet together to warm them, then settled at last into her pillows, drawing up the bedclothes to her chin.

For a while she stared at the canopy's deep darkness above her, then pulled her hand from inside the covers and drew Harry's feather across her cheek. She closed her eyes, imagining it was Harry touching her instead, and let the feather move over her lips. It had felt just like that, when he first kissed her. She sighed, and turned her cheek to the pillow.

Slowly she drew in a long breath, and slowly she let it out, and slowly she fell asleep. When she awoke the next morning, the feather was still clutched tightly in her hand, and she knew to her despair that none of it had been a dream.

When Artemis entered her own room in the Hathaways' house, she knew she had done her duty in warning Miss Hathaway from Eros, but she could not help feeling uneasy. For all the girl's agreement that a connection more than friendship was impossible, she could plainly see the despair in her eyes. Miss Hathaway was probably in love with Eros, but Artemis could not help that. It was important he continue his quest to find his wife.

She felt restless; more of her energies had returned to her now that she was away from the city. Though she had found Lady Blytheland to be an admirable woman, she could not understand how a woman of intelligence and independence should have consented to marry. Also, there had been little to do in London. Lady Blytheland had encouraged her to ride a horse in various parks, but Artemis despised the sedate pace she was forced to take, and the incessant comings and goings of various callers bored her.

Except Lord Eldon. His image flickered in her mind, her heart beat faster, and Artemis bit her lip, trying to control her imaginings. He had spoken to her kindly, even made her laugh from time to time. He had looked at her as if he knew she was a goddess; he had also looked at her as if he wanted to kiss her senseless, and she was senseless enough to want him to do it.

Artemis squirmed in embarrassment and began to pace the room. The clatter of hail on her window took her attention. She stared through the glass into the night, then suddenly opened the window. Rain slashed her face, the scent of cold clean air filled her lungs, and an exhilarating energy filled her. Her hands clenched and unclenched restlessly— she needed to run.

A snap of her fingers exchanged her round gown for her chiton. She jumped out the window, laughing, her feet briefly bounding from a nearby tree branch onto the wet grass below.

The beloved wildness of the countryside filled her, and though the night was pitch black, she could feel the moon above the clouds and its hidden light guided her feet along the fields and paths. The goddess entered a small wood, sensing the deer and the fox within, and they, called to her wildness, leaped from their hiding places and ran beside her. She cared not where she ran, but ran swiftly, and exulted in the power of the running and the wild animals with her. The chill rain seeped into her hair and her clothes, but the heat from her running caused a shimmering mist to form around her, a silver cloud in the night.

Always her feet had led her to forests, but this night brought a white building before her—a large cottage. She came abruptly to a halt, then cautiously circled the building. A dog barked furiously, not far from her, and the animals that had accompanied her scattered in fright, back to their homes.

Artemis went forward—it was a large mastiff, apparently a watchdog. She was fond of dogs, and loved the strength and exuberance of guard and hunting dogs in particular. She smiled and held out her hand. "Here, pretty boy," she cooed. The dog padded slowly toward her, giving a slight questioning whine and tentatively wagged its tail. She stepped forward and let the dog sniff her hand before bending and scratching behind its ear. The dog licked her wrist, and its tail wagged furiously. "There's my good boy, my good dog." He licked her face, and she laughed.

"Not much of a watchdog, I must say."

Artemis rose and whirled around—Lord Eldon. He was in his shirt sleeves and carrying a lantern and a shotgun. She had spent too long a time in London; it was a sign of her drained energies that she had not sensed his presence until he was just behind her. Rain dropped from his hair and soaked his shirt, making it cling to his arms and chest. She swallowed. She had thought all dandies wore padding to fill out their coats, or so she had heard it gossiped in Lady Blytheland's drawing room. But from the way his wet shirt clung to him, it seemed Lord Eldon needed no padding whatsoever.

"What are you doing here?" she asked.

He smiled slightly. "Just the question I was going to ask you, Miss Knightly." He gestured toward the cottage. "My hunting box. It's on the way to Hathaway's house—thought I'd stay here the night before I continued my journey. And you?"

"I was running, and I came here."

He gave her a concerned look. "Did you have some accident on the road?" He looked at her up and down, then frowned. "I thought you'd already arrived at Sir John's house."

"I did, but I was restless, so I—I ran. I always run when I am restless."

Lord Eldon cocked his head at her. "If I calculate it correctly, you arrived this evening at Sir John's house. Even if you had run steadily from that time to now, you could not have run that distance." He glanced at the sky, squinting against the fall of rain. "Especially not in this sort of weather." He hoisted the shotgun to the other shoulder and held onto it and the lantern with one hand. He held out his other hand to her. "Come with me. You may have warmed yourself with your running, but you'll become very cold in a few minutes. I certainly am."

Artemis hesitated, but then he smiled at her and she felt as if her bones had melted. She put her hand into his. He brought it to his lips and kissed it, then took her into the cottage.

She was glad of the brightly lit and warm fire in the parlor, for she had indeed begun to feel the cold. A warm blanket came over her shoulders—Lord Eldon had put it there—and she dug her feet into the thick sheepskin rug next to the hearth. He stood near the fire, holding his hands out to it, and she could see the outlines of his shoulders, chest, and stomach through his wet shirt. He shivered slightly.

"You should remove your clothes," she said. "You cannot become warm if you keep wet ones on."

He raised his brows at her, and she blushed, turning away.

"I mean, surely you have dry clothes? You should rouse your manservant—your valet—and get warm ones on. Indeed, I wonder why you bothered to come out this night. Do you not have some servant to look over your property?"

Lord Eldon smiled and shook his head. "Morton's the best valet I have ever had—the man's a genius with bootblack and the iron—but he refuses to come to the hunting box. He has an aversion to it and hunting, and has gone ahead to the Hathaways'. Dashed awkward, but I had a fancy to stop here and see if I could roust out some birds." He shrugged. "As for the property—I shall have to dismiss the game warden tomorrow. Blackie—the dog—barked enough to raise the dead, and since I was far from dead, and the warden was drunk enough to look it, I thought it best to load some shot and warn off the intruder." He looked at her curiously. "Good thing Blackie likes you—he could have torn you to pieces, and that would have been quite unfortunate." He pulled a low stool closer to the fireplace next to her, stretching his long legs in front of him as he sat. "Now, do tell me, Miss Knightly, what really brought you here?"

She stared at him, giving him her most haughty look. "I

desired to run, so I ran. That is all there is to it. That I happened here is . . . is purely accident."

"Ah. In the freezing rain, at night, dressed in nothing more than a shift."

"It is the truth!"

He took her hand, patting it kindly. "Miss Knightly, if something terrible has happened, please believe me, I am very willing to help you. Did robbers come upon you? Were you hurt? If so, I need to know, not only for your sake, but also for Lady Blytheland's if she was in the carriage with you."

Artemis looked into his kind eyes and nearly sobbed with frustration at her reactions of melting heat and yearning. She did not wish to feel like this, but the way he looked at her, with more warmth than the fire before them, and the way firelight flickered across his wide brow and lean cheek made her want to touch the contours of his face and press her lips against his lips so sharply outlined by light and shadow. She drew in a deep breath and drew in all her resolution, and turned away.

"No, I was not with Lady Blytheland. I tell you, I ran here from Sir John's house, simply for the pleasure of running."

He released her hand, and she felt cold, though she had not moved from the fireplace. "You can't have run all that way."

You should tell him. She remembered Psyche Hathaway's words. If she told Lord Eldon her true nature, perhaps he would believe, and not look at her so that she felt impelled to be with him all the time. She drew in a long breath.

"I am the goddess Artemis, Lord Eldon, not Miss Knightly."

He nodded wisely. "Ah. I suppose that explains it."

Artemis blinked. "You are not frightened? You believe me?"

He took her hands in his. "Of course you are a goddess. It's a dream—an intensely vivid one. It only makes sense. What reason could there be for such an impossible thing as having the most beautiful woman I have ever seen come running to my house, alone, dressed in almost nothing and that bit of nothing clinging like a second skin? And here"—he ran a finger over one shoulder of her chiton—"you are almost dry, whereas I"—he took one of her hands and put it on his chest, and she could feel the muscles beneath the damp cloth—"am still wet. How could it be unless in a dream?" He pulled at the bands containing her hair, and it tumbled to her shoulders. "It explains everything." And he pulled her close and kissed her.

If she had gained any power from running in the wild-wood, Lord Eldon's lips took it away: her legs lost their strength, and she clung to him to stay upright. She shivered as he kissed her mouth and her throat, shivering harder when he pushed aside the shoulder of her chiton and touched her breast with gentle hands.

"A dream." He sighed the words against her mouth and kissed her again, deeply. "An incredible, glorious dream." He pulled her down to the sheepskin rug.

She did not resist, and did not want to, for the wildness she had gathered during her run rose hot, and she seized his face with her hands and gave him kiss for kiss. She pulled at his shirt, and frustrated, snapped her fingers and it disappeared.

Lord Eldon breathed a deep and groaning sigh. "Definitely a dream. The best dream I have had in my life." He tugged at her chiton. "Make this disappear, too."

A faint alarm rang in the goddess's head. "No," she said frantically, then drew in a sharp breath, for he put his lips upon her breast.

"Mmm. No matter. Better this way," he said, and slid his hand from her knee to her hip, caressing gently. "Slowly." He closed his eyes and groaned slightly when his caresses made her move against him. "Perhaps a little faster." He slipped his hand between her thighs.

Liquid heat flowed though her, and a bright flash of sensation made her widen her eyes and gasp. She gazed at Lord Eldon's face above hers, at his eyes full of tenderness, at his finely carved lips she wished desperately to kiss, and knew she could not go through with this, for it would hurt him later when she left him forever, and she could not bear that he be hurt.

"No," she said, and moaned when he slowed his caresses but did not stop. "I—ah!—I mean, we must stop. Please!"

He kissed her again. "But this is a dream, so it does not matter, love."

"It is *not* a dream. I *am* here, and you are really—ohh!"

"Impossible," he replied and shifted on top of her. "Lady Blytheland is a very respectable woman. No lady she sponsored would come into a man's house and magically remove his clothes." He kissed her mouth before she could reply.

"I am a goddess!" she said when he moved his lips to her throat.

"I know. And I worship you with my body, my heart, my very soul," he replied, pressing himself tightly against her.

Artemis let out a despairing breath. He was convinced it was a dream and would not stop, and she was beginning to wish he would never stop, for the delicious wild heat was rising in her again. With all her remaining will and power, she shifted herself into silver mist and flowed quickly out from under him. Swiftly she ran for the door of the cottage, into the rain, then through the woods, back to the Hathaways' house.

Lord Eldon fell with a muffled thump onto the sheepskin rug. He closed his eyes and groaned. "This is the worst bloody dream I have had in my whole bloody life."

Chapter 9

Some of the guests who came to the Hathaways' house were delayed because the weather had destroyed some roads, and others because the estate matters to which they attended had taken longer than usual to straighten out. The strange weather and the havoc it had raised was the most common topic of conversation in the Hathaways' brightly lit drawing room.

Eros leaned against the drawing room mantelpiece, looking out the window to the clouds and the rain. It had rained steadily for at least two weeks, almost without cease. He glanced at the guests gathered at card tables; he was not the only one who cast worried looks outside. Kenneth Hathaway's friend, the Viscount Clairmond, looked grim and murmured he might leave early. Even Sir John dropped his scholarly fog, and had been busy interviewing applicants for the position of bailiff as well as going over the estate accounts and the muddy fields himself.

Lady Blytheland played a few airs upon the pianoforte, her sister turning the pages for her. Eros gazed at Psyche, certain she was aware of him, for she glanced his way once and a light blush entered her cheeks. He turned away, looking for someone with whom to converse; he should keep his distance, or else he would be tempted to find a way to kiss her again.

His eye caught two heads bent together—Artemis and Lord Eldon. Her face was flushed and she had an agitated air; Lord Eldon had a hungry expression, as if he were barely able to keep from devouring her on the spot. Eros grinned. Really, Artemis should let true love take its course; he was certain she would find it more pleasant than she was willing to admit.

"Do you think it will get any better for them?"

Eros almost groaned. So much for avoiding Psyche. He made himself smile and shrug. "I wished to punish Artemis for her presumption. I have seen no sign of her giving in to Lord Eldon; I suppose if she keeps resisting I might relent in time."

"But what of Lord Eldon?" Psyche looked at him, her brow wrinkling in a frown. "He is a very good sort, and I would not like it if he were hurt."

"I could turn his affections toward someone else, but I dislike doing that since his love arises from his heart." He shrugged again. "Artemis protests too much—I need do nothing more and all will be well between them." Eros looked at Psyche, at the careful distance she kept from him. So, she, too, was determined to overlook their kiss, he noted wryly. He felt discontented, then disgusted at himself. It was what he wished, wasn't it? How else was he to keep his mind on his quest?

He had come at Lady Hathaway's invitation because it would have been rude to refuse when he was such a close neighbor. Also, he was sure his wife was somewhere in Tunbridge Wells. He had remained in London after the Hathaways and their guests had left, and felt a gradual lessening of his powers. Now that he was here, his powers had returned. He was close, he was certain of it—it could be any woman in this company. He sighed. The sooner he was done with his quest, the better.

"Harry? Are you well?" Psyche asked, her voice anxious.

He brought his attention back to her. "Yes, of course. The weather distracts me."

She nodded. "Artemis told me about it, how it could be the beginning of chaos for us all." She took a deep breath. "And I am still determined to help you. It is not only for the gods, but for mortals as well."

"I prefer you do not," Eros said, but made his voice gentle to take the sting from the words.

She gazed at him, wide-eyed, and he saw the beginning of tears. "Please, Harry. In this one thing . . . I could bear it better if I had something to do with finding your wife."

He stared, inwardly struggling, at her. He understood of course. It would give her more control over the course of her life and her feelings. Surely he could respect her wish and could keep his desires under control—which reminded him he wanted to ask her to request a gift from him . . . it was the least he could do.

"I understand," he said. "Of course you may help." Her relieved smile rewarded him, and he was glad he had given her the right answer. He hesitated, then said, "In the time I have known you, you have asked me to exert my powers only for others—your family and friends. I wish to do something for you, soon. Whatever you ask of me, I'll do my best to grant."

Psyche was silent, and a stillness came over her. Then she let loose a deep sigh and looked up at him. "Please . . . when you find your wife, or just before . . . could you make me fall in love with some gentleman? A pleasant, kind gentleman, of course." Her clasped hands twisted together anxiously. "I have not"—she swallowed, then gave a slight, crooked smile—"I have not loved any of my suitors, and I don't think I could bear a marriage in which I felt no affection for my husband. So if you could make me fall in love with someone, I should be very grateful, and do my very best not to act in a silly manner."

He felt as if his breath had been taken from him, and dizziness made him grasp the mantelpiece for a moment. He'd thought he'd make a gentleman fall in love with Psyche, but to use his arrows on *her* . . . "You wish this?" he managed to say.

She gazed at him, her lips pressed firmly together for a moment. "Yes," she said. "It would be best." She hesitated. "Only . . . don't let me know when you do it. I would prefer to pretend it came from me, and not from your arrows."

Eros stared at her and a chill came upon him. He did not want to do it, but he'd said he would grant her wish. She was right, it was wise, for it would make her less of a temptation to him than she was now. Her attention would be given to another, and he never came between two lovers if he could help it.

"Very well," he said, and thought he did well keeping the despair from his voice. "As you wish."

She smiled at him, and almost put her hand out to him, but withdrew it. "Thank you, dear friend," she said, then returned to her sister at the pianoforte, turning the pages once again.

He watched her for a few more moments, then turned away, making himself talk to another guest. He thought about his promise, and looked keenly at the gentleman before him—a Lord Whelan. No, this one would not do. Amiable enough, but Psyche deserved a man of more wit. He continued to speak to the man, then went on to talk with grim purpose to another gentleman nearby. She asked him to select a husband for her—he had promised it, and he would do it, even if it killed him.

"Miss Knightly," Lord Eldon said, after entering the drawing room and bowing over Artemis's hand. "Do you enjoy running?"

Artemis cast him a quick, startled look, and felt her face grow warm. "On—on occasion," she replied.

"And do you run at night—whatever the weather might be?"

She glanced at him, but his face showed only polite interest. "On occasion," she said again.

"Mmm hmm." He took out his quizzing glass and trained it on the drawing room windows, then brought it around to her, gazing through it for a moment. "I imagine you run very fast?"

"Yes."

"Perhaps as fast as a deer?"

"Occasionally," she replied, raising her chin.

He began swinging his quizzing glass on its ribbon in a contemplative manner. "How unusual."

"Not unusual, if one is a goddess." There, she had said it again. Perhaps this time he would believe it since they were at the Hathaways', and not in the dead of night at his cottage.

"Ah. Yes. There is that." He nodded wisely, then smiled, bent toward her, and said in a lowered voice: "Miss Knightly, would you do me the honor of becoming my wife?"

Artemis's hand shook, spilling wine from the glass she held. She held it away from her, dripping, but Lord Eldon took it from her and whipped out his handkerchief. He set the glass on a table and mopped the drops on her hand, shaking his head. "I am afraid you will have wine stains on your glove."

His hand's warmth penetrated her glove, and she remembered how it had felt upon her body a few nights ago. He gazed at her for a long moment—she could tell he knew it was no dream.

"So . . . you know, now, it was not a dream."

He smiled, and a wicked gleam appeared in his eyes. "Yes," he said. She glanced away, not wanting to give in to his look.

"What made you decide it was not?"

Lord Eldon released her hand. She closed it, knowing she did it to keep the warmth he gave her for a little longer.

"It was *very* vivid for a dream," he said. He smiled at her. "I've had vivid ones before, but not like that. Dreams don't leave two sets of wet footprints on the floor—one of which was mine—and I haven't yet found where my clothes have gone."

Artemis's face grew hot again, but she made herself look at him. "But it could have been someone else—a thief, a robber."

His smile turned up one corner of his mouth higher than the other, and she wanted to kiss him again. She looked away.

"Definitely a thief, and a most comely one she was," he said. "One who has surely stolen my heart."

Her own heart beat fast as if she were running through a forest and not standing in a drawing room. But she could not let this go further. "Impossible—I am a goddess—"

"Didn't I say I worshipped you?"

Artemis looked up at him, and the kindness and warmth in his eyes nearly undid her. "Yes, but—but, what if I am mad, and not really a goddess?"

Lord Eldon looked thoughtful. "If you are mad, and not a goddess, then you could not have run all that way so quickly to my hunting box. In which case, I am delusionary for thinking you had, and we would be a well-matched pair, wouldn't we?"

A laugh erupted unwillingly from Artemis, then she shook her head. "It cannot be."

"Why?"

She sighed impatiently. "I have already told you!"

"Hmm." Lord Eldon pursed his lips, thinking in silence for a moment before saying, "No, I am afraid your protests have no basis. You say you are a goddess. Such an alliance has been done before, if my schooling was at all correct. If you are not a goddess, then it has definitely been done before, and most certainly must happen if a lady and a gentleman such as ourselves indulged in—" He stopped, the corners of his lips lifting slightly as if in pleasant remembrance. "Indulged."

Artemis swallowed, remembering also. "And if I were mad?"

"I shall take the utmost care of you, and perhaps go pleasantly insane along with you, for if that night was madness, I should wish it to go on forever." He paused for a moment, considering the matter. "With a different ending, of course."

"You are impossible, and no doubt crazed!"

"No doubt, but you have not given your answer."

She closed her eyes. She was insane even to consider it— all because of Eros's cursed arrow. She would refuse, and that would be that. Taking a deep breath, she looked straight into his eyes . . . eyes that gazed back with a deep tenderness, a fiery passion, bringing back memories of every word, every touch, every feeling she had had that night after her forest run.

"I—don't know." Artemis groaned in frustration. It was *not* what she meant to say. "I—need to consider the matter." She cursed under her breath, and Lord Eldon grinned. "That is, I won't—won't—know until you have proven your love for me." She sank into a sofa, near exhaustion with the effort of speaking against the compulsion to accept. Lord Eldon sat next to her.

"Name it, and I shall do it," he said simply.

She breathed a sigh of relief. She could put him off . . . and perhaps keep him from being so tempting and from offering her marriage. She searched her mind for something impossible, beyond his capabilities, and she gazed at his exquisitely tied neckcloth, gold-embroidered waistcoat, and Weston-tailored coat.

He was a dandy. She smiled, relieved. Perhaps he was good at some sport—he hunted, but with a gun, and no doubt rode a horse when he did. However, being good at one sport was no guarantee he could do any other, such as shoot a bow and arrow.

"An archery match," she said. Lord Eldon raised his brows. "Miss Hathaway has told you I am fond of sport, did she not? Well, then. I challenge you to a bout of archery. If you beat me in three tries, than I shall"—she swallowed—"I shall marry you." She summoned up a smile. It could not happen, of course. No one could best Artemis, goddess of the hunt, at archery.

A considering expression crossed Lord Eldon's face. "I expect you proposed this because you think you will win," he said, then nodded. "Very well, I accept." His lips turned up in a lopsided way again, making her clasp her hands together to keep herself from touching him. "It'll be devilish good sport, too."

Artemis relaxed at last, sure of her victory, and when Lord Eldon took his leave after a little more conversation, she did not even blush—much—when he bowed and kissed her hand.

News of the contest spread quickly among the house-guests, and Lady Hathaway consented to clear a spot in her very large and carefully kept conservatory. The skies still had not cleared, and rain had fallen steadily, preventing anyone from enjoying a ride outdoors, much less going on walks or an alfresco luncheon.

All the guests bet on it; it was an even match, everyone thought. Lord Eldon, though well known for his fondness of the hunt, did not engage in other sport that anyone knew of. Lord Blytheland smiled slyly and placed a fair sum upon Lord Eldon, but they were friends, and the marquess was known to be loyal. However, Miss Knightly was clearly used to sport; she walked with an athletic grace, and anyone who recalled her somewhat scandalous costume at the masquerade ball, also recalled how it revealed her broad shoulders and strong frame.

The clouds had lightened a little on the day of the contest, and servants brought a target from the attic of the house and set it up upon hay bales, the bull's-eye a good four feet above the ground. Artemis shrugged when she saw the bows and arrows brought for the competition; more bets were exchanged when the guests saw this—she clearly knew the sport well.

The conservatory was warm from the coal-fed braziers brought into it to preserve the rare plants and the hothouse flowers Lady Hathaway so prized. It was full of growing vegetation, and Artemis could feel herself strengthen from the presence of so many living plants. She smiled confidently. She would win this contest, and she would be rid of Lord Eldon; he was a man of honor, and if—no, when—he lost this game, he would realize his pursuit of her was hopeless, and he would leave her.

A hard, hot grief seized her at the thought, and she drew in a quick breath. It was the effect of Eros's arrow, not anything she truly felt. The sensation of gentle hands on her skin came to her, and her hand clenched on her bow. Stop! she told herself fiercely, banishing the feelings—at least for now. She looked angrily at Eros, who was leaning against a pillar with an amused expression on his face.

She glanced at Lord Eldon, whose valet was carefully removing his coat. She had more honor than to sneer at such frivolous care for clothes, but seeing it only confirmed her belief she would win. Someone so concerned with the cut of his coat and the folds of his neckcloth could not have enough time to spend on perfecting any sport.

"You may go first, Lord Eldon," Artemis said, once the target had been set up. The conservatory was a good sixty feet from one end to the other; it would be easy, even though the bows and arrows were not of the best kind.

Lord Eldon bowed politely. "Please do me the honor of going first, Miss Knightly. You must be expert at it, and I always like to learn." She looked at him suspiciously, but his expression was politely interested. He hesitated, then said, "I hope you won't mind if I stand next to you as you shoot."

Artemis gave a terse smile. "You may do as you please, Lord Eldon. My concentration has never been disturbed at this sport."

"Never?" he asked, his brows raising.

"Never."

"Even if I were to speak to you during your shooting?"

"Not even then," she replied confidently.

He nodded and stepped closer, and immediately she regretted her words. He would indeed be a distraction to her . . . but not for long. Nothing had ever distracted her from her shooting. She had even shot her arrows during wars—the most distracting of environments—and had always hit her target.

She nocked her arrow and pulled back the bowstring.

"You are very beautiful," Lord Eldon said in a whisper.

The arrow missed the bull's-eye by half an inch. Groaning and cheers arose from the guests.

"Thank you," Artemis said through gritted teeth.

"Not at all," Lord Eldon replied politely.

She gathered her concentration and nocked another arrow.

"However, I cannot decide whether you are more beautiful clothed or—"

Artemis uttered a curse under her breath—the arrow hit just on the edge of the bull's-eye. She let down her bow as Kenneth Hathaway inspected the target.

"More in than out," Kenneth called out.

The guests who had bet on Artemis cheered, and she caught a mischievous glint in Lord Eldon's eyes. She pressed her lips together. There would be no doubt about this last shot. She nocked her last arrow, and pulled back the bowstring, drawing in all the power she could and focusing it into the arrow and in the force contained in the taut bow.

"I love you, you know," Lord Eldon whispered again.

But he spoke too late; she had already released the string, and the arrow hit dead center. Artemis turned triumphantly to his lordship, thinking to see dismay on his face.

But there was only admiration in Lord Eldon's eyes. "Quite excellent," he said. "I congratulate you."

"You give up, then?"

He raised his brows again, smiling. "Not at all. Play or pay, my dear, play or pay." He took up his bow.

He nocked his arrow, his arm came back, and he released the bowstring in one graceful, effortless motion. The arrow hit the bull's-eye. Artemis turned and stared at him, aghast. The guests cheered, even those who had bet against him.

"Practice," Lord Eldon said modestly. "Dashed fine sport, archery." An image of him, naked, rose in her mind, and she remembered at last the strength of his arms, and how finely muscled they were—an archer's arms. She groaned. She should have realized it; one did not gain such strength by sitting on a horse or shooting guns. But she had been totally besotted, and had only admired, not thought. He took up another arrow.

"You lied to me," she whispered angrily.

"I? I did nothing of the sort," he said calmly, as the arrow hit the bull's-eye again. "I don't lie, my dear, not if I can help it." He took up his last arrow.

"Then you cheated!"

There was a pause in the smooth action of nocking, pulling, and release; the arrow hit the edge of the bull's-eye.

"More in than out," Kenneth called out.

The guests cheered and crowded around Lord Eldon. Lord Blytheland slapped his shoulder and grinned. "Hidden depths, eh, El?" He turned to the people around them. "Won first place in the Ancient Scorton Arrow tournament two years ago."

Lord Eldon looked alarmed. "No, no! *Not* first place—only second. Not as good as that, give you my word!"

"Well, you're a member of the Royal Toxophilite Society—no second-raters there," Lord Blytheland said. He turned to Artemis. "That was fine marksmanship on your part, I must say, Miss Knightly. I was half afraid you would beat El here to flinders. I don't think I've ever seen any woman shoot so well in my life. It was close—very close."

"Thank you," Artemis managed to say. She felt as if a stone had lodged in her throat—she could hardly speak over the indignation and humiliation that burned in her belly. She looked at Lord Eldon. No triumph was in his expression, only concern.

"Come, Miss Knightly, shall we celebrate?" He held out his hand.

She looked at it and then at him, wanting desperately to run away. But there was no honor in that, and the expectant looks of the guests stayed her. She nodded as graciously as she could. "Yes," she said, and took Lord Eldon's hand.

He put her hand upon his arm and walked slowly down the conservatory to the door, letting the guests go out first. As the last guest went out the door Lord Eldon pulled her behind a large fern.

"Well, Miss Knightly, have I proved myself worthy?"

She gazed at him and her heart turned in her chest. His eyes held only tenderness and admiration, and a deep intensity; she felt she could not look away. Her hand raised to touch him, but she forced it down again.

"You cheated," she made herself say.

"I, cheat?" His brows came down in a frown, then he smiled slightly. "Technically, I did not. You agreed I might speak to you while you shot, and you claimed you would not be distracted. In fact, you shot as if I were not there at all." His smile grew wider. "Are you saying that you *were* distracted?"

Anger flared. "Yes, by Zeus, I was, and you meant me to be!"

"Yes, I did—you need not be surprised I admit it," he said.

"So, none of the things you said were true," Artemis said.

"Of course they were true. I told you I don't lie." He sounded put out, then looked at her curiously. "You don't trust me. Have I done or said anything to cause this?"

Artemis fell silent. She could not think of one thing he had done, except— "You kissed me when I was not prepared for it, that time in the carriage."

He grinned. "I was overcome, and I did not think you would protest, which you did not, if I remember correctly." His expression grew serious. "Miss Knightly, you know the conditions of our agreement. Have I proved myself worthy?"

"I . . . I—yes, I suppose you have. As worthy as any mortal." Artemis closed her eyes—it was too much to look at him. She felt a touch on her chin, the smooth sliding of his fingers along her jawbone. She shivered, and opened her eyes again.

"I love you," he said, and kissed her.

She could not help herself; she leaned into him, kissing him deeply as she had that night she had run through the forest to his hunting cottage.

"It was not a dream," he murmured as he kissed her throat.

"No," she said. "No, not a dream."

He kissed her lips again, then drew away a hairbreadth's distance. "You will marry me—say you will."

"Marry—" *Marry.* She looked into his eyes, full of fire, and pushed him abruptly away. "I cannot."

Lord Eldon took in a deep breath and let it out again. "I don't care how you come to me, Miss Knightly, whether you are truly a maiden, a widow, or neither." He smiled crookedly. "Or a goddess. It doesn't matter, though I suppose it should. I only know I couldn't stop looking at you from the moment you appeared in that ballroom, and knew from the start I'd want to look at you for the rest of my life." He hesitated. "If it's me, then say the word and I'll never bother you again."

Artemis knew she did not object to him at all. He was as Eros had said: stronger, more virtuous and clever than she had given him credit for. A good man, in fact. She gazed at his hands that held hers—strong hands that could pull a bowstring with ease and grace, and touch her with a gentleness that filled her with wild heat.

But she could not marry him, and it was not for any of the reasons she had given him. She gazed at him, and knew to her shame that only one thing kept her from saying yes: fear. Overwhelming, abject fear of losing her heart and soul completely and absolutely after thousands of years of keeping it protected. She knew it, and if she was too much of a coward to agree to marry him, at least she would not deny the truth. Artemis lifted her chin and looked steadily at Lord Eldon.

"No, Lord Eldon, it is not you. You are a good man, and I know it." She bit her lip, then continued. "No, it is I. For all that I am a goddess, I am afraid. I am not sure if my feelings for you are—are all that you deserve. And that is why I cannot marry you." She covered her face briefly with her hands, then forced them down as hard as she forced down her feelings of grief and despair. "I am sorry." She looked at him, and saw an echoing despair in his eyes.

She could not stand it. Quickly she turned, and ran, out of the conservatory and into the house.

Lord Eldon stood, watching her leave, his hand half outstretched toward her. He sighed and dropped his hand, then wearily rubbed his face. "Well, you've missed the mark this time, old man," he murmured. He looked toward the door of the conservatory. "Celebrate? I don't know what for, but I might as well. At least Hathaway keeps a good cellar."

Chapter 10

It helped that Psyche could see the heartache between Artemis and Lord Eldon. Not that she wished them to be hurt, of course! But as long as she tried to think of a way to help them, she need not think of how Harry had promised to help her.

Harry had been too complacent about the effects of his arrow on Artemis. She was top over tails in love with Lord Eldon, and he with her, but after the archery contest neither approached or even looked at the other.

Psyche had tried to speak with Artemis, but to no avail. She knew she could speak to Harry and Lord Eldon, however; perhaps in that way she could make Harry try to help them. She was not sure anything could be done for Lord Eldon; he would love the goddess forever. But at least something could be done for Artemis. The goddess had drifted through the house, pale and listless, drawn to the conservatory—the place of her defeat—but avoiding it just before she entered. She was suffering, Psyche was sure of it, and it was not right.

The sun decided to make a miraculous appearance the day after the archery contest. Though the fields were still muddy and filled with small ponds where there should have been none, the Hathaways' visitors could not stand being confined any longer. Grooms and undergrooms took horses from their stables and saddled them, and at last the guests were free.

The horses tended to break into canters and gallops instead of sedate walks, and the only people not galloping across the fields were Lord St. Vire and his wife; Lady St. Vire was with child, and though his lordship had given in to her desire to ride a horse, he would not allow her to go beyond a slow walk.

Psyche could not blame anyone for riding fast, and allowed her own mare to have her head for a few minutes. It was wonderful, feeling the warmth of the sun on her face at last and the wind pulling at her hat, and she ignored the mud liberally splattered on the hem of her riding dress. She saw with concern that Lord Eldon seemed not to care about the black smears marring the white tops of his boots. Poor man! He must be feeling quite low indeed not to care about staining his boots.

She cast a glance at Harry, riding a gray, light-footed mare. He rode easily, as if he were part of the animal, and she could almost fancy wings sprouting from the back of the mare, for when they galloped across the fields, they seemed almost to fly. But when he came near, he clearly had not enjoyed the ride; his face was set in solemn lines, changing to amiability and interest when someone spoke to him, but resuming solemnity when alone.

Psyche pressed her lips together. Harry *would* listen to her this time! Surely he could not want either Artemis or Lord Eldon to continue suffering so. She turned her mare toward Harry. The mud dulled the sound of her horse's hooves, so he did not look up until the splish-splash of water alerted him to their presence. His face tightened for a moment, and she almost thought he would ride away. But he relaxed and put on a smile—a strained one.

She hesitated, then said, "Harry, I have mentioned it before, but I am very stubborn, so I will ask again: release Artemis from the spell of your arrow. You must see how miserable she is, and Lord Eldon as well. You said to 'wait and see' and nothing has come of it but heartache for the both of them."

He gave a sigh. "I saw the way they acted yesterday and today. You are right; there is not much I can do for Lord Eldon, but I can take away the arrow's effect on Artemis.

Perhaps she has made herself too hardened against love. I had thought otherwise. If she is a hopeless case, better that Eldon see it soon and find someone else."

Psyche looked at him, surprised. "Well, that was easily done!"

Harry shrugged. "How you underestimate me! I can learn, after all. Artemis is foolish not to accept love where she can, but I suppose forcing the issue will do no good. I feel sorry for Eldon. I know what it is to love and not be allowed—" He stopped and shrugged again, his lips twisting bitterly.

"You have not found her, have you, Harry?" she asked, her voice gentle.

He looked down at his hands clasping his horse's reins, then glanced at her. "You would be the first to know, I assure you." He closed his eyes briefly. "But she is near. I must be closer to finding out who and where she is." He gestured toward the sun shining weakly through the clouds. "The rain has stopped for now, as you see. My power weakened when I stayed behind in London, and I regained it when I came here. She *must* be here. I must have had some thought as to her identity—but I don't know which one it is! I can make nothing of the clues I had." He looked at her and sighed. "I am tired, Psyche. If I were not sure she is somewhere near, I would give it up. I wish I knew why she does not reveal herself to me, since she must be here."

Psyche reached out and took his hand—tentatively, then more firmly. She could not help it; her heart ached for him. "Perhaps she does not know it herself, Harry. I cannot imagine why she would hide if she knew you were looking for her."

The sun on her face grew warmer, and Harry looked up at it, squinting. He stared at her for a moment. "Perhaps you are right," he said, his brows drawing together. "It's doubly difficult now; I don't know what to look for anymore, and . . . it seems my memory has faded, the weaker the gods have become."

A sudden fear stopped the words Psyche wanted to say. All she could do was give a last squeeze of his hand, before she released it. They rode in silence for a while, coming up to a small wood. The leaves sparkled with a layer of glassy rain; the wind blew, and the drops sprinkled down upon them, splashing Psyche's face. She did not mind; for now it was enough that she was outside at last after so much confinement indoors, and that she was riding beside Harry.

They entered the wood, and when Psyche spied a spray of primroses in bloom, somehow protected from the bad weather of the past months, she insisted on descending from her horse to see them. It was difficult to get down by herself, since she was seated sidesaddle, and Harry alighted—that was the word, for he dismounted as light as a feather from his mare—to help her.

Psyche gazed at him as he held out his hand, at the way he smiled at her, and it sent a warm shiver through her. She almost refused—too dangerous, said an inner voice. But she had a fancy to see the flowers, and smiling in return, grasped his hand.

His other hand came to her waist as it did when he danced the waltz with her—long ago, it seemed, though it had only been a few weeks. For a moment Harry looked down at her, a hand still at her waist, the other clasping her hand. Then he let go and turned away to loop the horses' reins upon a low tree branch.

The primroses. Psyche unfroze herself from beside her horse and walked to the clump of flowers. She sighed. "I am glad there are flowers at last. The snowdrops that came out earlier were too delicate to stand against the hail." She scanned the arch of tree branches above, and smiled to see the sun peeping through the leaves. A flutter near her cheek startled her, and turning, she laughed. "A butterfly!" She held out her hand to it, a bright creamy white and black one, and it fluttered around her hand until it seemed weary of investigating it. "I haven't seen one at all this year—it seems ages ago—and they are rare enough without the weather keeping them away."

There was only silence, and for a moment Psyche thought

Harry had left. But when she turned around, he was still there, looking at her strangely.

"Harry, are you well?"

He strode up to her, then took her chin in his hand, staring intently at her.

"Are you my wife, Psyche?"

Her heart beat madly—oh, she wished it were so! She swallowed, and shook her head. "How can I be? I do not remember anything except my own life. I have known you since childhood. If I were your wife, wouldn't I have known it before now?"

"But you said perhaps my wife did not remember for some reason." Harry still held her chin, but then his fingers loosened their hold and slid across her cheek.

Psyche shivered, though she felt almost unbearably warm. He was only a hairsbreadth away from her, and he radiated heat. She pulled away from him, and a cold breeze ran between them. "It was only supposition," she said, trying to sound as reasonable as possible. "I cannot know any such thing."

"But what if it were true?" he replied, stepping closer. "How would you remember?"

"I—I don't know," Psyche said, a little breathlessly.

He looked at her speculatively. "I wonder if there is anything I could do to make you remember?"

A kiss. The words floated into her mind, and she gazed at his lips, remembering what they had felt like. If anything would make a lady remember her husband it would have to be a kiss. She closed her eyes and turned away. That's a bit of wishful thinking, Psyche Hathaway, so stop thinking it, for goodness' sake! she scolded herself. She needed to be *sensible.* "If I *were* your wife," she replied. "You can't be sure of that, and then your kisses would be for nothing."

A shout of laughter made her turn around and stare at him, then she realized what she had blurted. "Oh heavens," she groaned, and covered her face. "Oh, no." She ran to her horse, forgetting she could not mount it, but Harry was before her.

"Don't go, Psyche," he said. "I shouldn't have laughed—I was startled you guessed my thoughts—I am sorry." She stole a glance at him; he had a mischievous look in his eyes, but his smile was understanding and kind. "I suppose we have known each other so long, that our minds march the same way from time to time."

She relaxed and managed to smile. "I suppose we do." They walked silently back to the primroses under the tree. Then feeling daring, she cast him an impish look. "If we are to be honest, not only did I think about a kiss, but I thought it would be pleasant, too, because it *was* pleasant when we did it."

Harry laughed again. "Was it? I am glad. I hoped it would be." He gave her another speculative look.

"And no, Harry, we shouldn't kiss again, because I doubt I am your wife. After all, I haven't remembered anything after that first kiss, and I think it would have happened then, wouldn't it?"

"How inconvenient that you seem suddenly able to read my mind." He grinned. "Perhaps it's a matter of accumulation. If I kissed you more often, you might remember as time went by."

Psyche could feel her face grow warm, but she also felt more comfortable. Even though he talked of kissing her, Harry was teasing her in his old way again, something known and familiar. Perhaps they could talk this way for a while, and she could forget their relationship had changed and that they were only Harry and Psyche, old childhood friends.

"It is not a matter of reading minds," she replied tartly. "I can see it on your face. And I cannot believe additional kissing would do anything if the first one did nothing at all." She frowned briefly; a little niggling *something* entered her mind, but she could not bring it forth. No doubt more wishful thinking. She should dismiss such thoughts before they had a chance to bloom and disappoint.

Harry put on a morose expression. "Nothing at all! If the kisses of the god of love himself did nothing to you, Psyche, you are either a cold, hard woman, or I have lost my powers indeed."

"It did—that is, I am *not* a cold, hard woman, Harry!"

Harry theatrically put his hand to his forehead. "Alas! I have lost my powers."

"Stuff and nonsense! You know that is completely untrue."

His face brightened. "You did mention you thought my kisses pleasant. How gratifying to know you are neither cold nor hard, or that my powers are lost. I feared for a moment my judgment had gone awry." He cocked his head. "What *did* my kisses do to you? It must have been *something* to make you blush so."

"Oh, you—!" Psyche cried, looking about her for something to throw at him. But there were no sofa pillows at hand, so she had to content herself by throwing a primrose and some grass.

He dodged the grass, his eyes twinkling merrily, and Psyche felt so filled with love, she almost could not bear it. This was why she loved him—never because he was a god, or was magical, but because he was merry and teased her and was most of all, her friend. A rain of grass falling upon her head startled her; Harry had thrown a handful in retaliation. She remembered the games they had played when she was very young, and nostalgia overcame her. It was childish—but would Harry play them again?

She tapped him lightly on the chest. "You're it!" she said, and ran away, laughing. "The oak is sanctuary, and I shall get there first—no fair flying!"

A shout of laughter sounded behind her, and the wet squishing sound of running feet came closer. Mud would cover her feet by the end of this game, but she did not care. Exhilaration filled her from running and the joy of play and chase. She felt the swipe of a hand behind her and ran faster, laughing breathlessly. She ran around a small alder, and doubled back behind another, then saw her opportunity to run for the oak. She sprinted away before Harry could catch her, and then, somehow, her foot slipped—mud—and she was falling.

"Oh!" she cried, squeezing her eyes shut and stretching out her hands to break her fall. But at the last moment arms seized her waist, and she landed gently on her back. She opened her eyes and looked into Harry's above her. He grinned.

"I've got you now, and *you* are it."

She breathed heavily—from the run and the fall, she was sure—but as the silent minutes passed, her heart still thumped quickly. Harry still held her, but his smile faded and his eyes searched hers, then drifted to her lips.

"*Are* you it, Psyche?" he asked, looking into her eyes again. "Are you my wife? Tell me."

"I don't know—but, oh, Harry, I wish I were!" she said, her voice shaking in confusion and want.

Harry sighed, his lips came down to hers, and she could not, did not want to resist. His kisses were soft, as they were before; then as his lips moved over her mouth, they became firmer, tasting her upper lip, and then the lower.

She opened her mouth under his, closed her eyes, and let him kiss her slowly. The slowness was a torture she wished would go on and on, and she let out a small sighing moan. His fingers moved over her cheek, leaving a warm shimmering trail from there down to her neck, then plucked at the small pearl buttons of her riding habit. Harry made an impatient noise in his throat, and the buttons suddenly slipped from their buttonholes. With a satisfied sigh, he slipped his hand under her bodice.

Gasping, Psyche opened her eyes. Oh, she shouldn't let Harry touch her like this—it was wrong. Perhaps he believed her to be his wife, and that was why he was doing it. But she had no proof of it—with everything he was doing to her now, surely she would remember *something*. She lifted her hips to move out from under him, but it only caused him to groan and kiss her as if he were starving and she a feast laid out before him.

For a moment Psyche kissed him hungrily in return, but a

scattering of drops from the tree leaves above fell on her face, and she was suddenly conscious of the dampness at her back and Harry's weight on her. She could not sacrifice the fate of the world and his life for her desires, or his.

"No, Harry, stop! Pray stop!" With a sobbing breath, she struggled and pushed him forcefully from her. She heard a squishy splash and she sat up at last.

Harry rose from a small mud puddle into which he had apparently rolled. He breathed heavily and stared at her, a confused expression on his face. He began to move toward her, but Psyche put out her hand in warning and shook her head.

"No, Harry, you mustn't. I *can't* be your wife."

"But—"

"No!" Psyche drew in a deep breath, closing her eyes briefly. How she wished she was wrong . . . but it was not something either of them could risk. "Only listen, Harry, please," she pleaded. He stopped and stared at her, his eyes still confused. "I do *not* remember anything. Don't you think after all we have done just now, I would remember, if your kissing idea was true? But I remember only my own life, Harry. My *own* life."

The confusion in his eyes turned to despair, and he pressed his hands over them. "Gods, Psyche. I am sorry. I thought—" He pulled his hands down into fists and pounded the tree beside him. "I don't know what is wrong with me. I thought for a moment you were *her*—perhaps my powers are truly leaving me, though I don't *feel* like they are." He gave an awkward laugh. "Perhaps I am going mad. Sometimes I think I see signs of her presence, but they turn out to be nothing at all."

Psyche went to him and took his hand, pressing it against her cheek. "I am sorry, Harry. I—I wish I were your wife. But it is important for you to *know,* is it not?"

Harry stared at her for a moment in silence. "Yes," he said at last. "It is important that I know." He smiled wryly. "There is mud on your cheek, and on your nose."

Psyche rubbed her cheek, then noticed her hand that had

held his was quite dirty. She wrinkled her nose. "Your fault, I am sure. Your hand is very dirty, and"—she chuckled—"you are quite covered in mud."

Harry grimaced and glanced down at his trousers, almost all black from sitting in the puddle. Then he looked at her and laughed. "No different from yourself, my dear."

She gasped in dismay. "Oh, dear. This dress is ruined, I am sure." Drawing away the clinging skirt from her legs was difficult; it was heavy with moisture and liberally smeared with dirt, grass, and mud. "I dread what Mama will say when she sees me."

He smiled. "Perhaps if we look as circumspect and as innocent as possible," he said, "and tell her that you slipped in the mud and I slipped as well, trying to help you up, she will not mind it much." He began buttoning her dress and she blushed, but let him do it, for she was not at all sure her hands would be steady enough to accomplish the task.

"Oh, *thank* you for saying I am the clumsy one," she said.

"You are very welcome," Harry said pleasantly. "It always helps to tell the truth, after all."

"I am *not* clumsy."

Harry raised his brows. "I never said you were! You did slip and fall, however."

She stared at him, irritated. How he managed to get the last word, she did not know. It really was the most annoying thing about him. Just as well that she was not his wife! Indeed, she felt quite sorry for the poor woman, whoever she was!

But as she continued to look at him, her irritation faded, for his eyes had a smiling glint in them, and she knew he purposely provoked her, perhaps to keep her mind off what neither of them could have. She made herself smile at him and curtsied mockingly before turning to her horse. Harry helped her up, and she arranged her skirts the best she could. Then he, too, mounted his horse.

The rest of the guests had already returned to the Hathaways' house, though the sun was still shining through the clouds—shining brighter now. It was close to dinnertime, and both Psyche and Harry hurried their horses into gallops.

If Psyche had hoped to go up to her chamber and escape her mother's notice, her mother's presence in the hall struck down that hope as soon as her foot stepped over the threshold.

"Psyche!" Lady Hathaway shrieked. "Good heavens! Your face! Oh, dear Lord. Your riding habit!" She put a hand to her temple as if a headache had overcome her. "I do not know where I can find another cloth like it—you *know* we bought it because it was *not* like anything anyone else is wearing." She groaned. "Where am I to get another, now that we are away from London, child?"

Harry stepped forward, bowing politely. "I am afraid it was unavoidable, ma'am. Miss Hathaway slipped while viewing some primroses, and in my *clumsy*"—he shot Psyche a grin, which almost made her laugh—"attempt to help her up, I also slipped and fell into the mud and pulled her down again."

Lady Hathaway wrinkled her nose. "I can see that you did! Oh, dear me." She sighed. "There is nothing for it but both of you must clean yourselves up. I cannot push back dinner, for it wants but a few minutes until it is to be served, and it will take more than an hour for either of you to wash and dress. But I can have it brought up to you in your rooms if you wish."

"You are very kind, Lady Hathaway," Harry said gravely.

Psyche glanced at Harry, then smiled at her mother. "Thank you, Mama. I suppose I shall have to make do with my old riding habit if this one cannot be cleaned."

"*If* the old one fits," Lady Hathaway said. She waved her hands at them. "Go up and try not to drip mud on the way."

They went up the stairs quickly, saying nothing. Harry merely nodded as he left her at the door of her chamber, an oddly determined look about his mouth and chin.

Psyche waited until the servants brought up the water for her bath, then gingerly took off her clothes before sinking gratefully into the tub. Images of herself and Harry in the wood floated into her mind. What if she were wrong? What if she were somehow Harry's wife? Harry had talked of certain signs . . . she wondered what they were. They had come to nothing, he had said, so she supposed they were irrelevant now. *She* had no evidence of being his wife, and the consequences of making a false assumption were too frightening to risk. She felt a lump in her throat, but she shook her head. No, she was done with weeping. She was practical, and weeping solved nothing.

She had asked Harry to shoot her with one of his arrows, and she would keep to that course. Until there was proof that she—or someone else—was Harry's wife, it was best she look about her for a prospective husband. She frowned in sudden realization. Preferably one who did not get her muddy and not even try to magically clean her up so that her mother would not scold!

As she shook her head and washed, and her mind drifted into dreams, and she thought of the book she was writing. She sighed. If she could not have the love she wished for, at least she could spin perfect dreams and make them come true in a book. It was satisfying, sometimes, to do that.

But oh, she wished they could happen in real life!

Chapter 11

The guests danced and played card games that evening, but though Eros tried to be an amiable guest, he could not help gazing at Psyche, wondering if she were truly his wife, and if it was merely wishful thinking.

Was he going mad? He had joined Psyche's play of chase in the woods for the sheer joy of it. Then it had turned into something else . . . he had done the same thing with his wife. When he had caught Psyche Hathaway, for that one moment, he had lived that time again and had begun to make love to her, as he used to so long ago.

Then there were signs—the butterfly, symbol of his wife—the sun, and the air growing warm for the first time since the beginning of the year. Perhaps he had been in the mortal world for so long, he doubted them, and looked upon them as someone such as Sir John Hathaway did—unusual but natural occurrences.

But Miss Psyche Hathaway did not remember. He remembered the recognition in his wife's past incarnations, and he could not remember if it ever had happened in this Psyche. She was no doubt right; if none of his kisses made her remember her former life with him, she was, obviously, not his wife.

He sipped a glass of wine and watched as a guest begged Lord St. Vire to perform his magic tricks. Eros smiled, watching the viscount make a rose appear behind a lady's ear; the man had more than a hint of magic about him. He sighed and turned away. No magic would solve his problems, however. The best he could do was use his arrows to direct affections elsewhere, and that would not help him at all.

He caught sight of Artemis among the company, then looked for Lord Eldon. They were on opposite sides of the room, but if anyone was more aware of each other, he did not know of them. The goddess's interest in magic tricks was perfunctory, and it seemed her eyes were magnetically drawn toward Lord Eldon. Eldon did not look at her, but his jaw was taut, his mouth set in a straight line. But the moment Artemis looked down at her hands on her lap, Lord Eldon turned and stared at her. Anyone not watching St. Vire's performance would have known at once that Eldon was deeply in love with her.

But the goddess looked wan, and Eros could tell her godly powers were greatly reduced; Psyche was right when she said Artemis suffered. He did not wish suffering on anyone unless they truly deserved it. Artemis *had* deserved it, but she did not deserve the loss of her powers. No, Eros could not magically eliminate problems, but he could at least cure this one. He walked to Artemis, and bent near her ear.

"Cousin, I will release you from the arrow's effects anytime you wish," he whispered.

She turned swiftly, the gratitude in her weary eyes moving him to pity and making him wish he had told her sooner. "Please, now, quickly. I am tired, Eros, and grow more so every day."

He took three darts from a pocket of his coat. "I will even allow you to choose: The brown repulses; the silver removes the effects of the gold, which I used upon you. Then the gold, which you may choose if you wish to love Lord Eldon more than you do now." He smiled wryly. "I doubt you will choose that one."

Artemis shuddered. "No, indeed I will not!" Her hand hesitated over the brown and the silver darts, and she cast a quick look at Eros. "I am content not to be repulsed. It would be as unnatural as the gold."

Eros shook his head. "The gold is not unnatural—if you

understood its nature at all." He nodded toward the darts. "Choose, then look at Lord Eldon as you use the dart."

Her hand pounced upon the silver, she looked at his lordship across the room, then squeezed her hand tight. She winced, then sighed and her expression lightened. "Thank you," she said.

"Don't thank me," Eros said, his smile turning ironic. "You may yet regret what you have done."

Artemis looked at him suspiciously. "Have you tricked me?"

"No, by Gaia, I have not," he said, using an oath the goddess trusted. "The silver darts do reverse the effects of the gold." He nodded toward Lord Eldon. "See for yourself. At least you should tell him you are leaving—and you are, yes?"

"By rights I should not, for I think you are wasting your time." Artemis gave him an assessing look. "I suspect you would do well to use one of your darts on yourself if you wish to finish your quest." She nodded her head toward Psyche, who was watching St. Vire's tricks with round eyes.

Eros narrowed his eyes. "You would do well not to interfere, or I might change my mind."

"Do as you wish," Artemis replied, though she shuddered again. "I am too weary to bother with you—and may the coming chaos be on your head alone, because of your stubborn blindness."

"As you say." He shrugged, and Artemis rose, eager to leave now that her urge to stay near Lord Eldon was gone. Eros watched her cross the room to his lordship, then turned toward Psyche.

She wore the silver-embroidered gown again, the puffed sleeves just at her shoulders, the bodice a slight thing of gauze. It was not her favorite dress, he knew, and suspected her mother had made Psyche wear it, for it was a daring dress that begged to be taken off. Lady Hathaway had been casting quick looks at her daughter and at him. Clearly she wondered if he would ever propose; it had been obvious for a long time that she wished her daughter to marry him.

It was his fault. He had come to London out of rebellion as well as because of his quest, and had fancied a mortal style of life. He had gone too far. He had set himself up as an extremely eligible suitor, had attended Psyche at numerous balls, and had even bought Sir Matthew's dower house in which to reside.

Of course he could not propose to Psyche. She would refuse; she was certain she was not his wife. He opened his hand and regarded the remaining darts. The gold . . . he let out a long breath, and pressing his lips together in determination, he looked about the room for an unmarried gentleman.

His eyes fell upon Lord Eldon. Clearly Artemis had just spoken to him and left; the man's face was pale, and a hopeless look dulled his eyes. Had he not told Artemis of the man's virtues? Was he not kind, and intelligent? This was all that Psyche had asked, and he had promised to grant her wish.

Lord Eldon it is, then, he thought, gritting his teeth. But tomorrow, not tonight. It would be better tomorrow, after Artemis's absence had time to sink into him.

Somehow, though he was aware of his lordship's many virtues, Eros could not like him as much as he had before. He put away his darts, moving once more into company, chatting and jesting and staying as far away from Psyche Hathaway as possible.

The party went on late into the night; when the guests left for their rooms at last, Eros could not help looking at Psyche. He gave her a grave bow, and though he saw her hurt expression, quickly went up to his room without saying a word. He was not sure he could bear to speak to her now that his plans were set.

It was worse alone in his bed; dreams of Psyche, of his wife, and sometimes both of them as one person disturbed his sleep. His desires were getting the best of him. Now they were even entering his dreams. A distant tolling of a clock told him dawn had come at last, though it was still dark. Impatiently Eros pushed aside the bedclothes and put on his chiton. Thrusting open the windows, he leaped out and flew skyward.

Today would be the day he would turn Psyche's affections away from him, and it would forever be a cold day for him, colder than the freezing rain that slashed his face. The chill clouds covered him, then released him as he darted above them, and he could see the sliver of the sun at the horizon touch the mist around his feet with a pearl and coral sheen. He hovered there, pressing his hands into his eyes.

"I would give everything, my powers, my gift of flight, and my arrows, to be with Psyche Hathaway, so I could love her as I wish," he said. His voice dissipated into the rarefied air, absorbed, unheard. Was this the lesson he was to learn, to love greatly and to give it up? To give up his very nature?

He of all the Greek gods had kept his powers strong, while the others lost theirs. He did not know why—perhaps because his was a flexible nature, that could roam the world and still find work. Ares, the god of war, also roamed, but he was not as strong. The four goddesses had thought Eros had the answer for them, but for all his searching, he did not.

The sun was no longer a sliver at the horizon, rising to turn the clouds a shimmering white and gold. He focused his attention to the house far below. Sometimes, when Eros pictured Psyche Hathaway in his mind, he knew exactly where she was. It was, no doubt, because he had known her for most of her life. He closed his eyes and an image came to him of her moving uneasily in her bed, her red curls tousled on the pillow and her lips moving silently. His brows drew together in a frown. She had not slept well lately; her dreams disturbed her. He wondered what she dreamed, and hoped they were not dreams of sadness.

Determination made him pull a golden arrow from his quiver. If they were sad dreams, they would not be soon; he would do as he had promised, and she would fall in love with Lord Eldon, and be happy. It was the least he could do for her.

*　　*　　*

The next day brought rain again, but having had a taste of trees and warmth, Psyche could not bear to stay indoors. Her mother's scolding for ruining her riding habit still rang in her ears, so she thought of a compromise: she would go to the conservatory and perhaps sit on a bench and gaze at the orchids her mother had cultivated, or the roses which by this time should be in bloom. Quickly, not waiting for her maid, Psyche put on a simple ribbon-gathered dress, and ran out of her room.

When she stepped into the conservatory, Psyche closed her eyes. All she could sense was the warm humidity, the scent of earth, and the perfume of flowers. She would pretend she had been transported to an exotic land in the tropics—India, perhaps, or the Sandwich Islands in the South Pacific seas.

"The Sandwich Islands today," she said to herself. She had read of the way native women could sing like birds and danced with their hands waving gracefully about. It was said they were savages, but she could not imagine how anyone who could sing and dance so well could be a savage. How did they do it? She opened her eyes and began to wave her hands in front of her, humming the dance tune Lady St. Vire had played on the pianoforte last night, and moving her feet in the steps of the quadrille.

She stumbled, stopped, and wrinkled her nose. The Sandwich Island ladies could not be savages! One had to be quite civilized and intelligent, not to mention coordinated, to accomplish such a complicated thing.

A chuckle behind her made her turn and blush—oh, heavens! How long had Lord Eldon been there? He sat on a stone bench behind some ferns, which was why she hadn't seen him.

"Very interesting, Miss Hathaway." He grinned as he rose and bowed over her hand. "A new dance? I daresay it shall be all the rage should you present it at Almack's next season."

Psyche's face flamed hotter, but an image came to her of Princess Lieven dancing and waving her hands about, and she laughed. "I daresay *not*, my lord. If you must know, I was pretending I was a lady from the Sandwich Islands."

"Ah. And these ladies dance an exotic form of the quadrille, is that it? What was all that"—he waved his hands in front of his face—"about?"

"They are supposed to wave their hands gracefully as they dance, or so I have read." She sat on the stone bench and patted the spot beside her.

Lord Eldon thought on this, then shook his head as he sat. "I daresay it's nonsense. Dashed dirty place, the Sandwich Islands, or so I hear. They were probably brushing away flies."

"No, no! You must be thinking of Calcutta—Colonel Hanford told me it was horribly poor and filthy there." She had often thought the Sandwich Islands a most romantic place, and she did not like to think of it as dirty.

"That must be it." Lord Eldon nodded. "I remember him telling me the same thing last year." He sighed. "Wonderful thing, travel. Been thinking of doing some of it myself."

"Have you?" Psyche frowned. His lordship was very attached to his estate, and dandy though he was, he spent more time there than most of his set. "Since when?"

"Last night."

"Oh!" Psyche had seen Harry speak with Artemis last night, and seen him give her something that caused her to smile in relief. She suspected that Harry had done what she asked: given the goddess the antidote to the love dart.

There was silence. "Not to Greece, though. Couldn't bear that." He frowned for a moment. "Besides, I've already done the Grand Tour."

Psyche's heart melted, and she pressed Lord Eldon's hand. "Oh, I am so sorry!"

"Obvious, eh?" His lips twisted wryly. "The most beautiful woman I've ever met, and a devilish good shot with a bow, too. I was blessing every saint I could remember—what more could a man want?" He sighed heavily. "But Miss Knightly won't have me. My fault, I suppose—rode too fast over rough ground, I daresay, and for all her forth-rightness, she's as skittish as a colt."

"Perhaps you will find someone else?" Psyche asked tentatively.

"No," Lord Eldon said. "I knew the moment I set eyes on her. It's always been that way with us Fordhams. Happened to my brother Jeremy, as soon as he saw his Susan, wouldn't look at another after that, give you my word!" He sighed again. "There it is. Might as well leave for lands unknown."

Psyche bit her lip. Poor Lord Eldon! She wished now that she hadn't persuaded Harry to reverse the arrow's spell on Artemis, but what else could she have done? Yet, Lord Eldon was in a terrible state; his face was pale, his shiny boots scuffed, and worse, his neckcloth was awry. She had never seen him less than impeccably dressed—he must truly be heartbroken. And now he was talking of leaving his estate!

Did he know Artemis's true nature? Perhaps if he did, it would put him off the idea of wishing to marry the goddess.

"You should know something about Miss Knightly, my lord."

He looked at her, brows raised, all attention.

"I do not know how to say this . . ." She winced. "She is not Miss Diana Knightly, but the Greek goddess of the hunt, Artemis."

Lord Eldon looked thoughtful for a moment, then nodded. "That explains it."

"You believe me?" Psyche said, astonished.

"She told me," he said simply. "Then, too, she ran from your house to my hunting box, and she—" He stopped, and Psyche noticed with interest his ears turning a pink color that slowly traveled to his cheeks. "Well, never mind that. But no one could have run that distance in the time I calculated . . . unless she and Lady Blytheland had an accident on the road?"

"No, they arrived in the evening, in fine condition."

"As she said." He shrugged. "Therefore, she must have some special powers, ones I suppose a goddess might."

Psyche stared at him. "You are accepting this very easily."

"I've known other unusual people." He waved his hand dismissively.

"No, really?"

Lord Eldon leaned toward her in a confidential manner. "I imagine you think Lord St. Vire's tricks are sleight of hand?"

"Why, of course . . ."

He shook his head. "Magic."

"Truly?"

He nodded. "He showed me."

"No!"

"Truth!" Lord Eldon rubbed the end of his nose thoughtfully. "Although he was smiling in that way of his—I wouldn't put it past him to roast me, you know. Good friend and all, but devilish clever, is St. Vire, and fond of a joke now and then." He sighed again. "Whatever the case, Miss Knightly won't have me. I suppose she might look higher than an earl, being a goddess and all."

"No, that cannot matter, for she has not cared before." Psyche blinked, startled at herself. She knew nothing about Artemis's past, other than she was the goddess of the hunt. Perhaps it was something her father had told her. However, she could not imagine her father telling her stories about people having illicit affairs. Not that Artemis had committed adultery with Orion, of course! "Neither one of them had been married," she continued, still surprised. "Artemis told me long ago she would have married Orion, had it not been for . . ." She shook her head at an odd sensation in her mind, as if a door had opened and shut. When had Artemis told her this? She could not remember.

She heard a sharp gasp behind her—or was it a sudden gust of rain and wind upon the conservatory roof? Standing swiftly, she looked about her—no one. It was the rain, then.

Yet, a strange feeling, a sparkling glimmer in her mind, a presence . . . She wondered suddenly if Harry were about, and if—

She glanced at Lord Eldon and a dreadful thought came

to her: what if Harry were here, and decided she should fall in love with Lord Eldon? She had asked him not to let her know when he did it. The earl was a very worthy gentleman, but she had refused him already—could not Harry pick another one? She looked nervously about the shrubs and ferns.

"Could we sit elsewhere?" she asked. "I am a little chilled, and there is a warm brazier near that bench over there." Tall ferns and exotic palms blocked the bench in almost every direction. If Harry should move, she would certainly hear him. She listened for a while, but there was silence, and the odd glimmer in her mind was gone. Her shoulders relaxed; if Harry was here, he was at least not going to shoot her with any arrows. She breathed a sigh of relief. Another time, perhaps, and she hoped she would not be conscious of his presence when he did.

Psyche and Lord Eldon were in the conservatory; Eros could see them talking together. He took form behind a pillar atop which was a large fern, making sure to keep invisibility tightly around him. He watched as Psyche squeezed Lord Eldon's hand, and he felt a sharp ache in his chest. Her face held sympathy; they were talking of Artemis. Psyche had always been kindhearted and quick to show it—it was what he loved about her. He turned his eyes to Lord Eldon . . . he, too, was kind. It was probably the best match he could make for Psyche. He moved closer, nocked his gold arrow, and pulled it carefully back.

"Neither one of them had been married," Psyche was saying. "Artemis told me long ago she might have married Orion after a while, had it not been for . . ." An odd look crossed her face.

Impossible! Artemis had not spoken of her affair with Orion to anyone after he died—not to him, Eros, or even to her twin brother, Apollo. He stared at Psyche. She had said she wasn't—but she knew— His hands clenched and pulled with harsh force on bow and bowstring. His arrow shattered, sending splinters flying. A deep, searing pain shot through him, and he gasped.

He had almost shot his wife. Shock made him stand still, staring at Miss Psyche Hathaway: his friend, his love, his wife.

He'd been a fool, an idiot. The signs *had* been there: the fairy costume she had worn with the butterfly wings—the costume had been an almost exact duplicate of the one his wife had worn after she had been made immortal. She had loved butterflies, and yes—did not a rare butterfly appear that day in the wood just before they had kissed again? The weather—it had improved since the time he had wondered if she were truly his wife, and the sun had shone the brightest it had anytime this year that day in the wood. The rain had returned, however, as soon as he had decided to turn her affections away from him.

He remembered, suddenly, how Psyche had said things to him in exactly the way his wife had, so long ago. He had felt confused, wondering if, in his desire for the present Psyche, his failing memory deceived him. Now he was beginning to remember it, clearly.

How else was he to account for his increased powers ever since he had become Psyche Hathaway's friend? Was it not true when she had left London, he had suffered a loss of strength? He had weakened tremendously when he had gone to Spain to protect her brother in battle. But even in war he could cause love to happen, and it had not restored him as had his return to Psyche.

He had discounted all the signs, for Psyche had denied any significance to them, and said she could not remember. But didn't she herself suggest that his wife might have forgotten? Perhaps she did remember—somewhere deep inside.

"Are you well, Miss Hathaway?" Lord Eldon's voice brought Eros's attention back to the present. Psyche had risen from the stone bench; the pair had moved to another, farther away from him, shrouded in palms and large ferns. Psyche shook her head, then sat down again.

She smiled at Lord Eldon. "Quite well . . . I thought I heard something—but it was nothing." She hesitated.

"Artemis . . . I imagine the reason why she is so skittish is that she loved once before, and he . . . died. I think she is frightened of loving again." Psyche drew in her breath, and another odd look crossed her face, as if she did not quite understand her own words.

"Ahh," Lord Eldon said softly, and nodded. "Happened to Blythe. Then he met your sister and fell top over tails for her." He looked down at his hands resting on his knees, then pushed his fingers through his hair. "Wish I had known."

Eros watched as Psyche gazed at Lord Eldon, her eyes filled with compassion. She patted his lordship's shoulder in a comforting way. "If you would like, I could speak to her on your behalf. I cannot guarantee she will see you again, Lord Eldon, but I can try."

He brought her hand to his lips and smiled. "It's the best anyone can do. If you could convince her to talk to me one more time, I'll be your servant forever," he said.

Quick jealousy shot through Eros. He did not like seeing anyone kiss his wife—especially since he'd just begun to enjoy the pleasure again after much too long. He dropped his invisibility and strode forward.

Psyche's eyes widened and she stood. Lord Eldon's brows rose, and he pulled out his quizzing glass.

"Glad to see you and all that, D'Amant, but I don't think we've got a costume ball going this early in the morning." His lordship shook his head, putting away his quizzing glass after examining Eros from head to foot. "Not the warmest thing to wear, either, not in this weather."

"You can *see* him?" shrieked Psyche.

"Deuced well can," his lordship replied. "Dressed like a dashed Scotsman in that kilt, except he's missing a lot more than the color of his clan." He gazed at Eros's wings. "And added something else. Devil take me if I can see how you have those things affixed."

"You will *not* kiss my wife!" Eros said.

"I wasn't kissing her—well, just her hand, and anyone might do that. Perfectly proper, old man, perfectly proper." Lord Eldon's brows rose higher. "Wife?"

"No, no, I am not his wife!"

Eros stepped forward and seized Psyche's shoulders. "Psyche, only listen to me, I know it now—you must be her, my wife." She stared at him, shaking her head slowly.

"You know, D'Amant, if you are going to go about proposing marriage, you can't do it dressed like that." Lord Eldon shook his head in strong disapproval. "No wonder she won't agree to it; you've got to do the thing right, and what you're wearing would put anyone off, give you my word!" His expression turned mournful. "Not that Weston's best did *me* any good." He frowned thoughtfully. "Perhaps I should have tried Scott for a change. A bit military in cut, but who knows? It might have worked."

Eros shot him an irritated look, and snapped his fingers, making his wings disappear and a fine suit of clothes appear on him in place of the chiton.

Lord Eldon paled, but recovered admirably, and nodded. "Should have guessed—cousin of Miss Knightly—Artemis. Stands to reason you'd be one of those Greeks, too."

"How can I be your wife?" Psyche said, gazing at Eros anxiously. "What if you have made a mistake?"

"I haven't, Psyche. The signs—they were all there—your costume, the butterfly, my strength returning whenever you were near. I was a fool to discount them."

"I think a man would know his own mind, Miss Hathaway," Lord Eldon said. "Especially if he's known you most of your life. Childhood friend, didn't you say? I always did think the two of you were a matched pair—in fact, I recall I mentioned it to you some time ago."

Eros laughed. "You see, even Lord Eldon agrees with me." He drew her to him. "You'll remember—I shall make you remember." He bent his head and kissed her.

For one moment Psyche gave in to Harry's kiss, then she heard Lord Eldon clear his throat. She blushed and stepped back.

"I, ah, think I shall leave you both to your, um, talk," Lord Eldon said, edging away. "Dashed improper of me being in on a marriage proposal." He bowed elegantly. "You can depend on me to be discreet, whatever you decide. Your servant, Miss Hathaway, D'Amant." The sound of his footsteps faded quickly, and the conservatory door shut.

"Oh, Harry," Psyche said. "I don't know! How can I know?"

He drew her close to him again. "*I* know. It's all that's necessary." He brushed his fingers across her cheek, then moved his thumb across her lips. She looked into his eyes, and saw a light in them she had never seen before, full of joy and heated passion. "Beautiful Psyche," he breathed, and pressed his lips full upon her mouth. She moaned and closed her eyes, wanting desperately for him to be right. He must be right—did not Artemis say he would know? A tentative joy unfurled in her heart and she put her arms around Harry at last.

He pulled her down to the bench, and the ferns and shrubbery formed a shelter around them. His lips moved to her chin, then the soft, sensitive skin under it, and all thoughts fled. Harry untied the ribbon at her bodice, kissing each inch of flesh revealed as he pushed the sleeve off one shoulder. She shivered and wove her fingers through his hair . . . and felt a warm wetness. She opened her eyes and gasped.

"Harry, oh, dear heaven! You are bleeding! What did you do to yourself?"

"It's nothing," he murmured against her throat and slid his hand into her bodice. She drew in a long shuddering breath in response, briefly closing her eyes.

"It's not 'nothing'—it could fester if not cared for." She pushed herself away and sat up. A faint scratch from the top of his cheekbone into his hair bled slightly; she looked lower and noticed a few spots of blood on his neckcloth. She had not seen it at first because the scratches were along the far side of his face, and she had faced him all the while. "We must go in, Harry. Even slight scratches can become poisonous."

An irritated expression crossed his face. "It's nothing, I tell you. The arrow I aimed at you shattered—I overdrew the bow—a stupid thing that even an amateur would not have done. The splinters must have scratched me."

Psyche stared at him, her stomach suddenly leaden. "I was right, thinking you were here and . . . you were watching me, about to make me fall in love with Lord Eldon." She groaned. "And then you broke your arrow."

"I was a fool," Harry said, and pulled her into his arms again, pressing kisses on her lips and cheek and breasts.

Psyche pushed him away. "So that is why." She drew up her dress sleeve and hastily tied her bodice ribbon.

"Why I have this scar? Yes, I told you that."

"No. Why you are kissing me."

Harry looked mystified. "My love, I am kissing you because I adore you."

"No, you are not. You kissed me because you stuck yourself with your own arrow—and you must know what that does to people!"

"I am not 'people,'" he said haughtily; then his expression softened and he reached for her again. Psyche could not help responding, but the slide of her dress over one shoulder again made her struggle to stand up straight.

"No, stop it, stop it, Harry! Only listen to me!"

Harry finally moved away from her, but his eyes centered on her lips, as if he found them irresistible. "Yes?"

"Don't you see? You only decided I was your wife after you stuck yourself with your arrow." She seized his hand and turned it over, and pointed to a small splinter in his palm. "I *thought* I felt something odd when you touched me."

"Disturbing, indeed," Harry said, frowning, which made Psyche hope he was beginning to see reason. He plucked the splinter from his hand and tossed it away, then turned to Psyche and kissed her again. "Is that better?"

"*Please,* Harry, do listen!" she said, twisting from his grasp. "You are not yourself!" She quickly moved behind a potted palm tree, putting it between her and Harry.

"I am very much myself," he replied. "More than I ever have been for at least a thousand years."

"No, your arrow pierced you and you are now convinced I am your wife—but I am *not*."

He smiled. "Then marry me and you shall be."

"It is not that simple! Do you not remember your quest?"

"Of course I do. You are my wife. I found you. My quest is—almost—done." His smile turned into a wicked, sensual grin.

Psyche groaned. He would not be convinced until somehow the effects of the arrow were reversed. How was she to accomplish that? She bit her lower lip, thinking. At the very least, she could put him off.

"Very well, then! That may be what you think, but I am still a mortal, and I think it best to go about all of this in the usual way. For one thing, you have not applied to my father to ask my hand in marriage. For another, I do not think it is proper to kiss me before we are engaged."

"Your father has already consented to it, and since we have done much kissing before marriage was even mentioned, I suggest we continue what we have been doing." He reached for her again, but Psyche skipped away from him.

"No, Papa has not consented to your marrying me—he only said you were allowed to be with me because you knew Latin. You have yet to show proficiency in Greek or anything else he considers a requirement for courting me. As for kissing"—she swallowed—"besides, I cannot kiss you when you have blood on your face and on your neckcloth. At the very least you must have your cuts tended to. Surely you can see that."

Harry's face grew thoughtful; then he nodded. "It would be unpleasant to be kissed and bled upon. As for the other items"—he waved a dismissive hand—"they are easily dealt with."

Psyche moved warily from behind the palm tree. "Do you promise not to kiss me?"

"For as long as I am still bleeding," Harry said.

"And *not* when anyone might be looking, if you please! If I did not know I could trust Lord Eldon's discretion, I would have slapped you after you kissed me—as you said I should, if you remember!" She smiled grimly. "Indeed, there are many things you have taught me through the years that I can use to thwart you."

He frowned again. "How shortsighted of me to have taught them to you."

"No," Psyche said, taking his hand and pulling him toward the conservatory door. "It was very sensible, especially now that you have lost your senses."

"Perhaps I have," Harry replied in a contemplative voice. "In which case, I should test each one of them on you—sight, hearing, smell, touch, and taste. I think the last two should be especially gratifying."

"Oh, for heaven's sake, do be quiet!" Psyche blushed hotly, and took him to the drawing room to find her mother.

Chapter 12

Lady Hathaway was in her sitting room with her husband, having a companionable cup of tea and a few biscuits. "Just imagine, my dear—that odd Miss Knightly, called away so suddenly! I wonder what was so urgent that she felt she must leave? Cassandra had no explanation for it, and said her friend had wished to keep the matter private."

Sir John waved his hand, as if at a gnat. "A trivial thing. I suppose she will return when she feels it is fit to do so." He pushed up his spectacles and continued perusing the paper. "Odd," he murmured. "Snowstorms in late spring."

"Everything has been odd this year, John." Lady Hathaway nibbled another biscuit. "The weather, the guests—not all of them, but Lord Eldon has not been his usual self. Anyone with eyes can see he and Miss Knightly are in love, but then she left! He must be in abject despair, for he came to breakfast with his neckcloth awry! I have never seen him in such a state." She frowned. "Then there is Mr. D'Amant. I am vastly disappointed in him. I thought he would have asked Psyche to marry him by now, but he did not come near her all evening. There is something wrong, but my daughter will not tell me. How it is that I have such vexatious children, I do not know. They tell me nothing! It is not as if I were a dragon, for goodness' sake."

"Mmm," Sir John said, turning a page.

"Nor would I put anything in their way. I do not quibble about Mr. D'Amant's lack of title—being heir to Sir William is enough. I would even forgo that, for Mr.

D'Amant is wealthy enough to purchase his dower house—quite a tidy property!" Lady Hathaway eyed the newspaper that kept Sir John from her stern scrutiny. "Well, John?"

"A fool and his money are soon parted, my love," Sir John replied obligingly, showing that he had indeed attended his wife. "Mr. D'Amant has not shown me he has any more than adequate intelligence to support my daughter." He turned a page, showing a face of total calm. "What is a smattering of Latin, after all, if one does not know Greek, or indeed any sort of mathematics?"

"What does that matter? He replied to you very well, and said he knew Greek like a native. Is that not enough?"

A corner of the newspaper flipped down, and her husband gazed at her over his spectacles. "My dear, you asked me to make sure Psyche's suitors were not dullards. Firm knowledge of Greek and Latin, mathematics, and some knowledge of estate management is the minimum to qualify as an adequately intelligent man." The newspaper flipped up again.

"Surely you do not intend to give Mr. D'Amant a written examination!" Lady Hathaway laughed. "You did not for Lord Blytheland."

"I did not need to. Lord Blytheland graduated with honors from Oxford. His and his father's properties have always been well managed. Cassandra has said there is very little for her to do; all their tenants are well fed and healthy, and live in clean, warm houses, which proves what I had found out for myself." He closed and folded the newspaper. "I know nothing of the sort of Mr. D'Amant, other than he has traveled the world concerning various business endeavors and has served briefly in the army." He sipped his tea, then put it down, his brows drawing together. "I seem to be missing a page from the newspaper—do you have it?"

A knock sounded on the door before Lady Hathaway could reply. "Yes?"

"Mama, it is I, and Mr. D'Amant." It was Psyche, sounding agitated.

"Do come in, dear."

The door opened and Psyche entered, pulling Mr. D'Amant by his hand into the sitting room. "Mr. D'Amant has been injured, and I need some sticking plaster for him."

"Oh, my." Lady Hathaway peered at the scratches on Mr. D'Amant's cheek. "You were right to bring him, Psyche. We shall need to clean and patch it straightaway." She bustled to a basket to one side of the sitting room. "I have some gauze in my basket as well as basilicum ointment. We can use tea—I have read it is an excellent cleansing agent." She shook her head. "Tsk, tsk. However did you hurt yourself Mr. D'Amant?"

"He fell into some shrubbery in the conservatory, Mama," Psyche said quickly.

Lady Hathaway opened her mouth to rebuke her for speaking for Mr. D'Amant, but a glance at him stopped her. He was staring at Psyche with a dreamy—even besotted— smile. She transferred her gaze to her daughter and noticed the high color in her cheeks and how her bodice was just slightly awry. Lady Hathaway's heart filled with joy. At last! Their disagreement must have been resolved, and surely a marriage proposal was imminent!

Lady Hathaway quickly washed the wound on Mr. D'Amant's cheek. She frowned, noting some blood stains on his neckcloth just barely hidden by his collar. It was coming from *under* the neckcloth, not over it. How could that be, unless for some reason he had taken his neckcloth off? She shot a look at Psyche sitting with her hands clasped in her lap: her cheeks were quite pink, and she looked as if butter wouldn't melt in her mouth.

A bodice set awry, falling into shrubbery, blood from *under* a neckcloth—it did not add up to a respectable total. She gazed sternly at Mr. D'Amant, who looked back with a slight smile. "Shameless!" Lady Hathaway said under her breath, wishing at that moment she could dance in triumphant jubilation.

"Not at all," Mr. D'Amant said, also under his breath.

Her hand stilled over the plaster of basilicum ointment and gauze she had just applied, but she continued looking stern.

"You shall see," he said. He turned to Sir John. "Sir, if I may have a word with you in private?"

Sir John looked at him, then at his wife, who was casting meaningful looks in Psyche's direction. "Of course you may, Mr. D'Amant. Is there something you wished to say, Amelia?"

"No, no, not at all. Perhaps I should take Psyche to the drawing room downstairs—"

"I would prefer to stay," Psyche said, her chin thrust out mutinously. "I know exactly what it is Harry will say."

Mr. D'Amant grinned. "Very well." He turned to Sir John. "I would be honored if you would allow me to pay my addresses to Miss Hathaway. I wish to ask for her hand in marriage."

"I—" began Sir John.

"And I refuse," Psyche said instantly. "We shall not suit."

"What?!" Lady Hathaway shrieked. She put her hand to her brow and moaned. "No, no, I cannot have heard correctly."

"Of course we suit," Mr. D'Amant replied. "We are perfect for each other." He went to Psyche and kissed her hand. She pulled hastily away, blushing furiously.

"You see," she said between clenched teeth, "Mr. D'Amant is not in his right mind. That is why he is proposing to me."

"I cannot see that," Lady Hathaway said reasonably. "Any number of gentlemen have proposed to you, and I am certain none of them have been insane. Is Mr. D'Amant acting crazed? Is he ill and foaming at the mouth? No, he is not! Just because he wishes to wed you does not mean he has become demented." She eyed Psyche sternly. "Indeed, I would almost think *you* mad for refusing such a flattering proposal!"

"In which case, Mr. D'Amant should be happy not to

marry me," Psyche said. "He cannot wish to marry an insane woman."

"Of course I would," Harry said. "I am mad with love for you. If you are also mad, your contention that we do not suit is entirely wrong: we suit admirably."

Lady Hathaway gasped and pressed her hand to her lips, obviously suppressing a laugh.

A chuckle came from Sir John. "Well, Psyche, his logic is faultless, though I question the premise of his argument." He went to his daughter and held her hands. "My dear, the truth, please. Is this man odious to you? Has he harmed you at all?"

Psyche stared at her father, then shook her head. "No, Mr. D'Amant would never harm me and he is not odious to me."

"We progress, I see," her father said wryly. "Do you have any affection for him at all?" He bent down to her and whispered in her ear, "I shall know if you do not tell me the truth." She gazed at him, and saw a twinkle in his eyes. She blushed.

"I have—an affection for Mr. D'Amant," she said.

Lady Hathaway let loose an exasperated breath. "An affection! Why if anyone was top over tails—"

"Amelia," Sir John said softly, and his wife stopped and gazed at him for a moment before she nodded reluctantly. He turned to Psyche. "I am certain you have 'an affection' for Mr. D'Amant, my dear, and for some reason you do not wish to say why you have refused his offer of marriage." He released her hands and put his own behind his back, staring in hard concentration at the floor. "However, I think Mr. D'Amant must have his chance. How many offers of marriage have you refused, Psyche?"

"At least ten," Lady Hathaway said instantly.

"Ten!" Sir John's eyebrows rose high. "As much as that."

"I was not in love with any of them, Papa."

"And you are not in love with Mr. D'Amant?"

Psyche could only look away and say nothing.

"Very well, then." He looked thoughtfully at Mr. D'Amant. "I must determine if you are worthy of her, for I cannot wish her to marry a dullard. If you prove yourself, then my daughter will marry you, or give a good reason why she cannot."

"I accept," Harry said.

Sir John turned to Psyche. "Well?"

Psyche stared down at the floor, thinking hard. If she disagreed, Harry would find some other way of marrying her, particularly in his present state of mind. She needed time. If she could persuade him to give himself the arrow's antidote, then he would see reason and continue his quest for his true wife. She felt a weeping ache at the thought— she so wished what Harry had said was true. The state of the world was at risk, however, and she could not let him make a mistake in this matter, even if it cost him his love. If she agreed to her father's plan, then she would have that time.

She nodded. "Very well." Turning to Harry, she gave him a long look. "I shall make sure it will not be easy, Harry."

Lady Hathaway gave an exasperated groan. "For heaven's sake, Psyche—" She shut her mouth suddenly, then shook her head. "No, I shall not say more. I have done more than any mother might to bring the two of you to-gether—at least for now."

Sir John smiled at her, then turned to Harry. "So, the first thing: Do you speak Greek? You have demonstrated some competence at Latin, but I need proof of it in Greek."

Harry spoke rapidly in a language Psyche found vaguely familiar, but could not understand. It was obviously Greek; her father raised his brows and nodded approvingly. "Very good—impressive, in fact," Sir John said. Psyche almost groaned. She hoped the other tests would not be this easy. Her father hesitated, then asked, "You wouldn't happen to speak or read any other languages, would you?"

"But of course," Harry replied. "What would you like me to translate? Arabic? Sanskrit? Egyptian?"

Sir John stared at him. "You can read all of them?" At Harry's nod, he pulled out a handkerchief and mopped his suddenly perspiring brow. He looked at Psyche. "If you refuse to marry Mr. D'Amant after he has performed the task I give him, child, I shall be the most miserable man alive." He gave a deep and heartfelt sigh, then continued. "However, I must do my duty. I understand, Mr. D'Amant, that you are Sir William's heir?"

Harry nodded again.

"Very well. How well do you know his accounts and his estate management?"

Harry looked at him gravely. "I do not know them well at all. I have been busy with my own business."

"Well, I give you a week in which to become familiar with them, so that you may give Sir William a complete account of them, and your own, and you must send your reports to my solicitors so I may know the style of life in which you wish to keep my daughter." Sir John glanced at Psyche. "It is what any man might do when another asks to wed his daughter."

Psyche smiled. Certainly Harry had never opened an account book, and if he was bent on learning, then she would make sure to distract him.

Sir John looked at her over his spectacles, then at Harry. "However, if you can persuade my daughter to accept your proposal before you finish this task, I shall most willingly allow you a secretary to handle your affairs."

"Papa!" Psyche cried. "That is not fair."

"It is most fair, my girl," Sir John said. "If you were not so stubborn, I would have a prospective son-in-law who could translate all of my collected documents." He gazed hopefully at Harry. "Unless you might be willing to do so anyway?"

Harry grinned. "I am afraid not. I shall be quite busy with Sir William's accounts in the next week I believe."

Sir John sighed. "I thought not. Ah, well." He turned to his wife. "There, now, Amelia. Did I not do as I promised?"

"Yes, you did," Lady Hathway said, smiling. "I am sure it will be no trouble for Mr. D'Amant to do as you ask. Meanwhile, I believe there are more scratches that need tending. My daughter knows as much as I do about tending wounds."

She held out the basket to Psyche. "Do take him to the kitchen for more tea and tend to the scratch *under* his neck-cloth."

Psyche looked at her mother's stern expression and knew she was inches away from being forced to accept Harry's proposal to preserve her reputation. It was a very thin line to walk, but she would make sure that she would not be married, no matter what task Harry accomplished, what her parents wished, or what her own, aching heart wanted so badly.

Taking the basket, Psyche gave a challenging look to Harry before leaving the room. He gazed back, a slight smile on his face, then followed her out. The door shut, and she said, "I should let your cuts fester, I truly should. Then you would regret trapping me into marriage."

"Trapping?" Harry sounded indignant. "I did no such thing. I merely asked to marry you. Then you had your father set tasks before me—onerous ones, for you must know that I have never looked at an account book before."

"Oh, and speaking Greek to him was *so* difficult!"

"I haven't spoken it in almost a hundred years. I am a little rusty."

"Ha! I saw how you twisted Papa around your little finger. Sanskrit! Ha!" She went downstairs toward the kitchen.

"I only spoke the truth. I can read all those languages. Your father asked, I merely answered."

"Puffing yourself off. Putting temptation in his way. Now *he* shall begin to hint how you are a desirable husband for me!"

"Psyche, I am disappointed in you. I never thought you so disobedient a daughter as to go against your parents' wishes," Harry said in a mock-disapproving voice.

"Ha!" Psyche said, and pushed open the kitchen door.

Except it was not the kitchen door, but another room, one she recognized as the bedroom given to Harry during his stay. She turned to him indignantly. "What did you do?"

"I thought it best if we did this in private," Harry said. "I dislike disrobing in front of strangers."

"We are not going to do anything but clean and apply ointment on your cuts," Psyche said, remembering her father's words about Harry persuading her to marry him. She felt suddenly nervous, wondering how he might go about it.

Harry raised his brows as if in surprise. "Did I say we were going to do anything else?"

"No, but—" She let out an exasperated breath, and turned away, glad she had the excuse of taking out the ointment from the basket, for she was blushing furiously. "Never mind! This shall be quite awkward, for the tea is in the kitchen, not here."

She heard him snap his fingers, and turned to find a pot of tea, steam coming out of the spout. She eyed him sternly. "I hope you did not startle any of the servants below stairs by making it disappear when they were looking."

Harry shrugged. "I took it from the St. Vires' room. The maid in their room will suppose he did it."

"You are detestable!"

"No, practical. How else was I to get a pot quickly?"

Psyche closed her eyes and counted to ten. She opened them, then said, "I need to clean your cuts. Please take off your—" Her eyes met his. She knew exactly why her mother directed her to clean his wounds, although Lady Hathaway could not have known they would have missed the kitchen and come up to Harry's room instead. She was sure if she left now, she would find herself walking back to his room by some illusion or other. She ground her teeth. "I will clean your wounds and put ointment on them, and that is all. If you think you will compromise my reputation and thereby make me marry you, you may discard that notion now. You know I have no defense against your magic, and though I—I care for you, you may depend upon it that care will most certainly fade if you try your tricks upon me. You know I am stubborn, and not a butterfly so easily caught, believe me."

He gazed at her seriously. "I shall not attempt to trap you, love—I know better. Besides, your father said 'persuade,' not trap."

"No magic?"

"No magic," he said, then grinned wickedly. "Only my natural persuasive powers."

Psyche stared at him. She had known him a long time, and was fairly immune to his persuasion if she did not allow herself to become provoked. She nodded slowly. "Very well. And I shall do my best to make you see reason and think about how you are jeopardizing your quest."

"I am seeing reason, and have not jeopardized my quest, but have nearly completed it." He pulled off his coat and waistcoat.

"There, you see?" Psyche said instantly. "How can you see reason when you have stuck yourself with your arrow? Give yourself the antidote, then perhaps I shall believe you."

"I do not need to give myself the antidote, for I am not at all besotted or crazed." He gingerly took off his shirt, and Psyche drew in a deep breath.

His chiton had always obscured part of his chest, and Psyche had grown used to the way he had dressed throughout the years. But seeing him bare from the waist up, wearing only his trousers and stockings, was different. He was wearing more than when he wore his chiton, but somehow he seemed far more bare. She raised her eyes, and met his wickedly smiling ones, then uttered a growl of irritation. "Turn, please. You have a cut on your neck, and another on your—your chest and on your shoulder. I wonder I did not see them at the outset."

"We gods bleed slowly," he said. "And heal quickly. Ouch!"

"A splinter," Psyche said severely. "It serves you right. And here is another." There were quite a few splinters—she was surprised Harry had not complained of them earlier. It was proof to her that the effects of his arrow had caused him to ignore the irritation and pain he must have felt otherwise.

She took out as many as she could see, then dampened a

cloth with warm tea and approached him. Her cheeks grew warm again when she gazed once more at his muscular chest, and she shot a quick look at his face. He had a slight, devilish smile, and obviously knew she felt unsettled. Psyche clenched her teeth, dabbed at a cut, then went on to the next one.

At last she was done, and was able to gather some composure, for Harry was dotted with patches of sticking plaster, and somehow less distracting that way. Psyche sighed.

"You may put on your clothes again," she said.

She looked away while he dressed, trying not to think what he looked like half unclothed, and thus was startled when his voice whispered in her ear, "I am finished dressing."

She turned abruptly, opening her mouth to rebuke him for startling her, but he stood very close to her and the words died in her throat. Except for one on Harry's cheek, his clothes hid the bits of sticking plaster, and that remaining piece of gauze and ointment looked unreasonably dashing instead of distracting from his looks. He gazed at her for a long moment, and she wondered if he was going to kiss her, but he merely took her hand.

"I thank you," he said, and she felt oddly disappointed. She did not want him to kiss her, not while he was still influenced by his arrow. He brought her hand to his lips—he would kiss her hand, like any gentleman might.

At the last moment, he turned her hand over and pressed a kiss on her palm. She swallowed, and closed her hand, but it did no good; his lips moved to her wrist instead, and continued kissing a tingling trail along her arm until he reached the soft, sensitive skin in the crook of her elbow.

"Stop," Psyche said, her voice trembling. "You should not."

Harry rose and gazed at her. "Why not? I am not using any magic whatsoever. Your father has set me tasks to do to win your hand in marriage. But you? You are not allowing me to persuade you that you are indeed my wife. What if I am right?"

An uncomfortable sensation crept over Psyche. To be fair, she had to let him persuade her of his conviction, even though she was certain he was wrong. "Very well. What do you propose?"

"One kiss per day during the week I am working on Sir William's accounts."

"And you must reverse the effects of the love arrow on yourself," she replied.

Harry shrugged. "As you wish, though it will make no difference." He gave her a shrewd look. "I think you do remember you are my wife, but you do not recognize the remembering."

She glanced at him nervously. "You may not think much of it, but we mortals will be left in chaos if the gods fade away, and I must know for sure that I am your wife."

For a moment Harry looked somber. "Of course it matters." Then he smiled. "I am right, however; neither I nor the other gods will fade away, and the world will not descend into chaos."

Psyche sighed. It would be difficult persuading him, but agreeing to the kiss a day would give her an opportunity to distract him and keep him from finishing the accounts within a week. She would arrive when he was busy at it, and ask for her kiss ... unless he demanded it at another time. She gazed at his set and stubborn chin, and felt she was better off not mentioning the timing. A surprise attack was usually an advantage.

"We shall see," she said, and turned to leave the room. She halted, then looked back. "If you would so kindly make it appear that I have come up from the kitchens, I would be most grateful."

He bowed elegantly in assent, and Psyche could not help chuckling. She was just as stubborn as he, and she would win in the end. He would see.

Artemis sat on a large, low stump in the middle of the wood through which she had run only a few nights ago. A fox curled up at her feet, and a doe and her fawn cropped grass nearby. She absently rubbed her foot against the fox's furry side, and he stretched and smiled slyly at her, begging for a scratch on his belly. But she only sighed and drew up her feet on the stump, wrapping her arms around her legs.

The effect of the gold arrow was gone. She should go back to Olympus, but somehow, she could not. The image of Lord Eldon's face, strong arms, and body would not go away.

Especially his face, the moment, she told him she was going away. Despair had been there, quickly covered by an amiable and interested expression, but she had seen it. It had struck her to her heart, even though she knew she was no longer under the effects of Eros's arrow. She had hurt Lord Eldon, and it had sent a pain as sharp as a spear into her. She had not wanted to hurt him, she knew that now, but she had.

Lord Eldon had been good and kind, and had tried his best to help her when he thought she needed it. He did not deserve to be hurt, and if his feelings for her even approached what she had felt for him when she was under the influence of Eros's arrow, she could not help but sympathize.

No, she could not marry him, but he deserved something—it was a point of honor that she give him a wish, or grant him some request. It was the least she could do for him. Artemis stood, and raised her face to the moon, now shining clearly in the cloudless night sky. She felt the moon's strength flow into her, and the strength of Gaia flow up from the earth through the soles of her feet and into her heart. She had become stronger since the day after she had left the Hathaways' home. Eros. Had he found his wife? She could not account for her returning strength otherwise, and for the clear skies above. She gazed at the fawn nursing upon the mother doe, and smiled. Even the wild creatures had gained strength and had given birth at last, and none of their babies had died of cold and hunger.

Lord Eldon was still at the Hathaways' house and she needed to see him before she left. Artemis stood, and the animals gazed at her, alert. She gathered up her bow and quiver of arrows, slung them over her shoulder, and began to run.

She outran the fox and the deer, she ran until the heat of her running made a shimmer appear around her. The Hathaways' house loomed in front of her; then instantly it was before her. She leaped into the branches of an old oak, her feet dancing higher and higher among the new-budded leaves until she reached the one branch that touched the window to Lord Eldon's room.

The window was closed. Artemis frowned. She could return tomorrow, during the day, but she wanted to be finished with the granting of the wish tonight, and then she would be on her way. The branch did touch the window, however. She shook it so that it tap-tap-tapped a staccato rhythm. A muffled cursing came from inside the room, and the goddess grinned. He had awakened, and would surely come to the window now.

The window was flung open and Lord Eldon peered angrily out. "Damned bird," he muttered, and began to close the window.

"Lord Eldon!" Artemis called.

He started violently and opened the window wider.

"Here!" she called again.

"Good God," he said faintly. "What the devil—it's a dream again." He frowned. "But the last time wasn't a dream, was it?"

"It is not a dream, Lord Eldon." She held out her hand. "May I come in?"

He took a deep breath and pushed his fingers through his hair. "Damn." Tentatively, he reached out his hand to her. She clasped it—warm and firm—and leaped beside him, into the room.

He looked at her as if she were a miracle, a vision, and she could see his heart in his eyes as he gazed into her own. What was it that she was going to say? A wish.

"I—I came back," she said. "You were kind to me. I could

not leave without thanking you, and giving you something in return."

He said nothing, but raised his hand, touching her cheek with one finger. Artemis drew in a sharp breath. She remembered his touch; it had been gentle. "A wish. I will grant you a wish," she said.

"You know what I wish," he said. "But I asked you and you refused."

Artemis closed her eyes for a moment. If she were still under the arrow's spell, it would be difficult not to give him his first wish if she kept looking at him. He wore nothing but underdrawers even though the room was cold; the moonlight through the window and the light from the low embers in the fireplace outlined each muscle of his arms. "A wish other than that."

Anger flickered over his face, then it was gone. "One thing, then."

"Name it, and it shall be yours."

"A kiss," he said. "I wish a kiss from you. And then you may go."

An easy and quick wish to grant. She stepped closer and gazed long into his eyes. Her arms came around his neck and she tiptoed until her lips reached his and pressed firmly upon them.

A sigh, a groan, his arms were around her, and he pressed his lips on hers in a hard, fierce kiss. One kiss, she thought, only one kiss . . . and she pressed herself closer so it would not stop. His lips parted hers, and the delicious wildness she had felt before rose up in her until she, too, sighed.

He pulled away a little, but she would not have it. He said one kiss, and she could not bear that this one end. His lips touching hers still, he murmured, "One kiss."

Only one! Desperately she searched her mind for a way to continue the deliciousness. "You said *a* kiss. You did not say where," she whispered. "You could put *a* kiss in many places."

He laughed, a low, husky laugh that made her shiver.

"True. I could put *a* kiss here." He kissed her cheek. "I could put *a* kiss over here." He kissed her neck. "And *a* kiss here." He pushed aside the strap of her quiver and the shoulder of her chiton and kissed the upper swell of her breast. The quiver and her bow fell to the floor with a small crash. "Much better," he said. He untied the belt that held her chiton to her waist, and they, too, fell to the floor.

His wish did not include touches, Artemis thought, but she could not call them touches—a kiss of the fingers along her back and spine and upon her hip, gentle and warm. It circled up upon her ribs and then her breasts, and the fire that suddenly burned within her caused her to pull his head up for another kiss.

"One kiss," he said. "I already kissed you there." She groaned in frustration, then pushed him from where they were standing.

"There," she said. "We have moved to another place. You may give me a kiss."

Lord Eldon laughed, and when she put her hands upon him she could feel the rumble through his chest, warm and hard, then his wonderfully strong shoulders and arms—archer's arms—that quickly encircled her and pulled her to the bed. He kissed her again and moved against her, and thoughts of the number of kisses fled, for she must have as many kisses as he could give her.

They rolled and tumbled on the bed, and once fell off, returning to it, kissing and touching. When Artemis made his clothing disappear, he said, "This had better not be a dream."

She laughed. "No, not a dream, Lord Eldon."

He smiled dreamily as he moved into her, however, closing his eyes as she gasped. "Robert," he said. "I would be honored if—oh, God—if you would call me Robert—if this is not a dream, I've died and it's heaven, by God—or Robin." He breathed deeply. "Heaven. Absolute heaven."

"Robin . . . How appropriate," She laughed again, for an unfamiliar sensation—joy, and a strange fullness uncurled and flowered in her heart. "Robin. I shall call you Robin."

She moved against him, for she could not help it; the grow-ing fire in her belly forced her to move.

"Anything," he said, groaning. "Anything you say, just—just—" He pulled her to him and kissed her deeply.

Kiss for kiss she returned with wild intensity, moving below him and above, crying out once, twice, sobbing at last into his chest, his marvelous strong arms curled around her. He took her lips again in a kiss, breathing hard, and moved hard once more into her, then breathed out a long sigh. He opened his eyes and looked at her, then wiped the tears on her cheek with his hand.

"Not a dream," he said, kissing her gently. "And the most amazing kiss I have had in my life."

She chuckled, but when he began to move away, she held tight to him. "Don't go," she whispered. "I don't want you to go."

He took her face between his hands and gazed at her. "I am not the one who wanted to." Though his eyes no longer held despair, Lord Eldon's face was grave. "You love me, or you would not have come to my room. Will you leave me now?"

Artemis looked at him, at his handsome face and the love shining in his eyes, and an ache moved in her heart. She recognized it; the effect of Eros's arrow was gone from her, but it was the same, not as painful, but the same nevertheless.

"No," she said. "I will not leave you. I . . . I am not used to this." She touched his face, letting her fingers drift from his temple to his cheek and chin. It was hard to say it—she was used to holding tight to her pride and her loneliness. "Will you teach me? I have not loved like this for at least a millennium."

He laughed and kissed her again. "For as long as I live," he said, and she swore in her heart he would live forever.

They loved again, then fell asleep. When Artemis woke with the early dawn sun shining upon her and her lover, she gazed upon him and knew she had been a coward for too long. So when Lord Eldon woke, she smiled at him, and said, "Marry me, Robin."

And his joy gave her more strength than she had ever had in all the days she could remember.

Chapter 13

The next day had become suddenly warm, and the skies cleared into a shimmering blue, a bright intensity that made one's eyes ache if gazed upon too long. The fields were still muddy, but they began to dry in the warmth; the morning brought tendrils of mist hovering over the earth, like bright spirits rising up to the sun, dispelling all thoughts of gloom.

Even in Psyche, though Harry's claims that she was his wife still troubled her. She spent a restless night, full of vivid, even frightening dreams. In one, she had changed into a deer, and after running wildly through a forest, had come upon a strange dark man wearing ancient clothes and carrying a spear. He had savage eyes, and fear had leaped into her heart when he threw the spear. She had woken up with a start in the darkness of her room, her heart beating rapidly, and she was glad it had only been a dream. It was a strange one, unlike the usual dreams where she knew the people in them. She sighed. When she had finally gone back to sleep, there were dreams of Harry again, kissing and touching her. They were comforting after the deer dream, but just as bad for disturbing her sleep. She woke up at last clutching her pillows, feeling overheated, oddly on edge.

She rose from her bed, and rang for her maid. Perhaps if she went for a walk in the garden, it would refresh her and she would be rid of the edginess. Her maid came, and Psyche could not help fidgeting while she dressed, for the slide of the cotton over her skin reminded her of her dream and how Harry had—

She would *not* think of Harry, but the fate of the world, and how she should keep him from completing his task.

The flower garden near the conservatory was deserted. Psyche sighed with relief. She wanted to be alone to shake out the cobwebs from her mind. A cool breeze brushed her face, and she breathed it in, feeling invigorated. A few steps took her to her favorite rose bush, just beginning to bud. It was late in the year, but at least it had started. She could see a bit of red between the tightly closed green sepals; if the weather continued improving, it would flower soon.

"Psyche."

She jumped and turned around. "I do not know how many times I have told you I do not like it when you surprise me like that."

"But it makes you—" Harry began.

"I know, though why you should like to see me bounce, I do not know. We have had this discussion before, I remember." She noticed the plaster she had placed on his cheek was gone, and the cut had already disappeared, leaving no scar. He wore a fine Bath coat and fawn pantaloons, and his neckcloth was nicely tied.

He smiled. "It reminds me of when we first met, long ago, how I used to watch you hum and dance by yourself in your garden. That was before I made myself visible to you. Do you remember?"

"No—no, I do not." The odd open-and-shut-door sensation in her mind came again, and she began to feel frightened.

"You hesitate. It does sound familiar to you." His voice was eager.

"Familiar because—yes, I did it yesterday, before you came into the conservatory. So it is not at all a remembrance of some long-ago life with you, but one of only the day before."

"Ah, so you did the same thing yesterday." His voice held hope now.

Psyche swallowed down an echoing hope and growing fear in her heart. "Anyone might dance by herself. It is probably very common," she said, shrugging her shoulders. But if that were true, then Lord Eldon would not have laughed when he had seen her dancing and she would not have been embarrassed. She looked away, not wanting to admit she might be mistaken.

His fingers came under her chin, making her look at him. "My love, it is not common for anyone to dance by herself. You are just making excuses. Admit it, you told Lord Eldon all about Artemis's past love, with details she had told no one. I certainly did not tell you."

"She could very well have told me recently."

"Did she?" Harry looked deeply in her eyes, and she closed them, more afraid now.

"I—I do not know! I have not had much sleep lately, so it is hard to recall anything anyone might have told me." She felt confused, as if the ground was not as solid as she had always believed and she had suddenly lost her footing.

His fingers moved from her chin to the nape of her neck, massaging gently, and she drew in a long breath "Poor Psyche," he said. "I shall not bother you with any more questions today." He drew her to him and kissed her.

It was the promised kiss for today, Psyche told herself, and put her arms around him. He kissed her gently, comforting her, and stroked her back. The breeze blew again and she shivered. Closing her eyes, she moved closer; he was warm, and when he lifted his lips from hers, she put her head on his chest, rubbing her cheek on it. It reminded her of when they had cuddled together in each other's arms in the early morn—

Oh, heavens! She pushed against him, for the images in the dreams came into her mind again. Confusion made her stare at him and shake her head slowly. They were only dreams, puzzling, sometimes frightening dreams, and dreams sometimes so achingly wonderful they frightened her even more.

"You remember something," Harry said.

Psyche shook her head. "No—no, only dreams."

"Tell me."

She pulled away from him, her face heating. "You and I, we— No, they are only dreams." She put her hands over her face. "I am Psyche Hathaway, not your wife. I have parents, a brother and sister, here, now, not long ago. I have never married, we have never—no!" She shook her head again, and with one fearful glance at him, ran from the garden back into the house.

Eros took a few steps after her, then stopped. She was remembering. No doubt was left in his mind. She was truly his wife, her soul reborn in this Psyche. It was not a mere shape-change as he had thought long ago. Something had happened so that she had entered the cycle of birth and rebirth again.

Her newfound memories frightened her. It was not something Eros had expected. But of course it would—she had known herself as no one but Psyche Hathaway. He stared at the path down which she had run and slowly walked in the same direction. He would have to be careful with her, teasing her in his usual way, but not startling her. She would return tomorrow for the next kiss—Psyche was very honorable and kept her promises.

Pausing by one of Psyche's favorite roses, Eros smiled slightly, and touched a tightly closed bud. The green parted, and the rose unfurled. He was certain the kisses were not disagreeable to her, but he needed to be careful. His smile grew wider. Slowly, with a great deal of *loving* care.

He thought of her request that he take the antidote to the arrow. It would do no harm to agree. He would not change, and she would know he was in earnest and *knew,* not just believed, she was his wife. He wished there was someone else who could talk to Psyche and show her he was right. But the best he could do was try to convince her with every bit of persuasive power he had.

But first, Sir William's accounts. He had sent a letter to Sir William's solicitors and expected to hear from them soon. Sir William had been pleased, for the old man's eyes had become weak and he was glad to have Harry take over the accounts. He sighed. He could do it, but there would be much for him to learn, for he had never the need to account for anything.

He would pack his belongings—rather, he would make them go away—and leave for home soon. The dower house he had bought was close to the Hathaways', but it did not matter if it were near or far. If Psyche would not come to him, he would go to her.

He smiled again. And make sure he got his kisses every day.

Psyche ran to her room and shut the door, breathing heavily. She pressed her hand to her temple, feeling tired and confused. Was she Psyche Hathaway or Eros's wife? How could she be both? She had thought Eros's wife had shape-changed and hidden herself away. But later he had spoken of her as being a real person, and somehow that person contained the soul of his wife.

She could not deny the images that haunted her dreams, and now in Harry's presence when she was fully awake. They were at once familiar and frightening, for she knew they could not have all happened during her short life.

She went to the window, gazing out at her family's property, the fields and trees now bright green with the sun shining warmly on them. Harry had mentioned how the weather had improved and began to be restored to order because he had found his true wife, that his quest was almost done. But what if he were wrong?

Psyche shivered. That was the wrong question, and it was never the question she had feared, as she had tried to convince herself for some time. The question was, what if he were right?

It would mean she was not who she thought she was, that she was someone else, a stranger. She thought of the story her father had told of the original Psyche. At the time, she thought she would've liked to have been that lady, for Harry's wife had been brave, strong, and resourceful. Psyche was not sure she was like that. She suddenly wished she could remember all of it, so she would know the truth. It was much better than being afraid.

It was difficult . . . she had been Psyche Hathaway all her life. She did not want to be taken over by someone else. She wouldn't be *herself* and didn't want to be anything but herself. Closing her eyes, she made herself remember when she had the first memory-dreams. It had been after . . . Harry had first kissed her.

Of course, that was it. She had argued against it, but he had been right. She had not remembered right away, and only in dreams at first. With each kiss, she had dreamed more; then she had begun to speak of things she could not have known. How long would it take before she was not herself any longer?

She did not know, but the more Harry kissed her, the more she seemed to remember. If she got Harry to kiss her a great deal, she might remember everything at once. Psyche shivered and gazed out of the window again. It was frightening, but if it was going to happen anyway, she might as well get it done all at once.

Perhaps if she told Harry that she was frightened of the change, he would comfort her. She remembered the times since childhood when she had been frightened or sad, how he had listened to her patiently, had hugged her, or teased her out of her gloom. That would be the same. She felt a little comforted. Whatever happened, Harry would be the same.

The trick was to get him to do a great deal of kissing all at once. And what if that did not work? Perhaps it meant she would have to do more . . . Psyche thought of the dreams in which "more" happened, and she blushed. She would not think of that now. Tomorrow she had agreed to kiss him again, and that would be a good time to get him to kiss her more than once.

Psyche sighed. She had never tried or even wanted to seduce anyone, but if she wished to do her duty and help Harry finish his quest, she supposed she would have to. It was a very awkward thing, and she was afraid of turning into someone else, but if it meant saving the world from chaos, she would do it.

Lady Hathaway, working on her embroidery in the drawing room the next day, felt as content as a mother could who was within inches of having her youngest daughter married to a very handsome and eligible man. To complete her satisfaction, Miss Knightly had returned, and she and Lord Eldon had announced their intent to marry. It would have been better if Psyche and Mr. D'Amant had been first to announce their betrothal, but she would not quibble on that head! It had been hard enough to get Psyche to the point of even agreeing to give Mr. D'Amant a chance.

She shook her head. What a contrary child she was! The girl was top over tails in love with the man, but would she admit it? No, she would not.

The door opened, and Psyche wandered in, picking up small ornaments from the tables and putting them down again, casting glances at her mother from time to time. She sighed, gazed at a portrait of her ancestor, Sir Humphrey Hathaway, then sat on a chair across from her mother.

"Would you like tea, Mama?" Psyche asked at last.

Lady Hathaway gazed suspiciously at her. "Yes, that would be most refreshing," she said. Psyche pulled the bell rope and sat again, folding and unfolding her dress skirt on her lap. She cast more glances at her mother, then sighed. When the maid arrived, she ordered tea, then rearranged her skirts again.

"For heaven's sake, Psyche, if there is something on your mind, do speak up!" Lady Hathaway said at last. "Your fidgeting has quite distracted me, and I have mis-stitched this flower twice already."

Psyche stood up again, then went to the mantelpiece and examined a few china figurines there. "Mama . . . when does Mr. D'Amant arrive today?"

"He is invited for dinner and will stay for our musicale— your brother-in-law brought his violin, and Cassandra will accompany him on the pianoforte—so you will see him then." The tea arrived, and Lady Hathaway managed to hide her smile as she poured. Obviously in love, the silly girl!

"So he is probably at his house now, and learning about Sir William's accounts?"

"I imagine he must be."

Psyche nodded. "Mama, how does a lady entice a gentleman to kiss her? Aside from asking, that is?"

Lady Hathaway choked as she sipped her tea, spilling it onto the embroidery on her lap. Quickly she set down her teacup and dabbed at her embroidery with her handkerchief. "Heavens, child, a *lady* does not entice a gentleman to do such things!"

"Oh!" Psyche looked thoughtful. "Does one ask, then?"

"For goodness' sake, no!"

Psyche's brows furrowed. "Then how does one get a kiss from a gentleman?"

Lady Hathaway hesitated. No doubt Psyche wished Mr. D'Amant to kiss her. They were on the brink of becoming betrothed; surely it would not hurt for them to kiss, and she suspected they had done it already. But no, it was probably best just to leave it alone, and let their relationship unfold naturally. "It simply happens, Psyche. Discreetly, one hopes."

Psyche nodded. "I see."

"Not that you have done much of that, I hope!" Lady Hathaway said hastily.

Her daughter gave her a puzzled look. "But it says in the book *The Mirror of Graces* that one may kiss quite a few people, including one's friends."

"But if one has a great many friends, it could make one seem very undiscriminating," Lady Hathaway said, hoping she was leading her daughter down the right road where discretion was concerned. It would not be bad at all if she kissed Mr. D'Amant, but it would not be good if she did it with all of her friends—and Psyche had a great many friends, many of them male.

"Ah!" Psyche said, and smiled. "Only one's special friends, and no one must see it, I suppose."

"Very special, and absolutely no one must see," Lady Hathaway said.

"Thank you, Mama," Psyche said cheerfully, and gave her a brief hug before leaving the drawing room.

Lady Hathaway gazed at the closed door with foreboding. If she was not mistaken, her daughter was planning to kiss Mr. D'Amant. While it would not be a terrible thing if they should be found in a compromising situation, it would still be highly uncomfortable, and she should not like her daughter to be seen as someone forced into marriage to save her reputation.

She sighed. Being a mother was very much like being a tightrope walker at Astley's Amphitheatre, for she must balance furthering a desirable alliance for her daughter against short-term and very light scandal, but scandal nevertheless. She worried her lower lip before sighing again. She would watch them, though perhaps not *very* closely. Lady Hathaway shook her head. *Very* much like walking a tightrope! She should question Psyche more closely about the matter.

But when she went to find Psyche, her maid told her that she had left the house for a long walk and pointed in the direction of Mr. D'Amant's house. Lady Hathaway groaned, then pressed her lips together. Enough of this nonsense! Her husband wished events to unfold naturally. She had allowed it, and look what had come of it! No doubt her daughter was on the edge of compromising herself and would be stubborn enough to refuse to marry Mr. D'Amant, regardless of what anyone's feelings might be.

She called for her coat, asked for her husband, and ordered a coach be brought around to the front of the house. *She* would put a stop to this nonsense, if no one else was willing!

Chapter 14

Psyche walked for about a half an hour through the fields before coming upon Sir William's dower house—or rather, Harry's house. She felt awkward coming here. It was perfectly proper for her to walk alone about the grounds of her father's estate, but she was not sure about walking on anyone else's, even if he was a dear friend and one she supposed she would marry.

She had thought deeply about what she was about to do: though she knew Harry needed to work on the accounts, he still had enough time in which to go over them. It could not hurt to interrupt him for a little while. Her mother's advice about kissing must be true. Except for the one time she had asked Harry for a kiss, they seemed to happen involuntarily. However, Mama hadn't said anything about taking hold of a gentleman and kissing him that way. It seemed awkward—more like an attack than anything else.

The problem with kissing anywhere but at Harry's house was that they were too likely to be interrupted, and she didn't know how long she had to kiss before she had all of Harry's wife's memories. She shivered. If she were really Harry's wife, then she supposed the memories were her own. It was a foreign idea, an odd, invasive thing. She shook her head. *Very* confusing!

It was, however, necessary for Harry to complete his quest. But she would insist he remove the effects of the arrow from himself first. It was only fair, and she wanted to be very sure of his knowledge before she took the step to re-

membering fully all that she was supposed to. Psyche took
a deep breath, stepped forward, and knocked on the door.

When the door opened, the butler raised his brows, but let
her in immediately when she announced who she was. "I
shall let the master know you are here," he said.

Psyche hesitated, blushed, then shook her head. "No, he
expected to see me today." It was not really a lie—he did expect to see her today—later, at her parents' house. She did
not want Harry to come down, for she feared she would run
away before he did. "If you will take me up, I shall be grateful." The butler looked at her curiously, then turned and led
the way upstairs. She had half expected resistance; perhaps
Harry had directed that visitors be brought up immediately.

Harry was indeed busy; his head was bent over an account book. He was in his shirtsleeves, but wore a fine embroidered waistcoat, and his neckcloth was awry, as if he
had twisted it in frustration. He yawned as he wrote something on a piece of paper, then looked up, clearly surprised
when she was announced.

"What are you doing here?" he asked after the butler left.

"Oh . . . I thought I might see how you have changed the
dower house—I have only been in it once, and that a long
time ago." How awkward she felt! How did one go about
proposing any sort of kissing without asking outright? Psyche's eye caught the open account books—a diversion until
she could think what to do. "Are you doing your accounts?
May I see what you have done so far?" Harry gave her a
puzzled look, but bowed and gestured toward the books.

She sat at the table at which he had been working, and
frowned as she looked at the figures. She did a quick mental calculation. "Why, this is not right! Did you do this?"

He moved toward her and looked over her shoulder.
"Yes—what is wrong with it?" He bent close to her, and she
could feel his breath moving the curls of her hair. She held
her breath for a moment and then forced her attention back
to the accounts.

"You forgot to carry over the number from this column to

the next. And I must say, your handwriting is not very neat. I cannot be sure if this is a four or a nine!"

"It is a nine," he said, and rested his hands on either side of her, effectively trapping her in the chair. She drew in her breath, then let it out again.

"It should be fixed." She dipped the pen in the inkwell, carefully crossed out the nine, and neatly wrote a four.

"Why did you come here?" Harry asked, kissing her ear.

The pen skittered across the page and clattered on the table, leaving a line and a blot of ink. Psyche stood up hastily, bumping against a book, causing it to fall to the floor. "Now look at what you have done!" she cried. Heavens, it seemed she need do nothing at all to make Harry kiss her—it was the arrow, of course. She needed to tell him to take the antidote. She glanced at him, and he looked at her as if she were a feast and he were a starving man. "I came to ask you to reverse the arrow spell on yourself now, instead of later."

"And if I do not?"

"Then I will go away and not let you kiss me."

Harry laughed. "A terrible threat. Very well." He put his hand in his pocket and drew out a silver dart. "I will even let you administer it yourself."

Psyche looked at him suspiciously. "What if it's the wrong one?"

"You don't trust me." Harry gave a sad sigh, and Psyche tried not to feel guilty. "If you don't believe me, ask Artemis. She knows the effects of the silver dart—she used it herself."

"But she is not here to ask." Psyche looked at him. She so wanted to believe him! "What if I were to test it on myself?"

Harry raised his brows. "It would do nothing to you, since you have not been shot with the love arrow."

Quickly she seized the silver dart and thrust the point into her hand. It stung, and she cried out, for she had thought it would not hurt. She looked at the palm of her hand—it bled. Was it supposed to bleed? She had never seen either the arrows or the darts make anyone bleed, except Harry. But she brought her attention to her emotions—she felt no different.

She gazed at Harry; he sighed and took her hand. "There," he said. "Does that satisfy you?" He took the dart, then pressed it into his own palm. A small drop of blood formed where it pierced him.

"No one else has ever bled from your darts—why did I?" she asked.

He gazed into her eyes, then pressed his hand to the hand she had pierced. "Palm to palm, blood to blood, heart to heart. We are one, Psyche, and were from the first." He said it as if it were a marriage vow, and she remembered long ago it was. "That is why you bleed from them—because I do." He laughed, sadly. "Why I did not think of doing this before, I don't know. It has been a long time, and I have been very tired. I have forgotten much in all that time, and have made many mistakes."

Psyche's heart melted. She put her arms around his neck. "Kiss me, Harry," she said, even though her mother had told her not to. "I am afraid . . . but make me remember."

He let out a long sigh and put his lips on hers. All resistance fell from her; this was Harry, her friend, the one she loved with all her heart, and being in his arms felt natural and good. He kissed her gently, and just as gently pulled her to him, stroking her back and waist and hips. "Don't be afraid," he murmured, and kissed her neck at the collar of her pelisse. "Sweet Psyche." The coat came loose—he must have magicked off the buttons, for she felt a plucking at the ribbons of her dress under her coat and at the buttons behind, and it too came loose.

He pushed aside the sleeve of her dress and she heard the soft "whump" of the pelisse falling to the floor. "It will wrinkle," she whispered against his lips.

"I shall iron it," he murmured, then kissed her deeply. "And the dress, too."

She laughed. "Silly! You know nothing about ironing clothes—" then gasped as he slid one hand inside her bodice, and the other moved to her waist. Suddenly he was sitting, and she was on his lap, and his kisses were no longer gentle, but fierce. He parted her lips and she moaned from the sensation of silken pressure and raw sweetness. His hand was warm on her waist, then it moved across her belly and slowly down, like slow sweet warm brandy sliding across her skin. The movement made her bodice fall. She heard an indrawn breath, and his fingers softly moved under the muslin.

"Please . . ." Psyche's voice trembled, and her hand clutched his arm.

"Lovely Psyche," Eros murmured against her neck. He slid the dress sleeve down over one shoulder, following its descent with his kisses. The fabric clung to the tip of one breast, and he left it there, a hot trembling rising in him at the thought it might fall away at any movement she might make. She breathed a deep shaking sigh, the cloth fell, and he was lost.

Immediately, his mouth went to cover the exposed flesh, while his hand unfastened the rest of the buttons on her dress. He pushed his fingers through the opening; she wore only a light corset, and it made him groan and laugh against her breast. Why she thought she must try to seduce him, he did not know. He did not care. She was his wife, and she as much as admitted it, the way she had come to him and asked him to help her remember. She had always been stubborn, and it had always been a challenge to him, breaking down, seductively, that stubbornness.

Footsteps sounded in the hallway, and someone knocked on the door. Psyche stiffened. *"Harry!"*— she whispered frantically. "Someone is at the door! Oh, heavens! Quickly, I must hide!"

With a groan Eros moved her away. By all the gods, after more than a thousand years he had once again the chance to make love to his wife and now fate conspired to torture him. He was sorely tempted to make whoever it was disappear. The knocking sounded again, and he straightened, snapped his fingers, and Psyche gasped when her clothes straightened themselves on her. She looked madly about her, then ran and hid behind the thick velvet curtains at the window.

Another knock sounded on the door. "Yes, who is it?" Eros said, not able to keep a biting edge from entering his voice.

The door opened, and Lady Hathaway entered. Sir John followed in her wake, an exasperated look on his face. His wife gave a dip of a curtsy and Sir John bowed, then spread out his arms. "See, Amelia, Psyche is not here. I suggest we do not bother Mr. D'Amant, especially since he has clearly been busy with the accounts." He peered at an open book on the floor. "It seems you are doing well so far, young man."

Lady Hathaway gazed about the room suspiciously. "I have reason, Mr. D'Amant, to think that my daughter is here. For all that I wish a marriage between the two of you, I cannot allow untoward behavior until the engagement is announced." She stopped and bent a stern look upon Eros when he grinned. "Not that I would allow such behavior *after* the engagement, either! But I cannot have Psyche calling upon you at your house without any chaperonage. It is not done! Whatever foreign notions you might have picked up on your travels, sir, I would appreciate it if you did not encourage them in my daughter."

"Of course, my lady," Eros said politely. He moved forward to bow over her hand again, and kicked something.

Lady Hathaway looked down, too quickly for Harry to make Psyche's pelisse disappear, and he barely kept himself from uttering a curse—stupid of him to forget the coat. Her lips became a thin line as she bent and picked it up. She turned to her husband. "Do you still say she is not here?"

"Well, well," Sir John said, an interested expression on his face. "Very well done, my dear. Your deductive powers are better than I had thought."

The curtain near the window moved and Psyche came slowly out from behind it, her face the picture of guilt. Eros's heart turned in his chest—he had let this game go on too long, and he did not want Psyche to be miserable. He went to her put his arms around her protectively, then faced her parents.

"I am at fault, ma'am," he said. "It started out as a game—and I should have known better, I admit it."

Lady Hathaway's expression softened, but her lips were still pressed tightly together.

"No, no, Mama!" Psyche exclaimed. "I am at fault, truly. I know you said I should not kiss just anyone, but Harry is not just anyone, for he has been my dearest friend forever. So I thought . . ." Her voice faded. She had done more than kissing, and she could not go any further in deceiving her mother.

Lady Hathaway turned her gaze on her daughter. "I daresay you did not think at all, and in fact have been giving all of us a great deal of trouble. *I* have known for a long time you are in love with Mr. D'Amant, and yet you would not admit it, no, even though there is no opposition to it from any quarter! I cannot understand it—and no, John, I shall not be silent! I shall have my say, and I shall not stand for nonsense about accounts or Greek or anything else of that sort!"

Sir John remained obediently silent and sat on a sofa, folding his hands on his knee, obviously prepared to wait for a good while.

"And you, Mr. D'Amant! You may be able to charm your way past Lady Jersey, but not me, not where my daughter is concerned! I saw that not all was as Psyche said about the cuts you received in the conservatory. No, I do not wish to hear your excuses! I suspect I know very well what happened there, and I hope I shall not see anything of the sort again."

"You may be sure of that, Lady Hathaway," Harry said.

"And take that smile from your face! Indeed, I do not know why I wish for you to marry Psyche except I know she could not be happy with anyone else, and the love I have for my children could not wish for anything but their happiness, no matter how much I myself may be profoundly disturbed by how it may occur." She paused, sternly eyeing her husband, Harry, and her errant daughter. "Now, I do not want any nonsense from you, Psyche. Mr. D'Amant has proposed, and I expect you to accept immediately, and no nonsense about accounts and Latin, John!"

Sir John looked at his wife blandly, then turned to his daughter with raised brows. "Well, my dear? Your mother has spoken. What is your answer?"

Psyche looked at both of them, feeling the fear of the unknown again, then gazed up at Harry. She felt all tension leave her suddenly. He would always be her friend, and he would never change. Of that she could be sure. Had he not always been at her side, and helped her whenever she needed him? And she loved him. There was no doubt about that. She had known it for a long time.

"Very well, Mama." She sighed.

"Well, you need not sound so resigned!" Lady Hathaway said. She smiled at last, and patted her daughter on her shoulder. "I am very sure you shall be happy with Mr. D'Amant." She turned to her husband. "There! I have had my say, and we may return home, for all is resolved! I knew if I spoke to them all would be well, John, and there is no need for those silly accounts."

Sir John rose, then turned to Harry. "Well, my wife has spoken. You may continue with the accounts if you choose, of course." He hesitated. "Although . . . I imagine you will have a great deal of time to go over them at your leisure, whereas I was planning to present a paper in London when we return, and it involves translating a manuscript. You did say you could read Sanskrit, Mr. D'Amant?" He looked hopefully at Harry.

"Yes, I do," Harry said. He looked at Psyche, then back at her father, raising his brows expectantly.

"I am acquainted with a bishop, and he could procure a special license," Sir John said. If Psyche did not know any better, she would have sworn he sounded a little as if he were wheedling.

"No," Lady Hathaway said firmly. "We shall have banns read, and that is that." She turned to Psyche. "Come, my dear. We shall go home. Mr. D'Amant will join us later. I am sure he would rather have his entertainment with us rather than bothering with accounts."

"Indeed, Lady Hathaway," Harry said obediently, his eyes twinkling.

"Hmph!" she said, then smiled reluctantly. "I see you will be the most troublesome of sons-in-law." She beckoned to her daughter, and after giving one last look at Harry, Psyche left.

When Psyche arrived home, she sighed. She had received a great number of kisses—and more, in fact—but she supposed she would not remember more until the next morning. That was how it usually came about: kisses, dreams, then memories. She took off her coat and gave it to her maid to put away, then remembered how it had fallen from her at Harry's touch. Psyche moved restlessly. The fire that had coursed through her when Harry had pulled her on his lap still burned low, and she did not know how to dispel it.

It was worse when Harry came for a while to listen to her sister and brother-in-law play a duet. Though her parents had announced the betrothal before all the guests, and though they received congratulations from them, Harry kept a circumspect distance. Only once did he touch her, briefly running a finger across the palm she had pierced with his dart. She shivered, and looked up at him. But he had only smiled, a devilish light in his eyes, and passed by to talk with another guest.

Harry was up to something, but he gave no hint of what it would be, and she knew him well enough to know that he would not tell her, no matter how much she coaxed him. She frowned when he left early, saying he had more accounts to attend to. Lady Hathaway pursed her lips then shook her head and smiled ruefully, while Sir John reminded him he had said he might help with the ancient manuscript. And he gave Psyche only a brief, light kiss on the cheek before he left.

The room seemed suddenly dull when Harry left, and Psyche retired to her room at last, changed into her nightgown, and slipped into bed. She tossed and turned for a while, then sighed and rose from her bed. There was nothing for it but to read, perhaps, or better, write. She lit a branch of candles, pulled on her dressing gown, and padded to her writing desk.

Biting the end of her quill, she read over what she had written so far, then continued.

Cecelia opened the door, wondering who it was who came to her humble cottage, the cottage she had bought so dear with her small savings and the sacrifice of her virtue. She looked wearily at the man before her; it was Count Ormondo—oh, vile seducer!—whom she had thought loved her, for he had nursed her back to health, only to take odious advantage of her innocence. "Go!" she cried. "Go, you despoiler of—

Psyche frowned. She did not like the way this story was turning out. She scratched out what she had written, frowned some more, threw the paper into the fire, then began writing on a new piece of paper. Finally, she yawned, smiled, and put away her pen and ink, wiping her fingers on the rag she kept on her desk. There, a much happier ending. She climbed into bed again and closed her eyes, letting herself sink into the eiderdown mattress.

And opened her eyes again when she heard a tapping on her window. She frowned, then turned in her bed. A glow appeared on the other side of the glass, and her heart lifted.

She slid from her bed, flung open the windows and the glow drifted in. It brightened, grew larger, then solidified into the familiar form of Harry. He was dressed in his chiton, and had his wings again, just as she had remembered him from the time she had first met him. She ran into his arms.

"Oh, Harry, Harry!" she cried, bringing his head down to kiss him over and over again. "I am so glad you are here. I have been so afraid of not being me, but I do love you. And it has been such a long time—you have not come to my room since . . . since I grew up."

"Once," he said, kissing her in return.

"That does not count, for I did not know you came until after you left, and that only because you left one of your feathers behind." She sighed. "I did not know how much I missed your visits until now, although I should have known, for I have kept your feather under my pillow. I suppose it would have been improper then"—she shook her head at him—"as it is now."

"No, not now," he said, pushing aside the small sleeve of her nightgown and kissing her shoulder. "You are my wife. We have every right to do this." He pushed aside the other sleeve, and kissed that shoulder as well. "Besides, I refuse to wait any longer. I have been waiting more than a millennium for this"—he flicked the bodice of the gown that hung on the tip of her breast, and it fell—"and this." He did the same with the other one, and the nightgown pooled at her feet. "And this." He picked her up and placed her gently upon her bed. "And at last, at last, this." He moved over her and kissed her mouth.

Psyche moaned and pressed herself against him, feeling the soft cloth of his chiton sliding against her skin, and his bare legs sliding against hers. She reached down tentatively and tugged at his clothes, then slipped her hands inside, feeling his hard chest, then rising to trace the dips and mounds of sinew and muscle on his arms and shoulders. He gave a shuddering sigh, and his wings fluttered briefly, brushing a soft breeze across her breasts and belly. She closed her eyes at the sensation, then opened them wide, because the feeling continued, a gentle brushing up and down her body.

Harry smiled down at her, a wicked smile, with an equally wicked glint in his eyes. "I found the feather," he said.

"No!" Psyche said. "You know how ticklish I am!"

"I know," he said, and his smile grew wider. He kissed her. "But it has been a while since I've tickled you. You might have outgrown it . . . or perhaps not."

"I have definitely outgrown it," Psyche said firmly.

"Really? I wonder if you can possibly stay still and not laugh?"

"Of course," she said.

He took her hands in one of his and drew them above her head. "Let me try," he said, and drew the feather around her breasts and below. Psyche took in a quick gasping breath, and bit her lip to keep from laughing. "Mmm. Perhaps here." He brought the feather down to her hips, touching her thighs and circling around to her belly again. Another suppressed laugh made her squeak. "I wonder if I should give it up?"

"You should," Psyche said, her voice trembling from the shivers the feather gave her, and a seeping heat that had crept up from her private places.

He tossed the feather aside. "You are right. This is better." And he put his lips everywhere the feather had been.

Psyche moaned, for the heat flared into fire where he kissed her, and she clutched his shoulders and tugged at his clothes. The cloth melted from her hands and finally flesh met flesh, and his arms came around her, holding her tight.

"Ah, Psyche. Never be afraid. I will always be with you." He kissed her throat and ran his fingertips along the back of her leg, making her tremble and raise her knee to his hips. "Yes," he whispered, and moved upon her, and her heart opened in joy at last.

Her breath came quickly, as if she were running, and Eros slid his fingers through her hair spread on the pillow, fire hair, hair red as passion. His mouth returned to her mouth, and he inhaled the scent of roses that emanated from her, and her lips tasted of honey. She was rich with life and fire, and his heart drew it in and overflowed again, a tide of heat and love. He moved against her, harder, and his breath also came quickly as she moaned low in her throat.

"Harry, please," she said, her voice urgent, her hands trembling on his back, touching the feathers of his wings.

"Soon," he whispered, kissing her again. "Soon. Ah, sweet, move, like this. Like this." And he pressed himself into her.

"Harry!" His name burst from her in a breath of pain and pleasure, and she twisted beneath him, a hot and liquid tension. He closed his eyes, beyond words, and moved slowly, drawing out the tension. She trembled, and her hips surged upward; it pushed him over the edge and when he plunged into her he fell into heaven, into fire and ice, power searing through him at last.

The heat from where they joined burst, and Psyche arched into him again, clutching him tightly as he pressed deeply into her. A flood of sensation and images swept into her body and mind. She shuddered, gasping, and burrowed her face into the crook of his neck.

Stillness at last, the only movement his chest rising and falling against her. It was dark, but when Psyche stretched, she touched his wings arching above them, forming a protective shield as they always had in the past.

The past. She closed her eyes, and saw the memories of years she had not recognized until now. They were her memories, and mingled those of her family. She was Psyche, Eros's wife, and Psyche Hathaway, also. She smiled, relieved. She was mostly Psyche Hathaway, for that was what she was born to be.

She touched her husband's face gently, and he opened his eyes. "I remember now," she said softly, and kissed him. "I missed you, my dear love."

His wings folded, and the moonlight showed his eyes full of joy. A deep sigh escaped him, and he rested his head on her shoulder. A drop of wetness fell on her breast. "I have looked for you so long," Eros said. "At last." He sighed. "At last."

"I will never leave you again," Psyche said. "I didn't want to—I was killed while shape-changing, at the moment of mortality. And then I forgot everything in the cycle of birth and death. But something in me remembered." She sighed. "I suppose that is why I refused so many suitors. In all of my lives. I have been lonely, too."

"No more loneliness," he said. "No more. We will grow old together, then we shall leave what I have bought for our children, and you will live with me forever." He looked at her, and she kissed away the tears, and he kissed away hers in return. Soon the kissing turned into loving again, then softened into sighs, and at last they rested in each other's arms until dawn.

The marriage of Psyche Hathaway and Harry D'Amant fell on a day bright with sunshine, and no clouds marred the celebration. The wedding guests marveled at it, for in all other directions the horizon held clouds, both thick and light, but no wind blew them near.

Harry's two aunts and long-lost mother came to the wedding, three ladies of such immense grace and majesty, that it was whispered their veins held the blood of ancient kings. For a short time, they drew him aside, and Psyche could see them nodding. While his mother smiled brightly and Artemis left the group to walk with Lord Eldon, the other two looked thoughtful and nodded.

Harry returned, and took Psyche's hand, kissing it, then held it as they walked toward their house. "What was that conversation about?" she asked.

"I answered the question they wanted answered," he said.

"Which is—?" she prompted.

"What it is they should know."

"How very enlightening," Psyche said, and rolled her eyes. "You are a fount of information."

He kissed her. "It was the very last part of my quest," he said. "There was something the gods needed to know, to keep the world from falling into chaos again."

Silence, then: "For heaven's sake, Harry, I shall die if you do not tell me!"

He laughed. "Very well. I told them they needed to live among mortals again. It's the only way they would keep strong. It is why I stayed strong, and why Artemis had grown so weak until she fell in love with Lord Eldon. And why I will not be going back to Olympus, but living here with you."

Psyche sighed. "I am glad. I should not like our child to be away from my family." She shot him an impish glance.

He stared at her in shocked silence. "Already?" he managed to say.

"I only just found out, Harry. Artemis told me—she knows a great deal about midwifery. You are *very* persistent, you know, and for goodness' sake, what did you expect?" They walked around the corner of the house and through a garden door.

"Well," he said. "Well." His lips spread in a wide smile. "I wonder if he—or she—will resemble you or me?"

Psyche stood stock-still, staring at him. "Oh, dear."

"What is it?"

"I have not yet told Mama or Papa what you are. And if our child should resemble you—" She looked past his shoulder, where his wings normally would be. "Oh, good Lord."

He laughed, and his eyes gleamed mischievously. "Now that will be an interesting surprise."

"This is serious, Harry!" Psyche protested. "What shall I tell them?"

"The truth, of course," he said, and took her in his arms.

"But—"

Harry kicked the garden door closed and kissed her soundly, until her protests turned into long sighs. "They will be delighted," he said at last, pulling her down to the grass. "Your father will have all the knowledge I can give him about the ancient world, and as for your mother, you must admit, no title can be higher than that of a god."

Psyche gave it up. She could not find any way to argue with him, and his kisses made her remember other, more pleasurable things. But then, Harry's kisses always did.

ROMANCE FROM THE PAST

☐ **THE WICKED GROOM by April Kihlstrom.** It was bad enough when Lady Diana Westcott learned her parents were wedding her to the infamous Duke of Berenford. But it was even worse when she came face-to-face with him. First he disguised his identity to gain a most improper access to her person. Then he hid the beautiful woman in his life even as that passion of the past staked a new claim to his ardent affection. Now Diana had to deceive this devilish deceiver about how strongly she responded to his kisses and how weak she felt in his arms. (187504—$4.99)

☐ **THE SECRET NABOB by Martha Kirkland.** Miss Madeline Wycliff's two sisters were as different as night and day. One was bold and brazen and had wed a rake whose debts now threatened the family estate; but the other was as untouched as she was exquisite. Now Madeline had to turn her back on love and get dangerously close to a nefarious nabob to save her sister's happiness and innocence...even if it meant sacrificing her own. (187377—$4.50)

☐ **A HEART POSSESSED by Katherine Sutcliffe.** From the moment Ariel Rushdon was reunited with Lord Nicholas Wyndham, the lover who had abandoned her, she could see the torment in his eyes. Now she would learn the secrets of his house. Now she would learn the truth about his wife's death. And now she would also make Nick remember everything—their wild passion, their sacred vows...their child.... (407059—$5.50)

Prices slightly higher in Canada

Payable in U.S. funds only. No cash/COD accepted. Postage & handling: U.S./CAN. $2.75 for one book, $1.00 for each additional, not to exceed $6.75; Int'l $5.00 for one book, $1.00 each additional. We accept Visa, Amex, MC ($10.00 min.), checks ($15.00 fee for returned checks) and money orders. Call 800-788-6262 or 201-933-9292, fax 201-896-8569; refer to ad #SRR4

Penguin Putnam Inc.
P.O. Box 12289, Dept. B
Newark, NJ 07101-5289
Please allow 4-6 weeks for delivery.
Foreign and Canadian delivery 6-8 weeks.

Bill my: ☐ Visa ☐ MasterCard ☐ Amex_____(expires)
Card#_____
Signature_____

Bill to:
Name_____
Address_____City_____
State/ZIP_____
Daytime Phone #_____

Ship to:
Name_____ Book Total $_____
Address_____ Applicable Sales Tax $_____
City_____ Postage & Handling $_____
State/ZIP_____ Total Amount Due $_____

This offer subject to change without notice.